ACCESS ALL
AWKWARD

ACCESS ALL AWKWARD

BETH GARROD

■SCHOLASTIC

Scholastic Children's Books
An imprint of Scholastic Ltd
Euston House, 24 Eversholt Street, London, NW1 1DB, UK
Registered office: Westfield Road, Southam, Warwickshire, CV47 0RA
SCHOLASTIC and associated logos are trademarks and/or
registered trademarks of Scholastic Inc.

First published in the UK by Scholastic Ltd, 2018

Text copyright © Beth Garrod, 2018

The right of Beth Garrod to be identified as the author of this
work has been asserted by her.

Emoji by Madebyoliver, freepik and Dimitry Miroliubov at flaticon.com

ISBN 978 1407 18682 5

Printed by CPI Group (UK) Ltd, Croydon, CR0 4YY
Papers used by Scholastic Children's Books are made
from wood grown in sustainable forests.

3 5 7 9 10 8 6 4

This is a work of fiction. Names, characters, places, incidents
and dialogues are products of the author's imagination or are used
fictitiously. Any resemblance to actual people, living or dead,
events or locales is entirely coincidental.

www.scholastic.co.uk

To Gemma – who makes dreams become books, and strangers become friends.

CHAPTER

ONE

The correct name for "study leave" should really be "inventing-novel-ways-not-to-study leave". I was only in week one and had already managed to become an expert at identifying rare breeds of dogs (who knew the Norwegian Lundehund has six toes on each foot?! Well ... *me*, now I'd scrolled through every Instagram picture of them ever tagged) and had found thirteen legit reasons (2.17 a day) to go to my corner shop. Yesterday the owner asked me if I was "having problems at home". She looked unimpressed when I replied, "Yes, the problem of it currently not containing any Wotsits." I then went home, sat in the back garden and wasted another hour of study leave actually studying leaves.

"Erm, not entirely sure my mum's going to love

seeing your bum-ghost when she's having her morning coffee, Bells."

Rach looked accusingly at the spot where I'd just been leaning – the one black wall in her otherwise gleamingly white kitchen. Her parents had recently painted it with blackboard paint so they could write family memos to one another. Sadly their chalk "Home is Where the True Heart Is" now looked a whole heap more like "Home is Where the T art Is" thanks to a smudge mark in the undeniable shape of my leg cushions.

"Ah. Yes. Sorry…" I tried to rub the words back together but made it even worse – the T now looked dangerously like an F. "…And *that* is officially even worse." Rach laughed and threw a tea towel at me so I could wipe the whole thing off. But all she did was give me an open goal for my favourite joke.

"What's the most common owl in the UK…?"

Tegan smiled and rolled her eyes. "We know…" and together they both finished it off. "THE TEAT OWL. There's one in every home."

I grinned, still enjoying it ten years since Mum first told me. But the way Tegan kept looking at me for a millisecond after our laughing stopped reminded me of our conversation earlier. She was worried about me. And not just 'cos of my appreciation for dishcloth jokes,

2

or because she'd seen my dog-based internet history. She knew revision wasn't going well. Or more to the point, that my exams weren't. I just couldn't seem to get stuff to stay in my head (except things like *corgi* is Welsh for "dwarf dog", but I don't recall that being a major part of any syllabus). And the pressure was on – I'd messed up my mocks, so the grades I needed to get into Worcestershire College were way higher than the ones Rach and Tegan required. If the three of us were going to stay together into sixth form, I HAD to nail these exams. Everyone was counting on me.

I flumped down on to one of the bar stools, pretending not to notice Tegan clocking my change of mood, or her *quick-do-something* look at Rach.

"OK. How about this for a plan." Rach slid past us, using her socks as floor skis. "Quick snack break, saaaaay thirty minutes?"

"Twenty," Tegan jumped in.

"Twenty-five?" Rach bargained.

"Deal," I interjected, happy to be the middle ground between my two best mates.

"Then we do an hour's SOLID work. As in no chat. No phones. Not even a sneaky spot-squeeze break in the bathroom." I swear Rach gave me a knowing look. "Just high-level geography achievement." She stared out the window, all pensive romantic heroine. "Just think… This time tomorrow, the exam will be over, and we'll never need to look at a geography book or a map everrrrrr again."

I wasn't quite sure how she was intending to find her way round in the future, but neither Tegan or I wanted to burst her bubble. Happily humming away, Rach set the break timer and started to froth some milk. Yes, it might be one of the hottest days of the year but our hot chocolate consumption didn't play by the rules. Teeg clunked a capsule into the posh hot drink machine and I fished out the jar of mini marshmallows. Sure, we'd all grown up together, but Rach's home life was one of an ever-stocked supply of luxury hot drink accessories – mine was one with a mum who had texted me (more than once) to ask me to nab some school toilet paper 'cos she'd forgotten to get any in, yet again.

Teeg put her arm round me.

"C'mon, you. In three weeks this'll all be over."

Oh yes. I'd temporarily forgotten my real-life exam hell. I gave her my best doomed-zombie look.

"And my fate will be seeeealed."

She nodded firmly. "Yup – sealed that we'll all be off to sixth form together. You know your photography portfolio is a-maze."

4

An unauthorized half-smile popped out. Trust Tegan to be able to make me feel a bit better. She never said stuff she didn't mean just to fluff people's egos – she was too honest for that.

I'd spent weeks, months pulling my portfolio together – our art teacher, Mr Lutas, had gone out of his way to help me with it. They didn't offer Photography GCSE at my school, so he knew that getting on the college photography course all depended on me proving it's what I loved doing – and that I was any good at it. Goodness knows why I'd gone and made life even harder with my other subject choices. I blame watching *Planet Earth* the night before I chose them – and the resulting urge to become a professional photographer of penguins (and six-toed dogs). So one small tick of a form, and I'd added the small matter of also needing As in maths and science, to get on to the environmental science and biology courses I'd chosen. Thanks, Sir David Attenborough.

BLAM.

Rach, distracted by a message that had just come through, plonked down our drinks and caused a tiny table tidal wave of hot chocolate.

"Say what?!"

The more she read, the more her jaw fell (revealing

she'd snuck in some extracurricular marshmallow eating). "OK… *Right*." She gulped as if swallowing this new information. "Ignore the fact my dad still thinks texts are proper letters…" She held her screen out for us to read, which felt like an optician's test due to her hand wobbling with excitement.

> Hello, Rachel. How are you?
> I've been so impressed with your revision that as a treat I purchased two tickets for RebelRocks festival.
> Enjoy yourself! Don't do anything I wouldn't do!
> (Joke.) See you when I get back from the U-S-of-A.
> Love, Dad xx

Whoa.
Now I got it.

Rach had the same eye-glazed look she got watching the surprises on *Saturday Night Takeaway*.

"We've got t-tickets… Actual tickets."

We'd been talking about RebelRocks for ages. It was the first proper festival that had ever come to our town, and was happening the weekend our exams finished. aka, The Actual Dream. Music, talks, making stuff. New bands we'd had stuck on repeat all year, cool talks from some of our life crushes, even a headline slot from The

Session – Rach's favourite ever band. (They'd only had two albums out, but she was ob-sessed. At Christmas her mum had taken her to London just so she could get a glimpse of them turning on some shopping centre lights. We didn't talk about the fact she then went viral for a bit as "Wavy Crowd Girl" in some video they posted – seems the world wasn't ready for her 110 waves per minute [wpm] technique.)

So if there was one thing we knew, it was that RebelRocks was going to be BEYOND awesome.

And if there was another, it was that EVERYONE was going.

Well … everyone except us. Because despite a *major* campaign of parental begging, all I'd got was a big "no". I'd even washed the dishes six days running (Mum disputed that throwing away a takeaway pizza box counted towards this, but I argued it's the thought that counts). But the timing couldn't have been worse. Mum was looking for a more central location for her dog-ice-cream business, Give A Dog A Cone, and money was tight while she saved. And Tegan had put all her allowance towards some new gymnastics kit, so was flat broke too.

But Rach's text? This changed everything. And we all knew it.

But I also knew we were all thinking the same. Two tickets. Three people.

"Bells." Tegan was uber-calm. "I'll probs have training that weekend, so you should deffo take it." She was lying to make it easier for all of us. I couldn't let her do that.

"I… I might have to help out at the shop," I lied back. Rach's face fell. "Not that I wouldn't LOVE to come."

But it was too late. The damage was done.

"So, lemme get this straight…" Rach raised an eyebrow. "I have a spare ticket, to the festival we've been *dying* to go to – and no one wants to come with me?"

Well, this had backfired.

I panicked. "AS IF, Rach?! We'd both love to – right?" Tegan nodded so hard in agreement she looked like she was being fast-forwarded. "I mean … why don't I ask my mum again if she'll lend me the money to buy one?" I had an idea. "Or Teeg and I could try and go halfsies on the third?"

"Deffo – I'll ask tonight!" Tegan was also trying to stick an enthusiasm plaster over the awkward, but Rach was deflated.

"It's OK… I think we all know it'll be a 'no', right? It's not like you haven't asked one zillion times already."

She had a point. And none of us knew what to say next. So, to help deal with the silence, I did the wisest thing I could – slurped my hot chocolate really loudly.

"GUYS." Rach suddenly sprang up, pushing her stool back with a loud scrape, a look of determination on her face. "Panic no more! I KNOW what we should do. And I won't take no for an answer." It was harder to take her seriously when she had a pink/white marshmallow goop moustache, but now wasn't the time to point it out. "I'm going to give my spare ticket to …" She paused. Wait! Was she about to choose her favourite friend? This could change the world as we knew it! "… my brother. His boyf can have mine."

Sorry, what?!

"But, Rach?" I was actually spluttering. And not just because she'd mentioned HOB (aka Hot Older Brother). "You HAVE to go? The. Actual. Session will be there."

Tegan backed me right up. "Seriously – don't do this. You two go – it'll be amazing. I'd rather have FOMO than FAMO any day." Rach looked as puzzled as me. *"Friends Are Missing Out."* I nodded, knowing just how she felt, but Rach shook her head.

"Nope. It's the three of us or nothing." She was speaking extra quick to stop us getting a word in. "So instead, I reckon we throw our own fest." She looked around her. "HOUSEFEST! We can put tents up in my garden, play music and light one of those tiny BBQs you can get from the garage for a fiver. It'll be ace." She paused. "Although the name might need work."

"But…" I started to protest.

"But *nothing*, Bella." I'd never heard Rach so serious. Except the time she realized that it wasn't thin cows that made skimmed milk and larger ones that made full fat. "It's agreed."

And, as if it knew it was being symbolic, the timer buzzed. Rachel smiled sweetly. "End of discussion – the timer says so. So back to the plan – revision only."

A deal's a deal, so we sat down, putting our phones in the middle of the table for a phone amnesty – *phamnesty* – and opened our textbooks.

Quarter of an hour later, when Tegan ducked out to go to the loo, Rach banged her head on to her book.

"Bells – I think my brain might have shrivelled into a raisin."

"Same," I said with a wide-eyed stare back. "But mine's a dried pea. All I've learnt so far is that on page thirty-nine there's a chocolate stain shaped like…" I tried to think of a country. None came to mind. Not a good sign my geography revision was going well.

"Can we talk about something else? Something the opposite of this torture?" Rach pleaded.

A smile crept across my face. A naughty, happy, life-is-instantly-better smile that I had zero control over. Rach grinned. "Say no more. Your booooyfriend." She said it in the drawn-out, OTT way I deserved given the lame grin on my face at just the thought of Adam.

Boyfriend. *Boyfriend*. It had been seven months, but the word still felt funny. Could you have imposter syndrome in your own relationship? But it had been SO good. Adam had gone from massively awesome to even more awesome. *Mawsome*. Sure, there had been all the obvious amazing things about him at the start – his stone cold hottie-ness, the way he made everyone around him laugh, his forearms when he drummed – but as we spent more time together and I got to know the more secret bits, the things that he only shared with me – I liked him even more. I loved how he really cared what exam results he got. And what his future looked like. How he loved his younger brother. And how he had a weird Wednesday hobby of baking bread. As in real, actual pre-toast. With his own hands (well, with an oven).

The only thing that didn't feel so great was that even though my mum was a fully fledged member (potential president) of the Adam Douglas Fan Club, he'd never even asked me to meet his parents. Were they really always busy? Or, as I was beginning to suspect, was he more worried about what they'd think of *me*?

EURGH. Thinking about it again made me feel sick. Not sick enough to not drink my second hot chocolate (I'm a trouper), but sick enough to know that even the thought of him not liking me as much as I liked him was the scariest thing in the world. And these last few weeks, it just wouldn't stop niggling at me. Because – as much as I tried to ignore the evidence – he *had* gone off the radar a bit recently. Was it really just exams? I'd only seen him properly once in the last three weeks.

EURGH EURGH. How was I meant to concentrate on this revision if I was at risk of becoming so heartbroken I could never leave my house (most specifically kitchen) again?!

Tegan walked back into the room, looking her usual wise self. Hmmm… Maybe it was time to call in reinforcements.

"Teeeeg. Rach." I needed to get some cold, hard facts on my situation from my best friends (aka, totally biased advice based solely on what I needed to hear to make me feel better). "Before we get back to it, please can I get some advice?" I looked at Tegan. "I *swear* it will liberate my brain to extra-achieve proper revision after."

Teeg smiled. "Well, in that case…" As if she would have ever said no.

So, with them pulling up stools to watch, I divided the remaining space on the black wall into three huge columns to help us figure things out.

"OK, first one." I stretched up to write. "*Reasons Adam and Bella…*"

Rach heckled, "Adabella."

"OK, *Reasons Adabella are the Best Thing Ever.* Then –" I moved to the middle column "– *Things That Are Causing Me to Freak Out a Bit/Lot.* And finally, on the right – *Reassuring Things to Convince Me I Should Probably Stop Freaking Out.*"

That one took a bit longer to write, as however I spelt "reassuring", it didn't look right. As I corrected it, Tegan interrupted.

"We'll fill that one in, right, Rach?"

I grinned at them. "Legends. In that case, I'll start on the easiest one. Reasons Adabella are great."

Without having to try, I began scribbling away.

- Adam is so hot I'd follow him on Instagram even if I didn't know him.

- When we snog, it's so good sometimes I can only speak in vowels for 5 mins after.
- He makes me laugh. ALL THE TIME.

NOTE TO SELF: Maybe this is most hot thing of all?? I put two stars beside it to give it extra importance.

- He pats ALL dogs. Especially Mumbles.
- He insists we make up names for each other when we get a takeaway hot drink and can never let on they're not real (he didn't even crack when they shouted "Anita Shour").

Before I realized, I'd written ten more. (We have the same order of favourite songs on the 1975's debut album! He introduced me to cheese-and-marmite toasties!) Rach then pointed out we only had a couple of minutes before we'd have to get back to revising, so we should crack on with the middle column.

But my chalk seemed to not want to move, like committing my innermost worries to written words would make them more real.

"C'mon, Bells," Tegan said gently, "you've got this."

Slowly I began to write.

- Has he been avoiding me?
- Why doesn't want me to meet his parents? Is it me????
- He's so laid back, but I freak out when I'm within 20 metres of him, like I'm only just learning social skills. Is this normal?? (OR DOES THIS MEAN HE'S JUST NOT INTO ME??? DISCUSS!!!!)

But before I could get any further, Rach's alarm for the end of break part two went. ARGH. I hadn't even got to the good bit yet (i.e. the bit where Rach and Tegan tell me it will all be OK). All I'd done was create a life-sized worry cliffhanger.

"Maybe I'll just leave the chalk here." I placed it down right in front of them, hoping they might ignore the timer and fill in the positive thoughts I needed.

"On it like a car bonnet." Rach whipped the chalk away. Of *course* she wouldn't leave me hanging. "...Once we've done this next revision stint."

OR NOT.

Tegan sensed my alarm and pushed a packet of Skips towards me. A prawn-based peace offering. "Turn your back on it, eat these, and it'll be OK." She grinned. "Promise."

As much as I hated everything about studying, I

hated the thought of not spending the next two years with these two even more. And I wanted them to see how much I was trying. So I held off protesting and knuckled down.

The next two hours flew by.

If that flight was a turbulent, seat-belt-on-throughout, death-roller-coaster of boredom/fear for my future. I didn't even know those two emotions could happen simultaneously. Still, I managed to work my way through all the twenty-five little revision cards I'd made. Maybe I *could* get a B in geography tomorrow? And being so focused meant I totally missed Rach and Tegan filling in their newly titled "Reasons Adam Might Sometimes Act Weird But Is Definitely 100% Not Going To Dump Bella" list. They really were the best.

As we took our next break, I laughed as they read out their reasons. They ranged from the practical *maybe his parents always wear matching outfits and he's trying to stop anyone discovering this* to the wildly optimistic *sometimes he has to not see you as he gets too overwhelmed by his MAJOR LOVE FOR YOU.* Ridiculous or not, each and every one made me feel better, and as a result I positively smashed the impromptu quick-fire geography quiz they threw at me (never has one person yelled "Limestone!" "Flume!" "Boggy marshland!" with such

16

enthusiasm). We only stopped when Rach had to run off to answer the doorbell. As the door opened I heard some heavy breathing that I'd recognize anywhere. It got louder as a bundle of wagging tail and slobber tumbled into the room.

"Mumbles!" Mum must have been walking her and decided to pop in. My ever-happy boxer dog was so pleased to see me she ran in tiny circles, panting like she'd only just discovered oxygen. Thank goodness humans didn't do that, or I'd collapse with dizziness every time I even glimpsed Adam. Or a biscuit.

I crouched down to give Mumbles a cuddle, which switched into her pushing me down and jumping all over me. Standard. Her breath was a heady mixture of decayed fish and the smell of the water in the bottom of the toothbrush pot.

"Er, Bells?" Rach sounded weirded out. But I couldn't open my eyes, as there was a tongue attempting to lick them.

Mumbles slammed a paw down on to my chest, leaning in ever closer, now full-on breathing into my face, almost overcoming me with fumes

"Raaachhh. Help meeee… She's –" gasp "– squishing … my boooooob!"

But I felt no help coming, so wailing like a manic

17

squirrel, I used all the stomach muscles I had to push her off. Finally I was free to sit up and open my eyes.

To see Adam. Fit Adam. Fadam.

"WHAT THE WHAT ARE YOU DOING HERE?" Is something I probably should have thought quietly, rather than yelled in his face.

Adam blinked, unfazed – he'd had twenty-eight weeks, three days and 1.5 hours to get used to my ways (he was a quicker learner than me, as I'd had over sixteen years, but still didn't understand myself).

"Nice to see you too, Bells." Grinning, he put his hand out. Trying – and failing – not to gawp, I grabbed it, getting my usual tingle when our fingers touched. Was this normal?!

But what was he doing here? I hadn't seen him in weeks. I looked at Rach for some sort of psychic explanation but she just shrugged in a "Sorry, I have no idea what's going on either" way.

Adam sensed us all acting weird, and suddenly looked embarrassed, like he'd accidentally wandered into a girls' changing room. "Sorry – she got out on to the playing field while I was having a kick about." Classic Mumbles. Whenever she escaped, she always headed to somewhere that had the highest ratio of embarrassingly fit fitties. He looked at me. "So I walked her to yours…

And when no one was in, I guessed you might be here?"
He looked awkward. "But she's safe now, so I'll, erm,
I'll go."

Oh great, he felt like I didn't want him here. Nice
one me.

My insides = couldn't be happier to see him.

My face = complete shock.

If only there was a Google translate for my facial
muscles.

"No, stay!" I scrambled towards the breakfast bar.
"We have snacks and hot chocolate on tap, right, Rach?"

But as I looked in her direction, I saw what was
behind Adam. The entire, horrifying wall of my writing
saying things like:

The way he gets hiccups when he eats toast =
STRANGELY ALLURING (with no less than five
hearts).

*The mole above his eyebrow. DREAM/SWOON/
DROON.*

My heart sped up to the "intense panic/potential
fainting to save your dignity" zone. Whatever happened,
ADAM MUST NOT SEE THIS. He'd realize he was
going out with a list-making maniac who was clearly
head over heels in love with him. (And by realize I
mean read the bit that said, *I, BELLA FISHER, AM A*

"In fact. No. You should go!" I headed towards the door. Adam looked confused. "Now!" I accidentally shouted it. Mumbles gave me an "Are you OK, hun?" look. Great – my oddness was so intense, it crossed the species divide. I needed to be less weird. "You've got places to be and, er, people to see, right?" Yup, I'd unleashed a Mum phrase. "Although…" I looked around for something, *anything*, to distract Adam from what was behind him. "Have you seen Rach's garden recently?" I pointed out the window even though it was getting dark. Not a great time to remember I didn't know anything about gardens other than buying a potato in Asda seemed a whole lot easier than spending six months growing one. "Isn't it wonderful?" I flung my arm across the scene. "Such, er … bloom!!"

Adam looked at me like I'd gone a bit mad and politely said something about a cherry tree. I needed urgent backup. So, I gestured with my hand behind my back to the others and finally, *finally,* they got what I was doing. Immediately, they leapt into action, Rach throwing herself in front of the wall and Tegan manoeuvring herself between Adam and the writing. Even Mumbles ran head first towards Adam's trousers to sniff the area that must not be named (I'd like to think she was also helping with the diversion, but had to accept she just had terrible hobbies).

"So, erm, thanks for bringing Mumbles round." I tried to drag her head away whilst pretending it also wasn't there. Tegan saw how well things were going (not at all) and shuffled round to keep the wall blocked.

"No probs." Adam pulled on his backpack. He looked worryingly like he might be about to turn right and see everything. NO!! In the words of Beyoncé, *to the left, to the left!* (Although doubt that was because she'd ever written *The way Jay-Z casually throws sticks for dogs and they go impressively far* in giant letters next to his face).

I looked around for something else to keep Adam's attention to where I was. "Have you seen Rachel's mum's new phone charger?" I sounded positively hysterical. "It has three USBs!"

Wow. I was girlfriend GOLD. Once word got round about how much I loved gardening and chargers, I was going to be IN DEMAND. Adam smiled as enthusiastically as someone could when they thought their girlfriend fangirled over charging mechanisms.

"That sounds ... really useful?"

I had nothing left, and mouthed "Help" at Tegan.

With a firm nod to let me know she had this, she took matters into her own hands and sidestepped towards the kitchen door, nudging Adam round as she did. "Aaaanyway, thanks for reuniting the doggo with her rightful owner. But despite Bella being happy to chat about, er, USB chargers – great as they are – we better get back to the revision. Geography tomorrow and we still have Central Business Districts to get through." And to my relief (/guilt), Adam bought it.

So, with a quick bye, and a promise to arrange to meet soon, he stepped into the hall and out the front door. WE'D DONE IT.

There was only one thing for it – a full-on splat of relief on to the sofa. Followed by the three of us scrubbing every chalk speck of evidence off the wall as we relived how horrifyingly close I'd come to the total disaster of Adam discovering what I was actually like as a human. But as the laughter died down, and the other two began to plan meeting up for tomorrow's exam, I got stuck in my own thoughts.

Because as I rubbed away *He makes me feel like I can achieve anything*, a realization stung.

Even though I'd only written that an hour ago, right now I felt like I was only really achieving one thing: single-handedly screwing us up.

CHAPTER

TWO

"PENS DOWN!" Mrs Hitchman, our headmistress, yelled so loudly it was like she was alerting us to an approaching stampede of wildebeests. Nice to know that despite coming to the end of 1.5 hours of exam doom, she was her usual cheery self.

But who cared?! As I closed the paper for the last time, geography was officially over. BUH BYE, worst subject ever. Despite having that horrible panicked-hand-shake towards the end as I tried to write faster and faster, I'd answered everything – and hadn't even resorted to fake extra-bad handwriting to disguise the fact I was making some of the longer words up. Who knows how to spell ~~impearmeable impermable~~ waterproof anyway?

I POL-ed (phewed out loud) with such force I was treated to a Mrs Hitchman withering glare all to myself. I was already in her bad books from last week, when I'd got confused with the food rule about exams. I didn't realize when they said you were allowed snacks for "medical" reasons, that didn't include "being pretty sure my brain doesn't function without regular chocolate". So when ten minutes into English literature I began to crunch my way through some Smarties, Mrs Hitchman stormed over like she suspected I'd written the major plot points of *Julius Caesar* on them (although, retrospectively, I wish I had).

I gave Mrs Hitchman my best "don't hate me – at least I didn't bring Chipsticks this time" look – but all I got back was a cold, hard stare that made me feel like I was shrinking. In better news, my peripheral vision spotted two sets of thumbs up – one on my left, one on my right. That's the thing with having best mates with surnames beginning with A and W. Between us we covered a whole exam room – my F-ness being plonk in the middle.

Tegan grinned – good, it must have gone well for her too. She could fill me in when we got to the library. We still had a few more days of having to come into school every other day for "supervised revision". Then it was *goodbye, school* except for exams. And today Mr Lutas was supervising, so it would basically be a debrief and chill. As soon as we got the all-clear to file out, I gathered up my lucky pens and pencils into my clear plastic pencil case (aka a sandwich bag) and headed for the corridor. But I slapped straight into the one person who was worse than any exam. The evilest of exes. Luke.

"Heard your sigh of relief, Fishy Balls. Don't tell me you actually *passed* something?"

I raised an eyebrow defiantly. "The only thing I want to get *past* is you." Years of practice had helped me finally be able to stand up to him. "Please."

Well, almost.

I tried to push round him, but he was surrounded by his loser mates.

"Ahh, poor you. In such a hurry to see your fwiends. Is it because you don't think you're doing well enough to get to go to college with them?" His eyes were wide with fake concern. Don't feed the troll, Bella.

"As IF, Luke." Rach pushed her way between us. One of her superpowers was being able dodge through crowds five times quicker than anyone else. "So if you could get out of our way, that'd be juuust great."

She grabbed my arm and swished her hair as if she was in an American sitcom. The crowd parted like it

25

was a biblical sea and Rach was a beardy bloke. She had no idea this wasn't normal (and only happened to the extremely beautiful). Walking away, she flopped her head on to my shoulder (quite hard when I was at least five inches shorter).

"How awesome is it going to be when we don't have to see that *idiot* on a daily basis?"

I thought about it.

"Imagine if your full-time job was Chief Puppy Cuddler at Battersea Dogs Home, with a part-time position being a Ben & Jerry's taster… Well, more awesome than that."

Rachel laughed but stopped the instant we walked into the library and hit the brick wall of Mr Lutas's "I'm watching you" stare.

Muttering "Sorry", we headed to where Tegan had bagsied a table just as Mikey rocked up, his right arm still in a cast. He'd been skateboarding down the pavement and flipped his board on a rogue apple core. One small arm break later and he'd bagged a scribe for his exams – a Year Twelve with way neater writing and better spelling than him. He had all the luck.

"Soooo…" Mikey whispered. "How'd it go?" I noticed his good arm prod Tegan's leg under the table as he asked. And her give him a total look of love back.

All in 0.0001 seconds. Their version of affection was blink-and-you'd-miss-it, but somehow always there. Total goals.

"Kind of OK?" I looked at the other two. "Amirite?"

Tegan nodded. "I think the phrase is 'pleasantly surprised'."

Mikey nudged me. "Seeee, I told you things would pick up."

I couldn't help but grin at him. We'd had loads of chats about my exam stress. Mikey was in the same boat, but somehow kept his boat quietly chugging away, not like mine, which was called HMS AARGHHH and was sending out distress signals every two minutes.

"Total praise be to the Gods of Question Setters that there wasn't anything about coastline management." I stuck my hands in the air. "My midnight seagull sacrifice to them must have worked."

Rach and Tegan laughed. But then stopped and stared at me as if they thought I was going to say something else. Which I wasn't. Especially not now they were staring at me.

Tegan spoke first. "You're joking, right?"

"Noooo, I really did lure a flock into my room and sacrifice them while Mum watched *Long Lost Family* downstairs." But no one laughed.

Now, I'm used to that with most of my jokes, but this felt *different*.

Mikey caught my eye, as confused as me. "Have I missed something?"

I shrugged. If these exams had proved anything, it was that "knowing the answer" was not my forte.

"Bells…" Tegan looked concerned. "There *was* a question on coastlines…"

"Ha very ha, Teeg." I waited for her grin to crack through.

But all that came was pure concern. "…The final page? The essay worth fifteen marks?"

If this was a joke, it wasn't funny.

I looked at Rach – she could never keep a prank up for long. But she looked like she'd seen a ghost, and not the one of my bum on her kitchen wall.

My heart plummeted. "You're … not … joking, are you?"

They both shook their heads.

The exam flashed through my brain. The world felt like it was wobbling. I grabbed the table to steady myself.

"Tell me this isn't happening?!"

"Shhhhhh!" Mr Lutas hissed. C'mon!? I know talking's not allowed in the library, but surely acknowledging that you've just messed your whole life up is an exception?!

I HAD flipped the last page … hadn't I? Had I?

I hadn't. Had I?

As my last remaining glimmer of hope packed its bags and went on a gap year, I banged my head forward on to the table.

"I SAID QUIET PLEASE, MS FISHERRRR?!" But I was too miserable to lift my head, so mumbled my reply into the table.

"Soz, I'll try and keep the volume down on my total breakdown."

Rach rubbed my back.

"I'm sure it's OK," she whispered, sounding not sure at all. Well, this was a disaster. How had I not checked the whole paper? That was Exam 101.

I raised my head for a split second to take a discreet photo of my misery face, posting it into my stories along with the hashtag #IfYouDontReadAllTheQuestions DoYouEvenDeserveToPassAnExam along with two vote options: "No" and "No way".

Tegan was doing her best to say comforting things, but unless one of them was "I've discovered how to turn back time", no one could convince me it was going to be OK. Especially as I totally saw Mikey vote "No way".

"Ah, Fishy, bad news, is it?" Oh man. Could life not

cut me a break?! Luke was back, like a magnet to my worst moments.

"Get lost," Tegan said, not missing a beat. I remained totally still. He was like a painful chin spot. Sometimes if you ignored him long enough, he just went away.

"Fit Rach? Will you pass on a message to your weirdo mate when she stops pretending she can't hear me?"

Little did he know I was actually pretending he was a zit. 1–0 to me.

"Tell her I'm really sorry she's messing up her exams which also means her entire life and we'll definitely, DEFINITELY all miss her when we're celebrating at RebelRocks. Such a shame she's going to miss out."

I mouthed "douchebag" into the table. Luke *knew* we didn't have tickets. I'd seen him all smug happy when he'd caught Rach and me moaning about it. And this morning it had officially sold out. Luke had probably bought the last hundred tickets just so we couldn't possibly go.

But it was Mikey who replied.

"No need to pass it on – she'll be there. We all will." I sat up to look at him. He was lying so well even *I* almost believed him. Did he know something we didn't? He wiggled his eyebrows mysteriously. Luckily Luke missed it, too busy sneering at me.

30

"Oh – she *lives*…" he said. I rolled my eyes and huffed – but I did it harder than I meant, and made what sounded like a tiny moo. "Did I disturb you, snorter?"

"It was more of a moo, *actually*." Yup, classic burn there, Bella.

"Nice comeback, cowgirl." He sniggered. "Anyway, seeing as you are all magically now coming to RebelRocks –" he stressed the words with a smile so we knew he wasn't at all fooled "– make sure you check out Ska." Ah yes. Luke's model girlfriend, who was as pretty on the outside as she was pure evil on the inside. "She's playing the New Bands Tent. Going to be epic."

Epically avoidable.

The clanging brag-drop about his new girlf meant I needed to unleash a killer blow back. Something witty and bold and cooler than being in a band that gets paid to play festivals. This stage was mine. I breathed in.

"…Depends if there's a clash with someone else?"

Et tu, Mouth-e? My ex raises me the world's most intimidating girlfriend, and I hit back with calendar logistics?! But it was enough to end the convo and Luke sloped away. When he was out of earshot we grilled Mikey.

Tegan looked semi-annoyed, which, for Tegan, was full-on annoyed.

"Mikey – why did you say that? We haven't got tickets?" She threw Rach a reassuring smile. "Rach made an alternative plan, *remember*?"

Mikey unlocked his phone, making sure Mr Lutas didn't clock his unauthorized use of it. "But that was *then*…" He passed it to Tegan. "It's what I came over to say – someone signed me up for this random email list. And last night I got this…"

Tegan read the email out loud (technically out quiet given the setting).

"Thanks for your interest in working at RebelRocks."

Ahh – so that was Mikey's plan?! Getting in by doing super-cool backstage stuff.

I grabbed Mikey's arm. "You're a flippin' genius!"

He fanned his face. "As I've been saying for years." He winced. "Also, that's my broken one."

I apologized for potentially breaking his arm even more. Tegan carried on…

"The final opportunities have come through. We're looking for…"

My mind raced as Tegan paused. What could it be? Someone to get cups of tea for the bands? Someone to help assist all the stage setters-uppers? A celeb dogsitter?

I was so down for all of this!!!

"Litter pickers…"

Or not.

"To work Thursday–Sunday. You'll be required to work four shifts of four hours each. In return you'll get a ticket to the festival and backstage camping. Application deadline: Friday, 15 June. To apply please fill in the form below."

I tried to focus on the "backstage camping" part. This *could* be our way in. Sure, while everyone else was raving, we'd be recycling, but at least we'd be *in*. That was worth it, right? One look at Rach and I knew.

"Guys?! This is mega!!" She was bobbing up and down on her chair. As discreet as she thought she was being, the whole room could tell she was doing bum clenches of excitement. "We can all go after all! I can see The Session?! Witness the fitness of –" her voice got slower as she thought it through "– Brian … in the actual flesh." If there was one thing Rach loved more than The Session, it was their lead singer, Brian. She took a full minute to complete her Brian mind-perving. "Yes! It's time to say hello to the coolest festival cleaning crew Worcester's ever seen!"

Slash, the *only* festival cleaning crew Worcester's ever seen.

Mikey silently high-fived her across the table.

"Exact-o, Rach. I've applied already. Jay and everyone has tickets, so it's my only way of getting in."

Rach and Mikey both looked at Tegan and me, willing us to share their enthusiasm. This is how parents must feel.

"Well…" I looked at Tegan, trying to friend-lepathy what she was thinking, before I committed thoughts to words I couldn't take back. "It's a…"

I stumbled as I tried to bury the thought of wearing a high-vis vest in public to the back of my mind. But Tegan finished off what I'd started.

"It's a *hell yes!*" She was beaming as much as the others. "I'll send our applications tonight. If that's OK with you, Bells?"

It was more than OK. Now I'd dealt with the shock we'd be picking up other people's sandwich leftovers, I was TOTALLY up for it. I'd spent so long getting my head around not going that now I was allowing my brain to even think about getting a ticket, it was the most exciting thing ever.

"Rizzolt." Mikey raised his hands to the roof. "Only gutter is that at the end of the email they banged on about that new band thing Ska's doing. They had another slot up for grabs apparently." He looked at me. "I forwarded it to Adam, but the deadline was last night,

34

and I didn't hear back from him, sooo … guess that was a nonstarter." Mikey looked all blurry-eyed. "Imagine how awesome it would be having The Wet Donald Project playing?! Imagine Luke's face!"

That was the latest name for Adam's band. If there was one thing I loved as much as Tegan and Mikey's romance, it was Mikey and Adam's bromance. But I didn't have time to dwell on it, as Rach had pushed her chair back and, checking Mr Lutas was round the corner annoying some other students, was bundling us up into a hug.

"This is going to be THE best summer EVER!"

"Agreed!" I smiled back, feeling extra lucky to have the best mates in the world. Going to the festival meant this much to Rach, but she'd still offered to give up her ticket to keep us together. Althoughhh…

"Rach – don't *you* apply, you dingbat." It suddenly hit me what she was suggesting. "Or you, Teeg. I can work, then you two can have Rach's tickets." It was the least I could do after all their help with my revision.

Tegan looked stern. "As *if*. You already have a job at GADAC. I'll take this one for the team."

I shook my head. "Nope. No way. *Rubbish* idea."

Tegan brushed my words away with her hand. "Bin that thought!"

I tried not to laugh. "Pick-er a new idea."

Mikey waved his cast between us. "Guys – enough trash talking already?!"

Tegan folded her arms defiantly. I folded mine back, but accidentally punched myself in the boob just as Mr Lutas did a walk-by peer at us. We took the hint and pulled out our textbooks. We could all go – that was the main thing. So, with that amazing thought keeping me going, I got stuck into a solid hour of biology revision. I nailed the entire section on hormones. So much so that when I reached the end of four back-to-back chapters I rewarded myself by borrowing Rach's mag for a quick flick. The quiz about "Which food smells most like your dream boyf" was kind of biology, right? (Also, must urgently check if Adam *does* smell of Hawaiian pizza.)

"That doesn't look much like revision, Ms Fisherrrr?"

I leapt upwards with the shock of my art teacher's booming voice right above me. Mr Lutas. Part art teacher, part stealthy spy.

"Unless your syllabus includes…" He peered at the magazine. "Young men with dubious hairrrcuts messing around on inflatable unicorrrrns."

Shame. That's a syllabus I would have been well up for. I slapped the magazine closed. To reveal giant letters on the cover: "HOW TO MAKE HIM SIZZLE

BETWEEN THE SHEETS". I flipped the magazine fully over. Oh great, the world's biggest sanitary towel ad.

I tried to obscure everything with my arms. It didn't work.

"Please make sure you stay focused, Ms Fisherrr. It's not just you who has put a great deal of time into your porrrrtfolio."

My insides cringed. I wasn't sure what my face was doing, as it was so hot with shame, my nerve endings had temporarily deadened.

"I know – and I *promise* I'm still working on it." I looked him awkwardly in the eye. He made a noise which might have been approval, or just his stomach rumbling.

After school, we all slow-walked home through the warm afternoon to put Operation Persuade My Mum to Let Me Go to RebelRocks into action. As we turned into my street Rach nudged me.

"Look!" She gestured to the alley across the way, pointing at the girls leaning against the wall. "It's *THEM!*"

Rach and I simultaneously smoothed our hair and hoisted our bags up. Rach even managed a quick slick of lip balm. Tegan just looked bemused.

We'd first seen this group of girls in the Easter holidays. Rach called them "Future Us". She was clearly more optimistic about my future than I was. I called them MGC. Major Girl Crush. They always looked iconic. But in a no-effort way, which made them even more iconic.

The three of them had the most amazing style (Blue Hair Girl had three rings on every finger – proved after we zoomed in on one of Rach's surreptitiously taken photos). They looked like a girl band who were too cool to need to sing or dance.

"Hiyer." Blue Hair waved as we walked past.

What. She was waving. At us?!

I checked to make sure there wasn't someone behind us.

"Er, hiii?" the three of us chorused back, accidentally doing a synchronized wave. Could we be more tragic?!

What if they thought we practised it?!

"We haven't practised that!" I shouted before I could stop myself. Yup, they were effortlessly cool, I was effortfully uncool. I couldn't risk speaking again until we'd got to the next corner.

"They're even more increds up close…"

Rach looked all dreamy. "Did you SEE what Choker Girl –" we'd called her that ever since we once saw her wearing a nice choker "– had on her nails?! Some kind of actual mirror! Nail voodoo?!"

But I was distracted by a car parked on my drive that I didn't recognize. I dug my keys out, wondering if the car and the fact the lounge curtains were closed in the middle of the day were related. As I pushed the front door open, I got my answer. And wished I hadn't. Because there was a jaunty wooden "DO NOT DISTURB – UNLESS YOU WANT TO BE DISTURBED!" sign on our lounge door. And most alarming of all, a deep man-chuckle was coming out of the room.

Tegan looked concerned for my welfare.

"I'm sure it's not what you think, Bells."

I stared at the evidence. And tried to stay calm.

"First one up to my room..." Deep breath. "Puts my music on..." Breath. "LOUD."

Mortified, I pelted up the stairs as quickly as I could. Tegan still beat me. She turned the radio on, but instead of distracting me, it blasted out "Strip That Down". I turned it straight off. And flicked on my laptop to concentrate on concentrating on something else.

As Mum was otherwise engaged, I couldn't check with her first, so we filled in our applications to work at RebelRocks. We'd agreed that Tegan and I would both apply so we could do the shifts together. Rach's brother was up for taking her spare ticket, and it meant none of us would have to work on our own. As much as I needed Mum to say yes to this plan, there was no way I was going to knock on that door. So I pressed send and gambled on a yes for now – I'd work on upgrading it to a real-life one later.

Knock knock.

In a move that was almost subconscious reflex, I tabbed my screen to a different window. A spreadsheet from homework in Year Nine that I still had open at all times for moments like these.

"Hiyer, loves!" Mum came into my room.

Tegan and Rach replied "Hello, Ms Fisher!" all innocent, like we hadn't spent the last hour discussing what could possibly be going on behind that closed door.

"Oh, you *know* I don't like Ms Fisher. Call me … Mary, or Mum 2, or…" She did a little shimmy. It was horrifying. "International Woman of Mystery."

But I was not here for her friend-flirting. I needed to get serious. "Mother…"

"Daughter…" She plonked herself beside me on the bed and tucked a rogue bit of hair behind my ear. "How was your exam?"

"Erm." How could I balance the truth and still butter her up for the question I was about to ask? "Well, when

40

I finished, I was kind of happy." No need to tell her that ten minutes later I realized I'd ruined the whole thing.

Mum beamed. "That's my girl!"

Sometimes she spoke to me like she was a farmer and I was a well-turned-out cow.

"So, er…" It was time to turn the tables on to her life. "What's been happening in the lounge?"

The bed wobbled as Rach and Tegan shifted uncomfortably. It'd been years since Dad left, and Mum had never, *ever* had a "man-friend", as she called it, back here. Yes, it was bound to happen one day. But I was hoping that day would be when I was thirty-five and living at least 150 miles away.

I held my breath. Please let her be about to explain it was something totally non-alarming, and a reasonable activity for a mum in the middle of the day.

But no.

She did the worst thing.

She winked.

"Well, it's early days yet … just a bit of fun. But I promise you girls will be the first to know if it becomes anything serious."

Actual. Horror. Scenario.

"Erm, thanks…" Tegan replied to save me having to do it. "…International Woman of Mystery?"

Mum squeezed her knee. "That's my girl!"

So Tegan was a prizewinning cow too. All we needed was Rachel to join in and we'd effectively be a herd. Still, if Mum was in such a good mood (*moo-d*), it was now or never to ask about RebelRocks. I shuffled nearer to her.

"M-uuuummmm…"

"Whaddya want?"

"You know RebelRocks?"

She raised an eyebrow. "The festival I've already said no to on multiple occasions?"

"M-bee."

GULP.

I had to tell her straight.

"Well, if we could hypothetically maybe have an opportunity to sort of go in a way that maybe didn't cost any money, might you potentially think that would be, er … OK?"

Well, straight-ish.

"I think what Bella means is, can she please go litter picking at the festival? In return for a ticket," piped up Rach, with the optimism of someone who didn't really have any experience of parents saying no to stuff.

Mum's face scrunched.

Was she weighing up the ethics of sending her

teenage daughter off unsupervised for a weekend of extreme fun?

Was she wondering what on earth could go wrong with camping overnight and staying away from home?

Was she thinking how much more irresponsible this was than just letting me do extra shifts at GADAC to get the money together?

She sighed. "Will it be recycled?"

Tegan nodded, firmly. For some reason Mum had zoned me out of this decision process.

"Will you have gloves?"

Tegan nodded again.

Mum stood up and faced us all.

"Well, in that case … it's fine!" What?! Was this happening?! "Just you girls remember to eat, sleep and be *safe*."

Luckily sixteen years of these kind of comments meant I had a world-class gag reflex.

I couldn't speak with shock. Mum took this opportunity to pinch my cheek. "Love you, chickadee. But in return, I want to see some more positive thinking when it comes to these exams, OK?"

This time I managed a smile. "Sure."

And I meant it. Because I was totally positive that I knew I was messing them up. But picking up my results was three whole months away. So I decided to put stressing about them on hold and focus on RebelRocks instead.

The countdown to what could be the most fun weekend of my life was on.

THREE

So *this* was what freedom felt like.

Well, freedom give or take the 1.5 more hours of being legally required to be at school, and then six more exams.

Today was the day I'd been counting down to ever since I arrived at St Mary's. The day we could leave it behind.

It was the day my year left for good, and the whole thing had been surreal. Everyone who I'd spent the last five years with had spent it sauntering round the corridors like they owned the place. Like we were untouchable.

It had started off with a special assembly where Mrs Hitchman told everyone how proud she was of us (total lie, but she was high on the fact she'd almost got rid of us). Then we'd had to do a morning of "lessons" which turned out to be the best I'd ever had – teachers dishing out snacks as we handed in books and chatted about our best memories (I still wasn't over when Rach got a genuine crush on the illustration of "Axel" in our German textbook, but her face told me this wasn't the time to revisit it).

Lunch then consisted of zero eating, but the biggest water fight ever. Kind of regretted wearing my Minion-print bra under my now see-through shirt. Despicably bad choice, me.

And this afternoon, instead of sorting out our lockers, Rach and I had been in the sick bay helping Mikey inflate massive helium balloons and stuff them with glitter. We would have been loads quicker if he hadn't kept taking big glugs and singing "Let it gooooooo". I laughed so hard Rach ended up having to tuck me into one of the beds to try and regain normal breathing. Which didn't work, as seconds later Mikey started to write all over the balloons, things like "The time Mrs Hitchman got her skirt caught in her pants #NeverForget" and "The ultimate Maths puzzle? Why does the room always smell of gerbils?" One just said "Moist" – aka the most disturbing word in the English language. He and Jay then gradually let them loose around the corridors. When the teachers tried to burst them with the long window-opening pointy things, they got covered in total glitter bombs. Mrs Hitchman ended up looking like a cross between Dolores Umbridge and a disco ball (although she looked less shocked than our French teacher, who'd popped the only one Mikey had filled with, er, confetti people buy for hen parties).

Rach and I stepped outside the hall for fear of pulling a muscle from over-laughing. Which was good timing, as Tegan had finished helping with the locker checks she'd been roped into and was looking for us.

"Guess what I just saw?!" she said excitedly. Little did she know the superlative sight of Mr Roberts with a quiff full of peens was metres away. "There's a whole pile in the canteen."

Ahh. The yearbook.

The chance to see how misjudged people's ideas of themselves were. And whether they opted for a boring, funny or posey photo for everyone to remember them by (my choice was easy, as the only look I can achieve is "uncomfortable and startled"). We jogged along the corridor, Rach chatting even quicker than normal.

"Man, I've got ALL the feelings today. It's the right old end of an ear, isn't it?"

Tegan chose not to point out it was "era". "I prefer to

see things as starts, rather than ends." This was because she was the most positive person I'd ever met. But I didn't feel as relieved as I thought. Because I couldn't shift the nagging feeling that for me it *was* the end of even more of an ear/era. The era of tackling every day with my best friends. And possibly the start of one where we didn't get to spend all our time together. By the time we got to the pile of yearbooks, I was full-on freaking out about it. Why hadn't I studied harder for these exams? How would I cope with going to college without Tegan and Rachel?

EURGH.

Guess I was just going to have to stop fretting and start revising better.

And try to enjoy this last bit of school with them.

I grabbed a yearbook and flicked through. Rach peered over my shoulder. When it got to my page, she cackled.

"Bells, I *love* that you did that." She nudged Tegan to look. "Trust you to be next level!"

I mean, I didn't think my face was *that* funny, but Tegan burst out in hysterics too. Proper laughing, not just polite laughing.

I looked at where Rach's finger was pointing. At where my name should be. But really wasn't.

"Ermmmmm…" My voice got higher as I panic-scanned the other pages. Why was it only me who had been rebranded?!

"Guys – this *wasn't* me?!" My voice was now squeakier than Mikey's Elsa impression. "Has Luke been hacking stuff again??"

"Bells … what file name did you give your picture?" asked Tegan slowly.

I thought back but couldn't remember.

"You *did* see the instruction about it all being automated and calling your pic your own name, right?"

Ah. A cold wash of realization hit me.

"I *may* have missed that precise detail."

Which is why, in my hands, and in the hands of all the teachers and students I'd ever had lessons with, was a picture of my face – and underneath, instead of saying "Bella Fisher", in big, bold words it said "AWKWARD_BUT_ACCEPTABLE". What a legacy to be remembered by.

"Well, congrats me on being the only one to totally mess that up."

I hit myself over the head with the book. It actually quite hurt.

"Is now a bad time to say thanks for the photos you took of me and Tegan?" asked Rach.

My rage thawed a tad – at least I'd done *one* good job. I'd taken an amazing shot of Tegan mid-cartwheel, and a cool one of Rach where she'd dressed as full Hermione.

"Nah – it's allwaaaays a good time for an ego boost."

"OK. Well, in that case – and this might be the emotion or all the helium I inhaled –" Rach flung her arms around me and Tegan "– but can now also be the time I say how much I love you guys?"

"Luff youff too." Tegan's reply was muffled through Rach's armpit. "Dream team fffor ever."

And as the three of us stood in the school hall where we'd spent so much of our lives, I felt positively overwhelmed that the last five years were coming to an end, and so was getting to see these two every day.

OUCH.

Or did I feel positively whacked in the head? Something had hit me.

I rubbed at my scalp and looked down. Ahhh. The classic condom filled with custard. Lucky for me it hadn't burst. I looked up to see who threw it, and wasn't surprised in the slightest when I saw the culprit. Luke put his hands up to his mouth in fake shock.

"Sorry, didn't realize it was you, or would have explained what one of these was – seeing as you'll never have the chance to use one."

I shook my head at him.

"And you *still* can't give it up, even on the last day."

He blew me a kiss. "Never, Bells."

Sharpie in hand, he sauntered over. "Fit Rach – care to sign my shirt? For old time's sake…"

"Me?" She looked genuinely surprised. "That's nice…" She reached out for the pen. I was shocked, maybe a bit hurt, that she took it. "Just a signature, right?"

"Or your number. Whatever works." Wow, Ska was a really lucky girl. Rach stepped behind Luke, and after looking through some of the other messages, and a large variety of anatomical diagrams, found space to add her name. Luke smirked, pretending to be enjoying Rach making contact with him in all kinds of wrong ways.

Tegan uttered a "Gross", but he was lost laughing at my page in the yearbook.

"*Love* this pic of you, Fishy. Although not sure about the 'acceptable' bit. 'Below average' is more like it."

And right there, in the school hall, the last two years of sly comments, mean digs and making my life a misery finally boiled over inside me. The anger at the few weeks way back when, when Luke had been my boyfriend – before I knew what he was really like. Before he'd told everyone going out with me had just been for a dare.

It was the last day of school. Last day of having to see him. If I couldn't say what I thought now, when could I?

"Ahhh, Puke. I'm going to miss seeing you every day." I smiled. "Which, FYI, in case you're not 100% clear, is me joking." I felt so angry I didn't care that his mates were approaching. They could hear this too. "Once I'm not legally obliged to be in the same building as you, I will be BEYOND happy to never see your annoying, I'm-so-hot-yet-actually-NEWSFLASH-you-aren't-at-all face *ever* again." My brain gasped – was this actually coming out of my mouth? "Even your nose is annoying. And Ska? Who incidentally you go on about 24/7 – YAWN, WE GET IT – has my total sympathy. I can't believe I ever thought you were a decent guy." Time for the killer blow. "Now I can't look at a washing machine without thinking of our first kiss. You've given me kitchen-based PTSD."

Luke full-on spluttered – but before he could launch into a reply, his mates started sniggering. But not at me. At him.

Luke swivelled round. "What???" He spun back round again. "WHAT??!!??"

But he couldn't see what I could. Written on his back in some massive letters: "FACT: MY MUM STILL

52

CALLS ME LUKEY-POOKEY". Rach blew me a kiss. Of *course* she had my back. One of his mates took a photo and showed him the evidence.

I smiled. "Callllmmm down…" I tried to stifle a giggle. "Lukey-Pookey." If he looked cross before, now he was next level.

"HA VERY HA!" But the less funny he found it, the more hysterical it got. Seething with anger, he loomed over Rach.

"Bella's utter loserdom has finally rubbed off on you." He looked her up and down, his lip curled. "Such a waste – you could have been girlfriend material."

This time it was Tegan who couldn't hold back. "Like being your 'girlfriend material' is something anyone with a brain would aspire to?" She shook her head in total disgust. "Grow. The. Hell. Up."

Yaaasss. I gave a triumphant smile.

After all these years, I finally felt like it was game, set AND match to us.

This chapter of my life could now be closed.

"Goodbye, Puke." I waved my hand in a calm goodbye. "Hopefully for ever."

It was time to walk off with my head held high.

But as I put my foot down, I trod right on the custard-filled condom missile. Out of control, my front leg shot forward into almost semi-splits and I skidded full pelt across the shiny floor. Could a leg snap off from stretching too much? My right foot had never been this far away from my left foot in its life.

But the permanent groin damage wasn't the worst bit.

And nor was the wail I was making.

The worst bit was that the force of the slide crashed me straight into the leg of the table with all the yearbooks on. Which promptly fell over, landing straight on to me and the custard missile. Which then burst all over me.

As composed, confident finishes went, this was not ideal.

Luke was laughing so hard he couldn't speak. "Fishy Balls ... is ... covered in pudding gravy. Tell me somebody filmed that?"

I tried not to be momentarily impressed that he'd invented the phrase "pudding gravy".

"And not so quick with that goodbye." He tried to stop laughing. And failed. "'Cos with you messing up your exams, you're on course to end up at Shire Sixth Form with me."

He winked. I'd had NO idea he was going there. This moment couldn't actually get any worse.

Some custard dripped from my hair on to my chin.

Oh, it could. I would cry, if I wasn't petrified of diluting the pudding gravy even more.

Rach and Tegan, my rescue team, ran over.

"Loos. Now!" Tegan whispered. And looping their arms through mine, they dragged me to my feet and marched me away.

Fifteen minutes later, after using every bit of remaining toilet paper to scrub custard off me, I had mixed emotions.

Good news, I smelt kind of delicious.

Bad news, I looked like I'd had a fight with a yoghurt.

But with nothing else for it, it was the look I had to finish my school career on, until 3:50 p.m. finally rolled round and, bang on time, Rach's dad was waiting for us in his car. We plonked our stuff in the boot and piled in. He sniffed the air.

"You didn't tell me you were baking for the last day of term?!" He looked pleased.

Rach shrugged. "Nah, that's just Bella."

I smiled at him in the rear-view mirror. He gave me a nervous smile back, scared to ask questions and risk further details. "Sooo, how was your last day?"

Rach grinned. "Epic."

He peered over his glasses at her shirt, which was full of words and pictures. "Legit hot AF hashtag goals." He looked puzzled. "I know I've just come back from California, but is that even English?!"

Rach swivelled in the front seat and mouthed "Hellllp me".

Tegan stepped up. "Better than mine, Mr Waters." She extended her arm and showed him what Jay had written on her sleeve.

Mr Waters squinted and read it like he was learning a foreign language. "Most likely to ... get ... wified? Up?" He pushed his glasses back up his nose. "Don't tell me. Is that something to do with internet connections?"

Somehow Tegan managed not to laugh. She'd never make anyone feel stupid if she could possible avoid it.

"No – it means *wifey*. As in *wife*. As in, most likely to get married." She rolled her eyes. "As *if* I've spent all these years studying for that to be the one thing I'm most likely to achieve." She tutted. "As if it's even an *achievement*, not just an expectation from society."

Mr Waters' mouth opened as if yet again he wanted to speak but had no idea what to say in case it took him to an even weirder place. "I seeeee. Yes. And Bella? How about you?"

I shrugged and looked out the window. "Me? Oh,

you know… I officially got renamed Awkward but Acceptable and detonated a custard bomb all over myself. Standard."

With a frightened "Of course!" he put the key in the ignition and started the car as quickly as he could, suddenly very interested in the buttons on his dashboard, as if this excused him from all further convo.

Rach turned back round to us. "So when do you think you'll hear back from RebelRocks?"

We'd applied over a week ago, and hadn't heard anything.

Tegan bit her lip. "Sure it'll be any day now…"

I squeezed her hand. "Positive thinking – that's what you always say?"

She nodded, and squeezed back. And as we pulled away from St Mary's for the very last time, Rach turned up the latest Session album almost as loud as it could go, opened the sunroof and stuck her hands out. At the top of our lungs we all sang along. Well, all except her dad, who was shaking his head, but we could tell he was secretly enjoying it.

My foot vibrated. My phone was on the floor, all lit up.

MUM: So proud of my girls all grown up!!!!!

Oh no. Mum had posted about a zillion pictures of me when I was little into our family WhatsApp group. Mum had set it up and called it: "Messages WIthMy Two Daughters. Jo and Bella".

I don't think she realized everyone saw the description. Also, it was slightly alarming she felt the need to clarify who her daughters were.

I scrolled through the images. It was almost impressive Mum had been brave enough to give a real-life child a haircut that was so Lego-like. Lucky there wasn't the internet in those days or social services would have probably intervened.

JO: Soooo cute. Congrats on the last day of school sis 😁

My phone buzzed again. Jo had messaged me direct.

JO: THAT HAIR!!!! 😂😂😂

ME: OI.

ME: You were old enough to have stopped her?!
I was defenceless

JO: You were forehead-less too if those pics are
anything to go by 😊

I rolled my eyes. And clicked back into the family
chat. Why oh why had Jo ever shown Mum how to set
up a group? Just 'cos she was safe at uni. It was the bane
of my life.

ME: Thanks, Mum. Although remember the rule.
BABY PICS ARE NOT FOR FACEBOOK, OK??

MUM: Ofcourse sweetpea!!

Phew.

MUM: I'll definitely remembe r for next time.
IVE already posted these. Everyone lovesthem!
YOugot a thumbs up from Cousin MaTT.

JO: 👍👍👍

A direct message popped up from my sister.

JO: Fit Cousin Matt will never un-see those!!!
Ahahahhhahhahah

I sent her a potato emoji back. When we were annoyed we resorted to vegetables. But Mum hadn't finished.

MUM: Now all U habe to do is try your best with your exams!!! I believer inyou both!! Im a Belieber!!! 😗 😗

She still had no idea what that meant and used it liberally in all the wrong places.

ME: Thanks, Mum.

JO: What do you mean?

See what she did there.

ME: Think she's saying to love yourself. Have real Purpose.

The Bieber references went over Mum's head.

MUM: Yes! But pressure isn't food [Think she meant "good".] for the soul. So RElax andjust do your best Bellington Boot zzzzz

JO: We're all here for you. As Mum says, just do
your best!!! That's what counts xxxx

Jo instantly followed up in our one-on-one messages.

JO: And just try not to dwell on the fact I got 10
A*

I clicked my screen off. It lit up again instantly.

JO: Sorry.

At least she did have *some* remorse.

JO: It was eleven with the one I took a year
early.

This time I shoved my phone away where I couldn't
see it. Which is sometimes what I wished I could do
with my big sister.

"Ooh, Bella." Rach's dad turned the music down.
"Looks like you've got a male visitor?"

He said it in his best oo-er voice. I craned my neck
and got a glimpse of one of my favourite sights.

Post-school Adam. Shirt all untucked. Hair all

messy. Bag slung over his shoulder. Him leaning against my wall. If my eyes could talk they'd say: "Hello, fittieeeeeee." So probably best they couldn't.

I waved through the car window. When he realized it was me his face lit up.

DOES LIFE GET ANY BETTER?

I jumped out of the car and blew kisses to the others as they drove on to Tegan's house.

And then it was quiet.

Just me and Adam.

"So, er, this is a surprise?"

I'd only seen him twice since he'd brought Mumbles to Rachel's.

He smiled. And slid his arm around my waist. Waaaaaah.

"A good one, I hope?"

It was all I could do to nod. I was peak lame.

Adam kissed me gently on the lips. Not long enough to risk Mum banging on the window again (not to tell us to stop but to wave encouragement. Way more disturbing) but long enough to make me feel like the rest of the road had blurred.

"You smell nice…" He put his nose into my neck and breathed in. Errrr, why did someone sniffing you feel so nice?! Must Google if this is normal. "What is it?"

"Custard."

"I see."

"Think it ended up in my hair. Some *definitely* went up my nose."

"Right."

Silence.

"Aaaaanyway." His grin returned. "I can't stay long – I've got band practice, but…" He lifted his fists up and did a tiny on-the-spot dance. "I've got news."

"Oooohhhh!" What could it be? He didn't have an exam today, and didn't finish at his school for another week, so it couldn't be that. And he already had his place at the sixth-form college it fed into, so it wasn't that either. I'd seen him so little recently, it really could be anything.

"In fact no." He stopped jiggling and put his hands on my waist. "Question… Did you hear back about the RebelRocks job?"

I shook my head but couldn't help smile at how he made it sound like I'd applied to be the CEO, not rubbish picker-upper.

"Oh." He looked deflated – he knew how much I wanted to go. "That sucks."

"Oi. Enough about me." Without thinking I poked him in the stomach. If felt hard in a way that made me

63

want to turn to the nearest thing (in that case a shrub) and say, "Phwoar." I focused very hard on not doing that. "NEWS, PLEASE?!"

But his excitement had switched into something less comfortable.

"I dunno…"

"You came all this way – spit it out!" I threw in another opportunistic prod, purely for the benefit of my finger.

"You sure?" I nodded. "We, er…" He shuffled on the spot. "We … won a slot!"

BLINK. WHAT? "A slot?!"

"At RebelRocks. The Wet Donald Project. We won the new band competition."

"OH MY ACTUAL DAYS!!!!" I yelled so loudly five separate pigeons flew up in panic. "That. Is. A. May. Zing!!!!"

I stood staring at him, trying to take it in. Take him in. My amazing, competition-winning, festival-playing boyfriend. I always *knew* they were awesome, but he never believed me. Which was why, although he'd applied when Mikey had emailed, when he hadn't heard back, he'd assumed nothing had come of it. "You realize this makes you basically famous? This time next year you'll probably be playing Wembley."

He laughed gently but it faded quickly as he looked down at his feet. "Is it weird me telling you? I really thought you'd have got your job too so we could celebrate together?"

"As if?! I'm only mad you didn't tell me sooner."

He looked at his watch. "It's only been seven minutes."

I laughed. "Exactly! So, full deets, please…"

He grinned, excited to have full permission to talk about it.

"All I know is —" he was talking extra quick. It was incredibly cute "— they just rang, we get five songs, we play the New Bands Tent, the slot is TBC, I kind of can't believe it's actually happening and I'm about to go tell the others now. And, well … yeeeeeep."

I couldn't be smiling more. But as beyond brilliant as this was, there was something that wasn't good news. I couldn't miss this gig for the world. So if I didn't get a job, I'd have to find another way to sneak in. Could I camouflage myself as a tent?

Adam chewed his lip and looked down, suddenly shy. "I wanted you to be first to know."

My heart bungeed out of my mouth. Head, please save this moment to the Brain-Cloud so I can download it wherever, whenever for the rest of my life.

"Thanks," was all I could manage back.

"No probs, but…" He swung his bag back up on to his shoulder. "I really have to go."

As happy as I was for this impromptu visit, I was painfully aware we didn't have any other plans to see each other. If he wasn't going to suggest anything, I was just going to have to brave it.

"Don't suppose you're free this weekend?"

He shrugged but didn't give me an answer. Time to really put myself out there. "I could swing by yours if you're on revision lockdown?"

This time he did reply. But I wished he hadn't.

"Sorry, Bells – you know how it is." He sounded like an Adam robot. "Got to focus on exams … just for a few more weeks…"

He trailed off. I tried to ignore the fact he was about to go to band practice, which he still seemed to have time for, and said "OK, yeah, totally" with as much enthusiasm as I could fake. He ended up leaving with nothing more than an awkward wave between us – a disappointing alternative to the snog-my-face-off-goodbye I wanted.

But I'd taken the hint. I wouldn't ask any more about meeting up. Or about meeting his parents. He clearly didn't want me there.

EURGH. Why were feelings so hard to work out?

How was I meant to know what my feelings were feeling?

I loved being Adam's girlfriend. Him being my boyfriend. And I was beyond proud of him winning that competition.

So why did I feel like there was something he wasn't telling me?

CHAPTER

FOUR

Life post-school has been everything I've ever dreamt of.

If I dreamt of going to Tesco four times, watching five episodes of *Escape to the Country* (including the Ormskirk episode twice) and learning the names of forty-two more dog breeds. In better news, I did have one day where all three meals were crisps.

I wheeled my chair away from my desk and splatted on to my bed. Thinking was exhausting. My last day at St Mary's was a week and a half ago now, and as I'd promised myself, I'd been putting everything I had into revising for the remaining exams. I must have the equivalent of a brain six-pack right now. I'd even revised how to revise better. German, English language and history had gone better than geography. But I still had biology, chemistry and maths looming. Aka the big ones. I *had* to get As.

"Knock knock!" Mum opened the door, stopping in her tracks as she took in the scene. "Woooweee. It looks like a bomb site in here…" She scanned the mass of paper and highlighters all over the floor. "If that bomb had hit a stationery factory. You OK, darling daughter?"

I grunted, which seemed to sum up my life pretty accurately.

"Here…" She plonked a steaming mug on My bedside table. "This should help."

"Mmm, hot chocolate, thanks, Mum."

She puffed up, all proud. "Even better than that! Nettle, garlic and fermented bean." FACE, DO NOT REACT AT MUM'S DUBIOUS DEFINITION OF "BETTER". "Great to detox and get all those brain chemicals flowing."

Not sure *brain chemicals* was the correct technical term, but I appreciated the effort.

"Thanks." I took a sip. SPLEE. The only brain chemicals it induced were the ones telling me to "never ever drink this again". It tasted of herby mould puddle?! I remained mute until I could risk opening my mouth again. "Don't suppose the post has come?"

Mum shook her head. "Not a sausage."

Oof. We'd expected to hear back from RebelRocks by now, but with no email from them, we'd resorted to checking on the post too. People say no news is good news. But those people obviously forget all the bad news that just comes in late.

I was so glum I accidentally took another sip of tea. My stomach did a clench that was the organ equivalent of a computer error noise.

Mum plonked down next to me.

"Soooooo…" Oh lordy. She had her "I'm going to ask you about something you don't want to talk about" voice on. I braced. This was *so* going to be about boys. "What's the latest with Adam? *Things* going well?"

The way she stressed "things" alarmed me. I couldn't give her an inch. "Yes, *things* are."

But my vaguery did not satisfy the hunger of the Mum information beast. It was feeding time and it wanted fresh meat.

"Met the parents yet?"

I shook my head. She knew I'd been worried about it.

"Sure it'll come…" She flicked a bit of her orange nail varnish off, pretending she had nothing more to say. I knew this move – innocence before building up to a big finish. "Have you … said I love you?"

"Mum?!" This warranted a shout. She knew this was NOT acceptable chat. As if I was going to admit to her that we hadn't – especially when my biggest worry was that Adam never would. She ignored me ignoring her.

"And the *physical* side?"

This time I spat my unswallowed mouthful back into the cup. "Seriously?!"

She looked at me all innocent. But I wasn't being sucked in. One of us had to have reasonable parent-daughter limits. Alarming that it had to be me. "Too far, Mother."

She shrugged, as if I was the one in the wrong. "Well, with all the talk of that festival and Adam now going, I wanted you to know you can always talk to me. No boundaries here." More's the pity. Or I wouldn't have had to endure the show-and-tell she did with Tegan and the 3D results of her "Body Casting at Fifty" class. "A lot can happen in tents… I should know."

If I didn't already feel sick from the puddle drink, the knowing look in her eye sealed the deal. "I've, er, left you a little something in your top drawer." Please let her mean a White Chocolate Kit Kat. She smiled and patted my leg. "Condoms."

Oh, excellent. New top entry for "words I never

71

wanted to hear coming out of my mum's mouth". Didn't she understand that this was literally what the internet was made for? The end of parent-child conversations like this?!

Especially as all Adam and I had ever done was snog. Yet my own mother thought we were doing more than that.

I could never look her in the eye again.

Not to be dramatic, but I was probably going to have to move out.

I deployed emergency tactics: calling her out.

"And what about you, *Mother*? I heard all that giggling the other day."

But something weird happened. Her face sort of … changed colour. Was *she* … self-declared condom-pusher, who once rang into *GMTV* to talk about how she used to make macaroni and cheese using her own breast milk … was she blushing?!

She fiddled with her hair. "Well, you know I've been trying to scrape together money for Give A Dog A Cone?" I nodded, not sure how this was relevant. "I guess I thought a bit of something fun might help take the pressure off. Stop some of the worrying."

I had two options.

Say something supportive about her "fun".

Or drink more puddle drink even though it might actually kill me.

I gulped the puddle. Lots of puddle. So much puddle.

My mum's sex life was not something I wanted to think about. Ever. I didn't even like *thinking* those two words in the same sentence. Even in the same dictionary was too near.

BING-BONG.

Saved by the bell. Beyond relieved for the interruption, I ran downstairs, Mumbles leaping around my feet like she thought it might be a guest for her. I flung the door open to discover Tegan in her gymnastics gear, fresh from a training session.

I hugged her, the tails on my giant horse slippers swishing as I moved, driving Mumbles wild with excitement.

"Well, you look like a competent adult making me doubt every life choice I ever made."

"Hardly." She punched me lightly in the arm. "So, are we off then?"

I mentally scanned what I was wearing. Tracksuit bottoms. Jo's old *When I Grow Up I Want to Be Beyoncé* T-shirt. Zero make-up. Hair balanced on head. Potentially some crisp residue in the roots. Could the public see this?!

And then I thought of Mum, waiting on my bed, poised to unleash more excruciating chat.

Yup – the public was ready.

I kicked my slippers off and pulled on my Converse.

"Sozzy for my state. Wasn't planning on you being early."

We'd arranged our extended revision break/dog walk/Adam spot for one p.m. Rach couldn't come as she had been taken to a spa by her mum as another treat for revising so hard.

"And by *early* you mean…" Tegan glanced up at our hallway clock. It was one p.m. On the dot.

"I clearly mean on time." I tried to clip on Mumbles' lead but it was hard because she was bouncing with excitement – so much so that one of her large dribble strands splatted against the hall wall with an actual thud. She gave me a fleeting innocent look before fleeing the scene of the crime – running slap bang into the legs of the postwoman who looked minus impressed.

"Erm." I ran after Mumbles, lead in hand. "Sorry about that."

The postwoman shoved the post into my hand without saying a word. Well, not with her mouth. With her face she said, "I sometimes consider whether to sacrifice my own financial security just so I can move me and my family far, far away from you, your saliva-tastic dog, and your mum, who often forgets to wear an adequate amount of clothing when she opens the door."

As she walked off, I looked at Tegan. "Think I've made a real friend there…" But wait. I looked at the pile in my hand. There was an envelope addressed to me. And it had the RebelRocks logo on.

GULP.

This was too big for one person to deal with. Well, if that person was me. Tegan was more than capable, so I passed it to her. Calmly, she ripped it open and started reading, making noises like "Uh-huh", "Oh, OK", and "I see".

"Soooo…" She dropped her shoulders. "It's … it's not good news, Bells."

But it was too late. I was already smiling. From my insides out. Because if I knew one thing, it was when Tegan was lying.

Grinning with her whole face, she grabbed me. "WE'RE GOING!!!!"

"We're?" I asked nervously. This was just *my* letter.

She turned it so I could read. "Uh-huh! It has my name as your tent buddy?! We *both* got picked!!!"

I would have told her how amazing this was if I

wasn't too busy squeaking and jumping round in a circle with her.

My first festival. Our first festival.

It was really happening.

Immediately, we FaceTimed Rach. When we told her our news, she yelled "yes" so hard she cracked the clay mask on her face. We then had one of those conversations where there's too much to say, and not enough time, so everyone speaks at once with questions that never get answered, yet it still feels productive.

Do we have enough clothes to take?

Are Portaloos really that bad?

Does anyone have a tent?

Is trench foot a real thing?

It was intense. In-tents. I couldn't wait to tell Adam.

ME: GUESSSSSSSS WHHHHAAAATTTTTT?

He messaged straight back.

AARD: What what what what what what what what?

Along with a GIF of Professor Brian Cox doing a weirdly sassy eyebrow raise.

ME: 1 – that's AMAZING.

ME: 2...

Pause.

ME: ...

More dramatic pause.

ME: WE'RE COMING TO SEE YOU PLAY AT
REBELROCKS!!!!!!!

Then:

ME: HASHTAG ALL THE CELEBRATION
EMOJIS!!!

And then:

ME: 🎉👏🎉⛺🍾🎉🎏🎉

We both loved a good celebratory carp windsock
emoji, but only after I sent it did I notice I'd used a
Christmas tree instead of a hands up. I still felt it worked

though. But by the time Tegan and I set off for our now majorly delayed walk, all I'd got back was a thumbs up.

"Oi." Tegan put her arm around me. "I know what that face means. It means you're thinking too much about something. So…" She pushed her lips together. "Less fretting about what Adam may or may not be thinking, OK?"

"What about thinking about what my mum may or may not be thinking about me and Adam?"

"Banned too. Only thing allowed is more thinking about all the stuff we need to get ready for the festival."

So, taking her advice, we got right back into plotting RebelRocks. And soon we'd got our priorities in order. Priority one? Deprioritizing revision and getting all three of us together ASAP.

CHAPTER

FIVE

The spa was meant to have made Rach all chilled and Zen, but that evening she literally galloped across the playing field to meet Tegan and me – the entire twenty-second journey yelling something that sounded like "HELLOOOREBBELLLROOCCKKKK-EEERRRSSS." The over-60s cricket team that were mid-game looked genuinely concerned.

"Good eve, friends!" She dumped her massive bag off her shoulder, breathless. "Or should I say, co-festivalgoers!!" She did a celebratory wiggle, arms in the air. I whooped back.

She sat cross-legged on the grass, opened her bag and unfolded a massive bit of blank paper on to the bench.

"First things first." Rach passed us each a biro. "Which band's playing where and when." She got out her iPad. "My do or die is … The Session."

As if she needed to remind us.

Tegan opened her phone and made three lists: Friday, Saturday and Sunday. Underneath Sunday she wrote *The Session*. Yes.

Things I loved:

1) Making lists.

I peered at the long, upside-down grid of band names and panellists on Rach's screen.

"Mine is anyone who doesn't start before midday."

Tegan elbowed me in the ribs, knowing exactly what I was getting at. On further reading about our litter picking, we'd found out when our shifts were. One was a day before it started on Thursday, and the other three were the following days all starting at FIVE A.M., aka five o'clock in the Actual Morning.

"Thing is, with early starts…" Tegan was still trying to convince us both that this was going to be OK. "We can see all the bands."

"But will it count if we're having a standing snooze while they're playing?"

"We will not be doing ANY snoozing, my friends – well, except between the hours of 1 and 4.46 a.m., when we can deploy earplugs to the max." Rach said it with a knowing look at Tegan, who sometimes used them when it got too late at a sleepover. Because Rach wasn't working, she had major guilt over her free ticket, so was insisting on getting up and making us breakfast while we were doing our shifts. It all depended on being able to wangle camping in the same area though.

"Shall I check if any more line-up TBCs have been C'ed?" We nodded, and Rach wedged herself between us on the bench so we could all see as she Googled.

"There are three slots left, right?" I asked even though I knew the answer. "Am crossing everything that Velvet Badger are going to be one of them. Or The Helicans… Ooooh." A thought hit me. "Maybe they'll have announced Wet Donald's time too?!"

But when the search results for "latest RebelRocks announcement" came up, our faces all fell.

Our amazing festival had hit the headlines for all the wrong reasons.

And from her face, Rachel was taking it the worst. Stunned, she clinked the link.

Fancy getting your hands on merch for The Session's upcoming "It's Only Words" sell-out tour? All you'll need is £25 and zero self-respect.

For a band who preach that their fans always come first, their range of clothing has got some people raising their eyebrows. Brian was pictured rolling out of a female friend's hotel room this morning in what looked like one of their T-shirts, the words:

Never Ask. Never Apologize.

It's Only Words™

splashed across his chest. Hours later the full range made its debut in their online store, instantly crashing the site. Was that because of demand? Or disbelief?

With two ranges – one for guys and one for girls – take a look and see for yourself...

Rach shook her head, shocked. "The media are *always* after them ... bet it's not even that bad. Also—" She squinted at the photo of Brian, all scruffy hair and tattoos. "*Not the point* but he looks fit as."

I would have agreed if I hadn't already seen Tegan's judgy face. But Rach did have a point; gossip columns loved nothing more than speculating which new model Brian had hooked up with – and left heartbroken. Kind of the band's own fault, when their debut single had broken the internet for highest number of girls in bikinis in one video. They'd said it was "a celebration of empowerment of over 1,200 women". The internet wasn't so sure – lots of people reckoned that some of the women could have easily been celebrated while wearing actual clothes. Rach had given them the benefit of the doubt and been on one side. Tegan had been on the other. I'd tried to keep the peace.

And now I had a horrible feeling we were hurtling back to that very same place. We clicked through the gallery of the products they'd just put on sale. With a sinking heart, the pictures confirmed my fears. The new Session merchandise was item after item covered in sexist slogans that seemed like a bad joke gone wrong.

"So let me get this straight." Tegan was flicking back and forth through the pictures, as if looking for clues. "They think it's funny to make a guy's top that says 'Keep Calm and Date Models' but the girl's one says 'Property of The Session' right across the front?" She looked physically revolted.

I didn't understand. Surely no one would buy stuff like this? Could it be an elaborate joke that none of us were getting? There were loads of comments underneath of people finding them hilarious.

Rach shook her head as if she couldn't – or didn't want to – believe what we were seeing. She grabbed her iPad back. "We *must* be missing something…"

But as she clicked, all she found were more problems.

"Are you kidding me?!" Tegan was fuming. "Girls get 'Rockstar Girlfriend in Training' hoodies, but guys get 'Boys Will Be Boys … And Boys in Bands Will Be Worse!'" She was so outraged she kicked the ground. "Who do they think they are?!"

Despite it being a warm summer's evening the whole atmosphere felt frosty. With each picture Tegan was getting more furious but Rach was getting more heartbroken. She loved them, and all signs were pointing to the fact they'd let her down, big style.

Joke or not, I hated The Session for doing this.

"There *has* to be more to it." Rachel's voice was wobbly. "Here…" She opened up Brian's Twitter. "He *must* have said something. There must be an explanation. No one loves the Sessionites more than him. He doesn't think of his female fans like that."

Sessionites was the name of their fandom. Rach had been a proud part of it since they'd started. She knew her stuff because, like she predicted, Brian *had* said something. An hour earlier he'd uploaded a video, which already had over 12K RTs and 32K likes. Relieved, Rach clicked play.

"Oh, hi, guys." Brian was topless. And in bed. "Guess where I am?" He pulled a long section of pink, curly hair from off screen across his pillow and wound it through his fingers, laughing. "Or should I say, guess *who* I'm with?" A soft "Oi" came off camera and the hair disappeared. The rustling sound of someone getting out of bed could be heard. "Just wanted to let you know that although tickets for the It's Only Words tour went quicker than a bottle of Jack Daniels on our tour bus, later today you can get your pre-orders in for the merch. Have you seen it? It's proper funny stuff. All credit to moi. And let me tell you –" he glanced off camera "– this sexy *you know what* is already wearing it and she looks f-iiiiine… So –" he pointed down "– link below to get yours. And ladies? Don't forget to send us pics of you wearing it all. Hashtag 'em #ASessionPossession. And 'member. If people can't take a joke, tell them – it's All. Only. Words." And with that he blew a kiss at the camera and leant out of shot.

Rachel opened her mouth but before she could say a word, one final sound rang out.

The distinct thwack of Brian very definitely slapping a bum. And from the breathy cry of "Brian?!" I guessed it belonged to the girl in the background.

Rach flicked off the power. After a moment's silence she swallowed and spoke quietly. "Do you think there's *any* way it's not as bad as it seems?" But she already knew the answer. I might as well be the one to confirm it.

"From what we've just seen? It's really not OK." If we were hoping Brian was going to say it was a joke, what we'd actually got was him making us think he was even more of a sexist creep that we'd thought.

"Y-huh." Tegan slow nodded. "*So* far from OK."

It all felt so wrong. We'd just been working out which talks we were going to see at RebelRocks and had picked ones from people who were bold and ballsy and kick-ass. The kind who weren't afraid to shout loudly and proudly about what they cared about. About equality. People who called out idiots for being sexist, or for not treating everyone with the same respect. And now it seemed the headliners of the whole festival were a band who couldn't even respect their own fans enough to treat them as equal.

It sucked. They sucked.

Tegan broke the silence. "Sorry. But we have to do something, guys. HAVE TO."

But what?

Rach didn't say anything and leant forward to stroke Mumbles. She didn't even react as Tegan whispered "Sorry, Rach" as she crossed a line through where she'd earlier written "The Session". Tegan's gentle face had hardened into a look of grim determination. "OK ... the festival's called RebelRocks, right? So ... don't we owe it to the festival to stand up for what we believe in?"

I nodded, although wasn't sure quite what I was agreeing to. Was she seriously about to suggest the three of us could somehow take on the most popular band playing at RebelRocks?

The same band that was the very reason most people had bought tickets?

A band that had a fandom that regularly dragged people on the internet?

Who up until five minutes ago had been Rachel's hands-down favourite?

Tegan stood up.

"Here's what we're going to do." She folded her arms, and spoke calmly and confidently. "We're going to get The Session to realize what they're doing is gross."

Well, us pulling off what a zillion journalists had already tried and failed to do sounded 0% doable. She dropped her voice. "Rach, does that sound OK?"

Rach still looked in shock but managed a nod. With her blessing, Tegan carried on. "And we're going to get them to stop selling that ridiculous stuff." It sounded good – but near impossible. "And if they don't, we're going to get them kicked off the RebelRocks line-up."

Oh good. The *actual* impossible.

This was definitely the most ridiculous idea Tegan ever had.

But before I could stop them, three words emerged from my mouth.

"Count me in."

CHAPTER

SIX

AARD: SORRY. Can't make it on Tuesday. ☹
How about I get us an appropriate amount of
pick n mix (DEFINITION: AN ENTIRE BUCKET
OF) and a film for the week after?

Argh. I flopped down on to my bed as my stomach fled
on a misery mini-break to my knees.

Another plan I'd suggested to Adam. Another "no
can do". It was making the solitude of revising even more
painful. At least this time tomorrow my maths exam
would be over. My last one. They'd saved the biggest
till last – it was my deal-breaker subject for getting into
college, and I had to nail it.

And after that, we were off to RebelRocks.

Another message came through from Adam. Erk.

More bad news? I read it through half-open eyes, as if a slight blur could soften the impact on my emotions.

AARD: Your mum might let us watch it in your room again? Winky face.

My stomach repacked its travel bag and whizzed up to my head, down to my toes then ran out of energy somewhere in my middleish.

As *if* Adam could casually write those words?! Acknowledge in pixels that last time we watched a film in my room, we absolutely didn't. It was a two-hour snogfest of such epic proportions I had to apply lip balm every eleven minutes for the next two days to stop them peeling off.

IT'D BEEN BLISSFUL (the snogging, not the face-shredding near kiss-tastrophe). And when Mum asked what I'd thought of the film (*Beauty and the Beast*) I'd got away with "beautiful … and beasty?"

BLEURGH. Why did those heady days of full-on snogging feel like years ago?

All I seemed to get from Adam now was promises to do stuff another time.

For the fifth time that day, I scanned my memory for

more *does-my-boyf-definitely-still-like-me* evidence, but was stopped in my tracks as he sent me a picture of his sad face.

I *think* he wanted me to see he was disappointed too. But all I felt was morally questionable at how I could find someone's sad face so fit.

I couldn't keep up with myself. It was like every interaction I had with him (real, typed, whatever) made me feel even more out of control of my own feelings.

Is this what relationships are like? Months worrying someone doesn't like you, then as soon as you get together you spend the whole time stressing they're going off you? How is that enjoyable?!

GAH. Maybe I should just be celibate for the rest of my life.

I looked back at the picture of his sad face.

Or not.

I touched up my smudged eyeliner and sent him a photo of me giving a "no worries" thumbs up back. I wanted him to think I was busy and achieving loads, so spent the next thirty minutes arranging my revision notes and reapplying my gold nail varnish so I could casually hold my best pen in shot for a perfectly posed (to not look at all posed) Insta Story pic just in case he was checking.

I was meant to be phone detoxing today. The last few days I'd got sucked into endlessly refreshing the #TeachTheSessionALesson hashtag that Tegan had started the day of the merch scandal. Loads of people were on our side. And seeing them @ the band demanding an apology or tagging the RebelRocks organizers to ask them to take them off the bill was amazing. Buuuut, I wished there weren't an equal number of people totally slating what we were doing. Saying we couldn't take a joke. Making assumptions about us: saying we had nothing better to do with our time. That we must be jealous. Or from another fandom.

Or lonely. Or ugly.

Why were people so mean on the internet? Why does caring about something have anything to do with what your face looks like?

The worst stuff had come from an account called @HeyItsTheSessionHQ. They'd started their own rival hashtag #TeachTheSessionHatersALesson, and now there were pages and pages of posts of why we were bitter, desperate losers who didn't understand humour. Some of the stuff they wrote was so full-on, I was mega grateful Rach had persuaded Tegan to set up a general account to post everything, so they didn't have our personal ones.

Argh. Why had life chosen the most important time of my school life to throw everything at me? I dropped my phone on the bed, exhausted by everything. Exams. Adam. Now this.

But as I lay there, things got worse. An alarmingly familiar noise wafted up and out of the lounge. My mum giggling. And worse, the sound of a man voice doing the same. *Oh please no?!*

Their laughing was no laughing matter. I tiptoed to the top of the stairs. The "DO NOT DISTURB" sign was back up on the lounge door. My "I AM DISTURBED" feeling returned.

There was only one thing for it – flee. I packed my bag and dashed out to go to Tegan's. On the way I messaged Jo. She'd already broken up for uni so was doing loads of shifts at her garden centre job, which she hated.

ME: MUM IS BEING GROSS AND WEIRD AND I'M KIND OF SCARED TO FIND OUT MORE.
Do you know what's going on?

JO: All I know is I don't want to know.

"..." appeared. I waited.

JO: Sure you're not overreacting?

Argh. My sister could wind me up even from hundreds of miles away.

ME: OVERREACTING? HOW DARE YOU?! I
DON'T OVERREACT?!!!!!!

JO: Sure

ME: I hate you.

JO: Love you too. See you soon 👻

I'd reached Tegan's so didn't bother replying. Her house looked like mine – simple, brown, two windows at the bottom, two at the top, the kind you draw when you're a child. It was only Rach who had the mansion. Tegan had a younger brother and sister, so her house was a constant chaotic battle of them playing up, trying – and failing – to shift the blame on to each other, and their parents trying to tell them off. Tegan did her best to stay out of it, escaping to one of ours whenever she could. But today the rest of her family were out at some birthday party at a ball-pit park (why do little kids have the coolest birthdays when they have all the fun *every* day of the year?!) so it was just us.

"BELLLLLSSSSSS." She pulled the door open. "Come on in…" She pointed at the lounge. "Rach's already here."

I headed in to find a tidy pile of Tegan's books and notes lying next to Rach, who was sprawled out on the floor, face up, with a maths textbook open. Which would be more promising if it wasn't flat across her face.

"Bellsss. Thank cod you're here." She threw the book off her face. "My brain is on the verge of a walkout."

I plopped down on to a sofa, Tegan doing the same on the one opposite. I nudged Rach with my foot. "What does Bear Grylls always say? Positivity, positivity, positivity."

"But he only has to drink his own wee and wander around forests. I'd much rather do that than…" She rolled over and peered at a paragraph in the book she'd just thrown down. *"Translate simple situations or procedures into algebraic expressions or formulae."*

Tegan looked up from her notes.

"But he *is* called Bear."

I laughed and threw a packet of crisps at Rach, and one at Tegan. My peace offering for being ever so slightly late.

I was relieved there wasn't a weird atmosphere between them. Between us. I'd been a bit worried, as we hadn't seen each other since the bench night, and after watching the Brian vid, Rach had been worryingly quiet in our group. The exact opposite of Tegan.

"So, guys." I spoke above the rustle of Rach diving straight into the Skips. "I had a *really* busy morning."

"Yeah – we saw your story. That nail varnish must have taken forevs."

"Well, yes. Maybe." Damn them seeing straight through my attempt at fooling the world. "And maaaaybe I'm kind of ever so slightly behind on my revision schedule." It was an A3 multi-coloured planner of dreams I'd made at the start of study leave – but it had taken so long to make that by the time I'd finished I was already one day behind the schedule that was on it. "Sooooo." I held my hands out like weighing scales. "Opinion. The rest of the afternoon, whaddaIdo? Rush through geometry AND fractions? Or pick one and do it properly."

"Hmmmm." Tegan looked perplexed. "How well do you know fractions?"

"One eighth." I pulled my mouth into a sort of flat smile. "Which is half of a quarter, or two sixteenths … right?"

"And how well do you know geometry?"

"Inside angles of a triangle add up to 180°?"

Tegan shook her head. "That sounded too much like a question. So I'd say geometry. Rach?"

Rach nodded in agreement. "Totally. Fractions are easy. Just numbers with lines between them."

Well, that was one way of looking at them.

"Geometry it is." I tried to sound enthusiastic. "It's going to be SO useful for all those rhomboids I never have to draw."

Note to self: must look up what a rhomboid actually is before tomorrow.

But Tegan wasn't smiling. She had her hand to her forehead. Something was wrong.

"Teeg?"

"Look what just got posted." She dropped to her knees and shuffled across the carpet towards us, phone in hand. "Which, incidentally, SUCKS."

It was the search results for #TeachTheSessionALesson. The top post was a tweet from RebelRocks of a picture of their official statement.

We have seen the response to The Session's latest merchandise and subsequent social media campaign regarding their headline slot at RebelRocks.

Having spoken with the band their official comment is that their new tour range is "meant to serve as the ultimate reminder that people should always feel able to express themselves and to use their voice in whatever way they see fit. It's Only Words and we should use them how we want. Freedom of speech is the backbone of music, festivals and especially RebelRocks."

As organizers we agree. We are responsible for providing the best event for music fans, and with that in mind, are very much looking forward to hosting The Session for their first festival appearance of the year – and selling the merchandise as advertised. In doing so, we know we are keeping thousands of fans happy.

Here's to an excellent weekend – less than six days to go until kick-off!

For latest news please check out @WeAreRebelRocks

Whoa. In a couple of sentences the festival had brushed off ALL our effort. All those tweets and comments from hundreds of people around the world.

They'd just bought what The Session had said.

I felt like I'd been kicked in the stomach by a horse. A sexist horse.

"SERIOUSLY?? THAT'S SERIOUSLY IT?!" Tegan was at that rage level where you're so cross you sound like you're shouting even though your voice isn't any louder.

Rachel was quiet, staring at the statement.

"Seems so, Teeg." I felt stuck between them again. "Totally lame. Lamey McLame-ington."

"Sorry to ask, but do you think…" Rach sat up. She sounded nervous. "That maybe they have a point?" She darted her eyes between me and Tegan as if trying to suss out whether she was about to overstep some imaginary line. "That they're trying to show people you should be brave enough to say what you want? But we're putting all this time into trying to censor them?"

She sounded so un-Rach. And I knew why. It was a direct quote from one of the @HeyItsTheSessionHQ's criticisms of us. So, she'd been reading them too.

Tegan sat back down. I knew she didn't agree. She was totally up for a fight with The Session but at the same time was cautious about arguing with her best friend. She looked at me for help.

"Erm." I stabbed around in the brain-dark trying to find something to say that felt right. For the first time in my life I felt nervous around them. Well, this was weird. "Just, er, because they're a great band –" yes, start positive "– doesn't make them good people. And if they're all about free speech, then aren't we allowed to stand up for what we believe too? Which is not making their female fans feel like second-class citizens?"

"But…" Rach looked a bit tearful. "That's just it. You don't know them like I do. They love their fans. They're on our side."

As I suspected, despite Rach going along with Tegan and me the other day, her heart wasn't really in it. I felt like we were forcing her. As wrong as I thought she was, should we just agree to disagree?

"Erm, Rach." Tegan finally spoke up. "I've got something which you're not going to like. I, er, saw it a few weeks back." She looked at the floor. "I think maybe it's why I've been so unconvinced that they really are all about supporting their fans."

Rach looked at me as if I could explain. I couldn't. It was news to me too.

"What is it?" she asked, sounding more nervous than ever.

"I … I can't really explain. You need to see it. Unless you don't want to. It's…" Tegan looked uncomfortable. "It's some footage that was leaked of that shopping centre thing you went to."

The colour drained from Rach's face. "Wavy Crowd Girl one?"

Whoa. Tegan had gone *there*?! This must be serious.

"You don't have to see. Your call. But if you want to, it might, well, I dunno. Change the way you feel about them."

There was a pause before Rach answered.

"Show me."

Watching the original Wavy Crowd Girl clip with Rach had been hard enough – the comments section filling up with people taking the mick out of her.

But *this*? It was clear from the first few seconds, it was way worse.

It was a couple of minutes of secret filming that had been leaked to a blog, allegedly by one of their support acts, who'd had enough of the way The Session behaved backstage.

Footage of Brian, Q, Raf and Matt on their tour bus, drinking beer and flicking through fan footage on the internet. It was like a sport to them – scrolling through to hunt out the ones they could laugh at.

Some people got their dress sense pulled apart. Others got laughed at for camping outside a venue. One guy they nicknamed Mushroom Head because of his hairstyle (in fairness, it was very mushroom-like, but maybe that was the look he was going for?). But one person they'd really let rip on was Crazy Hand Girl. Or as we knew her, Wavy Crowd Girl.

Rach.

She blinked back tears as the camera zoomed in on her smiling face as Q, the drummer, burst out laughing and compared her to a "moron dolphin who can't stop flapping its dumb flippers".

"I think we've seen enough." Tegan clicked pause, not wanting to upset Rach even more. But Rach pushed her hand away. "No. I want to see the full thing."

She pressed play but clamped her hand straight to her mouth as Brian then looked her up and down, smirking, "But it's the kind of dolphin I definitely should have taken back after the gig. Should have told someone to go fetch her." He then licked his lips before they all laughed together at Rach's happy face waving away. On stage, the band were all happy gestures back and smiling at their fans. In real life they talked about them as objects, not caring that it was because of people like Rach and Mushroom Head that they even had a career.

She was shocked.

So was I.

Tegan just looked more determined than ever.

It was proof The Session had no respect for anyone.

And when it finally ended the first one to speak was Rach.

"Two things." She stood up and looked at Tegan. "One, thanks. I *needed* to see that. And two…" She pointed at the screen, paused on the smug faces of The Session. "This. Is. War."

The two of them were a force to be reckoned with – but I still had no clue how the three of us could actually make any difference.

"So now the organizers have gone down the 'don't blame us, we're keeping thousands of fans happy' route, anyone got any suggestions of what to do next?"

Tegan's eyes lit up. "That's it, Bells!"

"What is?"

"You're a genius!" She shook my shoulders with excitement.

"Er – *how* exactly am I a genius?" (Exactly the

kind of question an actual genius would never have to ask.)

"Because *that's* what the organizers are bothered about. Keeping thousands of fans happy…" Tegan was waving her hands with excitement.

"Sooooo…?" I asked, hoping I wasn't being too slow.

"So that's what we have to do next. Convince the festival that even more people will be unhappy if they DO play!"

But how? I felt like it should be so obvious I couldn't really ask.

Luckily Rach didn't feel the same, and asked just that.

Tegan pulled her pen lid off and scrawled on a piece of paper.

PLAN: GET THOUSANDS OF SIGNATURES ON A #STOPTHESESSION PETITION.

Ahhh. A petition. That's what she meant. And it made sense. So soon the three of us were hurling ideas around about how to make it happen. First thing we needed was a proper social media campaign – not just a hashtag.

Tegan paused in her note-taking.

"Bells – long shot, but could you get Jo on the case to make us something official? Logos or animations or something?"

To say my sister was ever in the mood for helping me out was a long shot. As in, a shot so long it would probably lap round the world and be catchable by the original thrower. But I was down to try.

"Sure – maybe some posts for Instagram, something to set up a site with?"

"Which I can do," Rach jumped in. She'd just finished making a website for her mum's new vintage tea-set hire business. "I'll set up it now actually. Will only take me a minute and we can update it with some of Bells' photos as we go."

Tegan jotted it down. "And I'll register some more @StopTheSession accounts. Message some official people from somewhere official." She looked like she was processing a million ideas. "If we can *really* get thousands of signatures they'll HAVE TO listen. And respond." She looked up, determination all over her face. This was the Tegan I loved best. Pure thunder, all wrapped up in polite, measured calm, just like when she competed in her gymnastics. "Although…" She caught sight of the time on her TV box. "Look, we should get on with our revision. Just till tomorrow." She looked a bit guilty, remembering how important this last exam was. Especially to me. As fired up as we all were, we HAD to prioritize tomorrow's exam. So after messaging Jo, I pulled out my geometry textbook. But before I'd even read through the first paragraph about complementary angles (I could only hope they were the ones that said nice things about you), I'd got a reply.

JO: COUNT ME IN. I can't believe they're letting them get away with it! Scumbags. Lemme know what you want.

I fired back a massive, genuine thanks, and a list of everything we'd need. She replied with a 🖕

Jo studying graphic design was one of the greatest things that had happened to me. Mainly 'cos it meant she left home. But also because since she'd started she'd been my go-to designer – my profile pics had never looked so good. But just as I was getting dangerously close to thinking she might actually be OK, she messaged again.

JO: Btw, don't think this means that I don't think you're really annoying.

JO: I just really like Tegan and Rach and hate The Session.

I sent back the emergency picture I kept of Jo when she was twelve. She had a terrible fringe, and had just been horse riding. The saddle had given her a big dark patch on her pale trousers, making it look like she'd wet herself, but she had no idea and was grinning gormlessly. I pulled this beautiful image out whenever she got too annoying, just to remind her I still had some element of power in this relationship.

But despite receiving the normal flurry of abuse back in return, I was happy. Although the reason was gross, I loved being on a mission with my friends. And as I read my revision notes it turned out some of the stuff I'd learnt had miraculously stuck in my brain – it had just been hiding behind layers of song lyrics and dubious dog facts (the Besenji dog doesn't bark! It yodels!) But soon it was time to go home, as I'd promised Mum I'd be back for dinner. And as we tucked into a jacket potato with chips, I told her all about what we were up to.

"Oh, Bells. I'm SO proud of you." She beamed at me. "It sounds just like when me and my college friends had to protest about the road widening in our local forest. We really stuck it to them."

I grinned back. It *was* kind of cool when she put it like that.

"Like mother, like daughter, hey?"

She smiled. "Sure is. I found protesting naked so raw yet SO powerful!"

Or not. I prodded at my potato, trying not to let that thought linger. "Saw you had a visitor again earlier?"

Thanks, brain, for latching on to "disturbing topics" as this evening's theme.

"You saw right." She looked a bit sad. "It was all over very quickly though. Not sure I'll see him again now."

She looked fed up. And when push came to shove, I'd much rather Mum was happy than I was spared a few alarming man-noises from downstairs.

"Don't worry, Mum – just remember what you always say to me … everything happens for a reason." And with one generic motivational quote her smile returned.

We spent the rest of the meal chatting about a new shop space she might have found for Give A Dog A Cone. Being spared the washing-up, I headed upstairs to get back to my revision. When half eleven rolled around I decided to call it quits. I'd done a mega-stint only stopping when Jo's awesome artwork came through. She'd done an amazing job. Tegan and Rach were absolutely buzzing. I guess sometimes having a sister could be cool. Although I would never, ever say that to Jo.

But when I got into bed, desperate to get as much sleep as possible, I couldn't switch off. My mind was racing and my body felt full of nerves.

Was it the exam tomorrow? I couldn't mess it up.

Or was it taking on The Session? Could we really do it? If people found out we were behind it we could be absolute heroes – or completely hated.

What if their fans came after us?! What if the band themselves did?!

Argh. Why was it so hard to know what doing the right thing was?

If this was the right thing, why did I feel so unsure?

And why hadn't Adam replied to me asking how his rehearsal was? Or even liked my picture of Mumbles asleep with her tongue out? Even as an impartial viewer, it was a classic.

When I eventually fell asleep, I got stuck in a nightmare of chasing Luke around school to ask him to sign the petition, only for him to answer in quadratic equations. When I woke in a panicked sweat, it was seconds away from my alarm going off and there was a message on my phone.

Adam had replied.

Forcing light into my sleepy eyes, I opened it and read.

And what it said made me spring straight upright.

Forget the biggest exam of my life.

Twenty words meant it was now nothing compared to the fresh terror that had just been unleashed.

CHAPTER

SEVEN

The message was from late last night but I'd had my phone on silent and had missed it.

It had started strong.

AARD: Hey Beefy.

Adam's nickname for me. It may appear bovine, but had started off as my initials, BF, which morphed into beef, and now I was Beefy. At first, I wasn't sure how I felt about it but:

a) I loved that he had a nickname for me
b) I was happy to have something in common with his favourite flavour of Monster Munch.

AARD: Practice was OK. So much to do!
Wanted to say good luck for tmorrow. Am
thinking of you (zero change there!).

Obvs I screengrabbed this and saved to my "FOR
BELLA'S EYES ONLY" folder.
But… Well, then it took a turn.

AARD: Don't suppose you fancy coming round
for dinner after? Mum's making veggie lasagne
and it has your name on it.

Dinner tomorrow?! DINNER TOMORROW?!

AARD: I mean, your name's not exactly *on* the
lasagne but if that'll help convince you to say
yes, I'm sure it could be arranged.

Then a couple more:

AARD: Soz I didn't ask earlier. My brain's all
over the place.

AARD: I totally get you might have other plans.
So no pressure. But also. YOU KNOW I WOULD

LIKE IT REALLY LOADS VERY MUCH LOTS.

And then a final one.

AARD: LEMME KNOW IN THE MORNING COS YOU'RE PROBABLY ASLEEP DREAMING OF PYTHAGORUS (not in that way) (I hope) [maths emojis]

Erm. What?! I'd spent five minutes reading and rereading them, checking I was actually awake and this wasn't one of those half-awake-sleep dreams where you think you're on a sinking ship that's repeatedly honking, only to realize the honking was your actual alarm, and school starts in an hour and you wish you were on the sinking ship after all.

I perched at the edge of my bed, dealing with the carousel of emotions spinning round my head, no idea which one I should land on.

Happy? Adam wanted me to meet his parents!! He wasn't trying to hide me from them after all!

Terrified? This meant actually meeting his parents?! I should be more careful what I wish for.

Even more terrified. 'Cos I HAD to do well in my maths exam but now all I could think about was

113

$B + AP = D^2$ (Bella + Adam's Parents = Disaster^2).

Argh. This was monumental. Mum-umental. (And dad-umental, but that didn't work as well.)

My instant reaction was to contact Tegan and Rachel for reassurance, but out of maths-exam respect, I decided to wait until after it was over. So after composing ten different replies to Adam, I settled on a thumbs up.

I HAD to compartmentalize. Push Adam panic down underneath the things about triangles.

Exam first.

Then meal stress.

Then actual meal.

C'mon, Bella. You've got this.

And I didn't know if it was Mum's camomile tea, or me being so worried that I'd gone full circle into calm, but when I entered the exam room I had the focus I needed. Maths was something I *knew* I could do OK at. I'd revised everything. Well, everything except fractions, but they'd come up in our mocks, so I wasn't worried.

Steadily I made my way through the paper, my confidence growing as I got question after question I could answer. Algebra. Trig. Even a rhomboid! What was the probability of *that*? (Answer: 0.0000001✔). I even had time to do readable handwriting.

Until all that was left were the last two big questions. Fifteen marks each.

I turned the page.

Interpreting graphs.

I couldn't help but grin. I could do this in my sleep. I answered it quickly, leaving plenty of time for the final question – the only thing now standing between me and the decent mark I needed.

I flipped the booklet.

And gulped so hard I induced a hiccup.

IT WAS THE WORLD'S HARDEST QUESTION ON FRACTIONS.

I didn't even know what one of the words meant?!

I blinked. *Please when I open my eyes let it say something different.*

But it didn't. It said the same thing, just more blurry.

This was my big finish?!

How was this fair?! Yesterday I'd spent three hours revising congruent shapes and they hadn't even been mentioned once!

Could I add an NB with all the spare stuff I had in my head that they were never going to know that I knew?

But I had to answer it somehow. So I gave it my best shot, but when I'd finished I still had two whole pages left for workings out, and I'd only used six lines to come to the answer "12", which didn't make me feel massively reassured. As I stared at the page, willing my brain to find the cheat code to open up a secret hidden bonus level of knowledge in it, the buzzer went for the end of the exam. My GCSEs were officially over.

Everyone cheered.

But I didn't. I couldn't. I'd messed it all up.

I was going to spend the next two years at college without my best mates.

I hardly noticed walking out, too lost in wondering about whether they'd move on without me. Whether they'd forget me for their new, clever friends at college. How I was going to cope with results day.

OOF.

A human cannonball almost knocked me off my feet, long red hair and waving arms flying in all directions.

"WE'RE FREEEEEEEEEE!!!!!!"

It was Rach, closely followed by Tegan, who weaved through our noisy classmates.

"WE DID IT!!!"

I swallowed down what I was really feeling and forced a smile. This wasn't about me being a sad sack; I owed it to my amazing friends to be happy.

"We sure did!"

116

Tegan gave me a hug. "And, as if that's not already the best thing EVER, I just checked and we've already got four hundred and four signatures on our petition… At this rate we really could hit two thousand by the end of tomorrow?!" Two thousand was the target we'd set to get before sending it to the organisers. Tegan looked round and leant in, dropping her voice right down. "You-know-who's been up to their usual though…" She glanced in Luke's direction. "Here's this morning's effort."

It was a comment from him under an Instagram Tegan had reposted about the petition.

> Quick, guys! Sign up and make sure your name is counted as being one of the totally lamest people!"
>
> Or, if you're not a massive loser, check out @ska_city 2 p.m. on the main stage @RebelRocks. It's going to be 🔥🔥🔥. I'll be watching from backstage in the vip area.

"Humblebrag city." I ignored that both his comments had tens of likes.

Rach shook her head.

"Surely the most pathetic thing to do is follow

someone just to talk crap?" She clicked on the settings icon and looked at Teeg. "May I?"

Teeg nodded and Rach pressed at the screen, smiling sweetly. "B to the L to the O to the C to the K." She waved at Luke, even though he was busy having a fake scrap with his mate. "Buh byeeee!"

But as she did it he turned round and mistook it for something it wasn't. He bounded over.

"You waved?"

"I waved bye." Tegan folded her arms. "Yup. No more school with you. No more comments on our social."

He smiled. "Oh, that? I was only saying what everyone's thinking."

"Not four hundred, and …" Tegan refreshed her screen. "… seven people?"

Yes! It had gone up by three just in the last minute.

He smirked. "Big time?! Sure, you're going to make some real headlines with that." He pressed a foot up against the wall to give him extra height, putting his hands up to his mouth and shouting across the groups of people.

"GUYS! ANYONE WHO WANTS TO PUT THEIR NAME TO THE WORLD'S MOST POINTLESS PETITION, THESE ARE THE PEOPLE YOU NEED TO SPEAK TO." I tried to look stern and powerful but felt my cheeks freestyling with their own brand of bright red. "AND BE QUICK! YOU STILL HAVE AT LEAST A DAY TO TRY AND RUIN OUR UNOFFICIAL END OF SCHOOL BLOWOUT!"

But Tegan wasn't going to take this lying down. Or even standing-awkwardly-blushing.

She shouted back even louder.

"WHAT HE MEANT TO SAY WAS, ANYONE WHO HASN'T YET SIGNED THE PETITION TO STOP THE TOTALLY SEXIST AND INAPPROPRIATE SESSION PLAYING REBELROCKS, THEN THERE'S STILL TWO DAYS TO DO IT." No one knew what to say. "SO LET'S SHOW THEM NO ONE CAN GET AWAY WITH TREATING WOMEN AS LESS IMPORTANT THAN MEN AND ADD YOUR NAME TO TEACHTHESESSIONALESSON.COM!"

My old netball friend Sarah whooped a "Yes, gals!" and we got a few other whistley cheers, but the main reaction was confused stares.

I needed to back up my best mate. Show solidarity in numbers. Jump in with a big finish. I took a deep breath.

"I … er…" But nothing came. "WHAT SHE SAID!" I put my arm lamely in the air. "Yeah?"

A smattering of claps punctured the cloud of cringe. And one shout of "Classic 'Awkward But Acceptable'!"

Oh good. The yearbook wasn't forgotten either.

"What IS all this commotion?" Mr Lutas's voice bellowed.

Luke sniggered. "Don't you know you can't yell at us now you're technically not our teacher?"

A disbelieving "Oooh" went up from the crowd. Mr Lutas didn't flinch.

"And do you, *boy who probably doesn't even rrrealize he has pen on his face*, know you are still verrry eligible for detention? Every night for the next thrrrree weeks until the official end of terrrrm?" Luke's smirk made a sharp exit. "So, any other pearrrls of wisdom you're keen to share?"

Luke stared at Mr Lutas, but his bushy eyebrows and wrinkly mouth didn't shift a millimetre. Defeated, Luke turned and walked off.

Yesssss, Mr Lutas.

He turned and glared in my direction.

"You do know you said that out loud?" Rach whispered in my ear.

I did not. I smiled at Mr Lutas. And promptly spun round and scurried as fast as I could away to safety.

"Classic Mr Lutas." Rach was laughing as she caught me up. "Although, rrrrevelation." She tried to roll her r's but sort of just spat quite a lot on my arm. "I almost might miss him."

I snorted. "I wouldn't go that far?!" But I only half meant it. Mr Lutas had come through for me and my friends in a couple of ways over the last few years. And although I'd never, ever tell him, and he'd never, ever want me to, I kind of agreed with Rachel. He even let me borrow the proper school camera on the d-low.

She looped her arm through mine. "You never said! What was the life-changing news you were bursting with?"

Tegan looped her arm through my other one. "Yes, Bells. Spill?!"

I took a deep breath. And told them everything about being invited to Adam's parents for dinner. And as they asked a billion questions – from what I was going to wear, to my talking/chewing strategy, to conversational dead-end rescue tactics, to how firm a handshake I would attempt – my brain re-sorted itself from exam worrying, past Luke-hating, through Session-stressing, and firmly into full-on meltdown about this evening.

CHAPTER

EIGHT

I stood at the end of the path up to Adam's house. It was time to Meet The Parents. Adam's mum and dad. Aka, Mr and Mrs We-Copulated-to-Produce-the-World's-Fittest-Human (although I'll probably call them Mr and Mrs Douglas to their faces).

They were about to basically put me through a job interview, but the job I was going for was dater-and-snogger of their son.

I stepped up to the door. One small step for Bella Fisher, one giant leap for girlfriend-kind.

Rach had FaceTimed to help me pick my outfit, but now I was wondering if the necklace saying "I Can't Even" was too much. I mean, *I Could Even*. I was right here. Make-up-wise I'd gone for black eyeliner, clear lip gloss, and extreme coverage of a forehead spot which was almost at the flaky stage. Not ideal, but other than wearing a low-brimmed hat, which isn't traditional meet-the-parents attire, I had no other option.

Deep breath, Bella. You've been alive for sixteen years. You've met loads of old people. You know how to make conversation. They are the people *most like Adam* – your favourite person.

Although. FEAR. If Mr Douglas looked *too* much like Adam was I going to auto-fancy him by accident?! Same for his mum?!

My heart sped back up. I flicked my phone on for a final look at my emergency conversation topics list. Tegan had helped compile it, based on all the times she'd met Mikey's parents.

It was short, but to be deployed at key points.

- You have a lovely house.
- You look lovely, Mrs Douglas (ONLY IF SHE LOOKS LIKE THE KIND OF PERSON WHO WANTS TO BE TOLD THAT SHE LOOKS LOVELY). If not, compliment a random thing like a vase.
- Say the food is delicious (even if so terrible you can hardly swallow).
- Try and drop in key life achievements:

- ° Successfully completed GCSEs (kind of – leave till last in case).
- ° Grade 3 Piano – merit (don't mention you haven't played in four years).
- ° Young entrepreneur (Aka, job against my wishes at Give A Dog A Cone).
- ° Winner of both Year Nine art AND maths prize (although they might take it back after today's performance).
- ° Once made a pencil sharpening 62cm long that is on the noticeboard at home (ONLY IF DESPERATE).
- ° Once grouted half of our bathroom (ONLY IF DESPERATE *AND* CONVERSATION HAS STRAYED INTO DIY).
- Say nice things about Adam. Unless they seem like the kind of parents who enjoy it when you tease their child (WARNING: don't commit to this too much in case they think you actually hate him, and are only going out with him due to a personality disorder).

I'd tried to hint to Adam that this might be the most terrifying evening of my life, and did he have any tips, but all he'd given me was, "It'll be ace." (In fairness,

all my message had said was "See you later" – but I
was expecting him to understand the true meaning as I
hadn't added a single kiss due to intense panic.)

My phone lit up. Probably Tegan or Rach reminding
me it's no big deal. Not to panic.

JO: Mum says you're meeting the parents?!
WHAT A MASSIVE MOMENT!!

Or not.

MUM: LuckYy them!Just BEYour usual
wonderful self!!! 👻

My sister then messaged me direct.

JO: Remember...

Did she have some calming words of advice?

JO: If they don't like you, this could RUIN
EVERYTHING. DON'T MESS IT UP!!!

I typed back.

ME: Thanks for that.

JO: Anytime.

JO: Just think – what would your big sister do?

ME: Hand out totally unwanted advice at completely the wrong moments???

JO: 😄 😄 😄

I wasn't joking.

JO: Srsly though. Don't stress. Be yourself. You got this 💪

I waited for the mickey-taking follow-up, but nothing came.

Tucking my phone back in my pocket, I took a deep breath and pressed the bell.

And waited.

Nothing happened.

Which was a relief, as I felt some rogue crisp stuck in my teeth. I lifted my phone up and used the front camera for a quick mirror check. It looked like I was taking a really close picture of their door. But it was worth it because there WAS a tooth morsel. I wiggled my tongue out to try and nudge it away.

"So the moment is finally here."

Oh. My. God.

The door was talking!

I looked up.

Even worse/more logistically possible – a man was talking! A man who had opened the door. A man with a confusing facial hair configuration. Who looked like Adam. And I was frozen. Tongue out.

I was face-to-face with Adam's dad!

"I'm not taking a picture of you!" *Was I shouting?!* "I was looking at myself." *Please stop talking.* "And I didn't think the bell had worked…" *Someone stop me. A rogue pigeon. Anything.* "Maybe I just can't use one properly?!" *I was still holding the camera in the air.* "Which is bad considering my name is Bella. Bell … a." *Should I call it quits and go home already?*

Adam Dad, *Dadam*, mustered the bare minimum of smile.

"I see." He opened the door ever so slightly wider. "You must be the 'The Girlfriend'." He did air quotes. Did I need air quotes after seven months? "Probably best you come in."

My first impression = someone who is bad at first impressions.

I followed Dadam into the hallway, trying to think of something to say to win my first proper smile. But nothing came. Except facts about triangles.

I'd been in Adam's house a couple of times before, but it had always just been the two of us. Now it looked all different. *Felt* all different. Like an obstacle course I had no idea how to navigate.

As my fear began to spiral I heard something that calmed me right down. Adam's laugh. His dad looked in the direction it came from, the kitchen.

"Ready to meet the clan?"

Real answer: No.

Suitable fake answer to appease parentals: Yes! I cannot wait!

Actual answer: Terrified nod.

This wasn't going well. I tried to muster something from Tegan's emergency list, but it was all jumbled in my head. "You have a lovely…" I looked around for an end to a sentence I didn't mean to start. "Carpet."

Dadam looked down at the bog-standard beige carpet beneath our feet. "Erm … thank you?"

Yup, he thought I was unhinged.

"Great, er…" Why had I chosen carpets?! I knew nothing about them. "Shag pile?"

OH GOD WHY HAD I JUST USED THE WORD SHAG? HE WAS TOTALLY GOING TO THINK THAT I WAS A SORDID SEX PEST WHO HAD DESIGNS ON HIS POOR, INNOCENT SON.

I felt dizzy.

This was awful. At least if I fainted it really was an incredibly soft shag pile to land on.

"BELLA! Is that you?" A lady's voice came from the kitchen.

A voice that wasn't Adam's shouted back, "Nope. Dad's talking to his alter ego Michelle again."

Dadam strode into the kitchen, inviting me to follow. "Lewis. What have I said? Not when we have guests." I'd met Adam's younger brother before, but it was hard to get a word in edgeways, as all he did was scattergun insult whoever was nearest.

"*She's* not a guest, *she's* Adam's girrrrlfriend," he said in a super-annoying way.

I smiled as much as I could. Technically it was true, but him saying it like that made me want to disappear through a large crack in their wooden floor.

Adam had been leaning up by the stereo, trying to make his phone play through it, but as soon as he saw me he gave me a massive grin and walked over, giving my hand a secret squeeze. I knew the rule – no touching. He'd warned me yonks ago, PDA-ing was not a thing in this house. Not like at mine, where Mum would switch sofas to make sure we were "strengthening our relationship with everyday intimacy".

"So awesome to have you here," he whispered in my ear. I gave him a weak grin back. He was my safe space.

His mum was at the hob, perfect hair, wearing a red body-con dress, Ugg slippers on, an apron tied round her neck.

Determined to try and make one parent like me (or just not hate me), I stuck my hand out in her direction. "Pleased to meet you, Mrs Douglas."

Which I immediately regretted, 'cos she was clearly wrestling a blazing-hot tray out of the oven.

"Just a minute…" It wouldn't have felt *quite* such a painfully long minute if I hadn't kept my hand awkwardly dangled towards her throughout the process. When she eventually stood up, I lunged for the shake, forgetting she was wearing an oversized oven glove, which I then pulled off mid-hand-jiggle.

"Erm, sorry." I held it out limply. "The lasagne smells amazing."

"It's actually chilli. *Someone* didn't tell me until the

last minute that we had an extra guest." She looked accusatorily at Adam, but I couldn't help but feel the full brunt of guilt.

"Yeah, yeah, Mum. You just forgot." He pulled a chair out. "Grab a seat, Bells."

I shuffled into position. Lewis was opposite me. He kept winking. I had no idea why. But then again, he also kept hitting himself on the head with a spoon, and that made zero sense either. I cleared my throat.

"Thanks for the invite." My voice sounded tight and unnatural. "It's really nice to meet you all. I've heard loads about youuuuuuu." I didn't mean to sing the last word, but Adam gave my knee a secret squidge and it turned me into a human accordion.

"All good, I hope?" Dadam asked as he put the plates on the table.

"Of course!"

He sat down. "And we of course have heard lots about you too… The infamous girlfriend." He didn't do air quotes this time but I could tell he was thinking them.

I smiled back. "All good, I hope?!"

No one replied.

Well, this was going well. Adam gave my knee a reassuring rub.

"As if you needed to ask, Bells?" I clearly did, considering no one would give me an answer. "You're nothing but good things."

Hello, temporary wave of happiness. I loved that he'd invited me here, and loved even more that he'd say something like that in front of his parents. I *so* wanted to make the best impression for him.

Mrs Douglas slid a steaming-hot dish of rice on to the mat on the table, followed by the biggest vat of chilli I'd ever seen.

"Mmm, that smells delish," I said. And meant it. Had to hope it wasn't hot though. I couldn't even eat spicy Nik Naks without my eyes watering.

She pushed the ladle in my direction. "Dig in."

Argh. My first test! Too little and it would look like I was a fussy eater. Too much and they might think my mum forgot to feed me (she did, but that's what snacks were for).

All eyes were on me. I spooned a large splodge of rice on to my plate. Silence. What did this mean?!

"Is that *all* you want?" Adam's mum sounded disappointed.

"No, of course not?!" I immediately put another large spoonful on my plate. I was the proud owner of a rice mountain.

"We like a big eater." Aka, I'd definitely taken too much. "Chilli?" This time she was waving a ready-loaded spoonful in my direction.

"Ooh, yes, please."

His mum looked pleased. Yes! I'd done something right. "Our first ever vegan one. Just for you."

It looked all beany and Quorn mincey and nice. Didn't need to mention I wasn't actually vegan. NBD.

"You know Bella isn't vegan though?" said Adam.

From the looks he got, he might as well have emptied the food on the floor and then sat on it.

"I did NOT know that," his mum said through gritted teeth. "*No*, Adam."

As much as my mum was totally inappropriate and wore an apron with a naked man's torso on it, at least she wasn't this passive aggressive. I wanted to help Adam out.

"But this smells *amazing*." I took an overly large breath in. "And I looove veggies." I looked at his dad, who was just staring at me. "And vegan stuff. We have it all the time at home. I once invented a Quorn-ish pasty." Still nothing. "Like a Cornish pasty?"

"We get it," Adam's mum said, taking her first bite.

"It's actually dead nice," Lewis said, rice flying out of his mouth.

Their mum shook her head. "Manners, Lewis! Don't want Adam's girlfriend thinking we're animals."

I tried not to worry whether she actually knew my name and concentrated on holding my knife and fork extra properly as I took my first bite.

Oh. My. Kidney. Bean.

It was SO spicy.

Was my mouth actually bleeding?

Owwww-eeee.

Could. Not. Cope. I reached for my water and tried to swallow the entire mouthful without any more chewing.

I looked down at my plate. Thanks to the rice mountain, I had at least forty mouthfuls left.

"So, Adam tells us you're off to RebelRocks too? We're SO proud of him playing there."

I took a glug of water to quell the rising inferno in my mouth so I could answer.

"Yes – he's amaaaazing." Sip of water. "As in, musically." Didn't want them thinking I was being creepy.

"Ah. Guyyyyys." Adam fanned his face like he was blushing. The through-draught cooled the fire in my cheeks a bit, but my mouth was still alight. "But Bella's doing something way better than me. She's socking it to the man!"

Lewis looked confused.

"Which man? Why does he like socks?" His mouth was hanging open – giving us a delightful view of a load of half-chewed beans.

"*THE* man. You know, the patriarchy!"

"Pay tree what?"

"We don't want to see your mastication, Lewis!" Dadam sounded stern. "Shut that mouth."

Man. This was stressful. And now I was dwelling on how mastication sounded like a word that really wasn't helpful to have in my head in this situation.

"So what's happening, Bella?" His mum prompted me for an answer.

I'm desperately trying to think about words that don't rhyme with mastication.

"Erm…?" I took a politely small mouthful of food. And regretted it. Were my eyes watering? Had I used my waterproof mascara?!

"You're heading down earlier than Adam, aren't you? He's got exams until Friday."

I nodded. "Yup, I finished today." I was heading down tomorrow, a day before it started, to do my first shift with Tegan.

Dadam jumped in. "And how did they go?"

I grinned. Time for the safe ground of a mum joke. "Well, the main thing is, they *went*?!"

Only Adam and Lewis laughed. Their parents just looked at each other, unimpressed.

"That's the thing with all these *extracurricular* activities…" His dad stared at his plate like he'd never seen beans before. "Revising is always the last thing on the list."

Was that directed at me or Adam?

Adam rolled his eyes. "C'mon, guys. Enough nagging already."

His mum didn't get the memo.

"In fifteen years' time, what's going to matter more? Your results or…" She looked at me, as if I'd back her up. "Girls?"

OOF.

I thought they were slagging off his band practice, but they were slagging off *me*. To my face.

"MUM!" Adam was properly annoyed. "I've hardly spent any time with 'girls', as you so nicely put it."

By "girls" he did mean me, right?! Was I now a plural?

"And I'm NE. VAH. going along with the stupid phone box thing when I'm older." Lewis looked over at a wooden box on the side, a label stuck on it that said "NO ACCESS BETWEEN 7–10". They'd been confiscating Adam's phone?! The humanity! "We're not both as much of a pushover as Ad."

Adam went to flick a bean at his brother, but his dad saw and he instantly stopped.

Still, at least I now knew why he'd never invited me round before and had been weirdly absent lately. He had the world's most terrifying parents on his back.

"So as you were saying, *Bella*." Adam stressed my name to shut his parents out and move the convo on. "Tell everyone about the amazing festival thing you're pulling off…"

Mustn't react to him saying "pulling off".

"Oh…" Game face back on. Prove that both Adam and I were fine at life. "Just the world's most gross band are acting like sexist pigs. So my friends and I are trying to get them to own up to it and stop treating their fans like rubbish. At the very least we want an apology."

Adam looked so proud, it almost brought tears to my eyes. To join the ones that were already there thanks to this meal, which was hotter than the sun.

"Bell's got a petition and everything. She might get them kicked off the bill!"

Should I take the hint and follow through with the brag? I looked at Adam's sexy proud face. Yes I should.

"We've got over eleven hundred signatures already." Tegan had updated me on the latest figure just before I arrived.

Adam's dad looked … impressed. YAS ME.

"Well, good work, you. Bands like that don't deserve a place on the stage." We finally had common ground! "Not when you have wonderful artists like The Session playing."

Oh.

Should I tell him that is the exact band I was trying to stop?!

"I've seen them live FIVE times. Got their albums on *lockdown*." I had no idea what that meant but he said it like it was a cool, current word that I should be impressed by. "Such vibes." I swear I heard him using a z instead of an s.

So *this* was the midlife crisis Adam had warned me about? Adam looked mortified. I stifled any form of reaction by taking another mouthful of the chilli (which was the least chilly thing I'd ever tasted and should really be called "hotti"). I was now sweating with the heat.

I dabbed my eye with the material napkin they'd laid out (so posh! At home we mainly used loo roll). But when I put it back down, it had black on it. Oh god, had I smudged my eyeliner?

I tried to kick Adam's ankle under the table. Did I look like a panda?

He mouthed: "You OK?"

I used my knuckle to discreetly point up to my eye. But I still had hold of my fork, and instead of being subtle, flicked an extra-large bean across the table and into my water. It splash-landed with a massive plop.

Adam's family stopped chewing and looked towards my glass. I grabbed it and tried to chug the rogue bean down before they spotted it.

But I was still mid-chew. And as I swallowed, I accidentally forced a bit of food down the wrong throat compartment.

Oh. My. Chilli. Bean.

I couldn't breathe.

I tried to inhale.

Nothing.

I tried to exhale.

Nothing.

I made the sound of a sink emptying.

Still nothing.

I didn't want to cause a scene – but the alternative was death (and surely that would be a bigger scene?!).

What could I do?

My breathing stopped for so long that my body decided for me. My hands hit the table, as if the force might dislodge the bean.

Nothing.

The colour drained from Adam's face as he realized what was happening.

"Oh my god – *she's choking.*"

I could feel my eyes actually bulging, blood rushing to my face.

Yes, I was facing a "dying on Adam's parents' floor" situation, and my focus should be survival, but part of me still found time to be horrified by what a good look this wasn't.

Lewis's mouth was hanging wide open. Full mastication on show.

NO BRAIN NO! NOT THAT WORD AGAIN!

When other people died their lives rushed before them.

My final moments were going to be thinking about not thinking about that?!

Adam was whacking me on the back. I was dimly aware his mum was screeching things like "Bend forward", and "Ring 999".

Life felt like an alternate reality. I felt hands grip round my ribcage, lifting me into a standing position.

With a massive pump, they pulled me back.

Air rushed into my lungs.

The bean rushed into the air.

I felt invincible!

Until the killer bean landed right on Adam's mum's plate, making an actual *ping* as it landed.

I could breathe!

I was alive!

Nothing else mattered!

Although…

Yes it did. Was it OK that I was now very much in a backwards-cuddle formation with Adam's actual dad?

I disengaged and spun round to say thanks, make this less awkward. Which absolutely failed as I brushed my left boob straight into his hand. He looked shell-shocked (by the choking and the boob). As did everyone.

"I am SO sorry!" I was a sweaty, black-eyed mess but Adam broke the PDA rule and gave me a massive hug. Quietly, we returned to our seats, except Lewis, who hadn't moved and was still staring at me, chewing slowly.

"That. Was. Epic."

I *had* to try and regain some dignity. Win back some girlfriend points. "All's well that ends well." Did that sound vague and adult enough?

He pointed his fork at my head. "You've still got some rice there."

"Oh. No. That's an old spot." Maybe I should have just thought that.

It was time to scrape the conversation barrel. Bring out an emergency maths fact. "Did anyone know that if you write out pi to two decimal places and reflect it in a mirror it says 'pie'?"

"I did not," muttered Adam's mum. And slowly we polite-conversationed to the max and finished up the world's most awkward meal. Although it only took half an hour, it felt like four weeks.

It wasn't until I was on the doorstep to leave that I got another much-needed cuddle from Adam.

"Sorry that wasn't exactly the most fun evening ever." He kissed my forehead (carefully avoiding rice/spot). It did kind of make it better – although the slight waft of chilli in his T-shirt gave me PTSD. "Now you get why I always come to yours, right?"

I nodded, not needing him to explain anything. With perfect timing, my mum arrived in her car, singing along way too loudly to the pan pipe CD which was stuck in the stereo. She waved at us both, genuinely happy to see us.

I hugged him goodbye. "I had a nice time." I lied as best I could, but I wanted him to know I was on his team. "Thanks for inviting me."

"Thanks for not dying."

I shrug-laughed. "Any time."

"Hopefully *all* the time please…" He took both my hands in his. "You know I think you're ace, right?"

Well, this alone almost made tonight's near-death worth it. Plus it was the perfect opportunity to tell him how I felt too.

That I really, really, really liked him. Maybe even more-than-liked him.

Could I tell him?

"Thanks." No, I couldn't. "And good luck in your exam on Friday."

He had no idea that behind my smile I was silently screaming at myself for being a wimp.

"More like good luck with the petition! And your first shift tomoz. Can't wait to see you there!"

I couldn't wait to see him either, even if he was having to miss the first half of the proper first day. After an awkward cheek-kiss in case his parents were watching, I waved bye and got in the car.

Mum stroked my face. "So how was it, chickadee?"

She looked so positive and excited I couldn't tell her about bean-gate and burst her bubble.

"Eventful…"

She didn't press me further, and as we drove off, I

zoned out as she chatted about all the packing I needed to do tonight, letting my mind drift into the horror of the inevitable post-meal analysis that would be happening in Adam's kitchen.

I had made quite the first impression.

And from the way his parents had said goodbye, my suspicion was, if they got their way, it would also be my last.

CHAPTER

NINE

"So let me get this straight." Tegan pushed the trolley round Tesco while I tried to perch on the end. "You spat on his mum's plate, accidentally placed your, er, breasticle in his dad's hand, then almost choked to death in front of the entire fam?"

I shrugged. "That's about it, yeah." She nodded, letting the story seep in as we turned down a new aisle. We had £23.21 between us for all food and drinks to buy for the festival – and it had to last from this afternoon to Monday morning. Five days. Four whole nights.

We could only afford necessities. Tegan had gone for fruit. Vegetables. Water. I'd thrown in a Haribo and Jaffa Cakes. She could always rely on me to cover the most important food groups. Snacks and nibbles.

"On the way out, I tried to convince them I wasn't a total lost cause by redeeming myself with some hardcore geography chat but accidentally called it the Specific Ocean."

Last night's sleep had done me good.

Given me perspective.

Perspective that I could never see ANY OF ADAM'S FAMILY EVER AGAIN.

But today wasn't about moping. It was about getting ready for the weekend of our lives. The only bummer was Rach couldn't join us, as she was out with her dad at Shire Hill Shopping Centre, getting some festival clothes. She was going to meet us there on Friday morning, when RebelRocks opened to the public.

I did an involuntary upper-body happiness shimmy as Tegan turned us down the loo roll aisle.

I jumped down and threw in some wet wipes. I also grabbed a twelve-pack of extra-value loo roll, just as Tesco Matt Healy walked past the end of the aisle. He waved at me, box in hand. I waved back.

"Nice bog roll." He grinned.

"Nice." I looked at what he was carrying. Just my luck. It was *always* mozzarella with him. "Balls." An old man shot me a weird look. "CHEESE BALLS."

TMH smiled, a whole heap less fazed by me than

in the early days. We didn't really chat as much now nothing had happened with him and Rach, but it was always nice to see him. His attention switched as a group of girls walked up to him, hugging him like they were old friends. They all had perfect hairstyles, and outfits that made them look like they were some sort of Insta squad. I lost natural control of my limbs as I realized who they were. Our MGC. *Of course* they were close friends with TMH, aka, the most eligible man in supermarket history.

"Teeg," I hissed. "Loooook."

She was mildly appreciative of this in-the-wild spotting. Even though they only seemed to be buying … I strained to see … a butternut squash (of *course* it would be an experimental vegetable), they looked like they were having the time of their lives.

They must have sensed a dishevelled girl frozen to the spot, clutching loo roll and staring at them, because Blue Hair looked over.

GULP. I didn't want her to think I was obsessed with her and was totally staring (I was). I dropped the loo rolls in the trolley and grabbed the nearest thing off the shelf. Toilet unblocker. Amazing.

"So, Teeg." I tried to put it back without anyone noticing. "You reckon we're at two thousand signatures yet?"

Last night while I'd been choking at/on Fadam's family, Tegan and Rach had put in a sterling effort emailing, posting and tagging anyone and everyone to support the petition.

"1,876. So we need 124 before we set off."

The response had been MAJOR. And had made us even more determined. Our plan was to email the organizers and the local paper and radio station as soon as we hit two thousand. They wanted to keep thousands of people happy? Well, we were going to show them thousands they'd made incredibly unhappy. Then they'd HAVE to take us seriously – unlike the band, who were reposting our stuff along with snarky comments. And snowflake GIFs.

But we only had four hours before we had to leave – not much time.

"Sooooo, let's get home and get back on it." Tegan peered in the trolley. "Have we got everything?"

We looked at the list. The only thing we didn't have was Coco Pops and toothpaste. We headed to the health and beauty aisle and I grabbed a tiny travel-sized tube of Colgate. I was worried how cute I found it.

"19p?! Done." I gave Tegan a knowing look. "Sure you don't need…" I gestured to the family planning area. "*Anything?*" I was enjoying going full my-mum on her, now Mikey had a ticket too. His mate Big Ben (he was 5'3", people are mean) had got glandular fever – bad for him, great for Mikey getting his ticket.

Teeg raised an eyebrow. "If you mean condoms –" AS IF SHE COULD CALMLY SAY THAT WORD IN PUBLIC. SHE KNEW I WAS MORE COMFORTABLE WITH PEENCOAT "– I'm all sorted, thanks. Mikey grabbed some yesterday."

Mind.

Blown.

How was my best mate someone who could calmly say these contraceptive-based facts as if they were NBD?! And how could Mikey and Teeg talk about it openly enough that she already knew he had some?!

Terrible. Thought. WAS IT BECAUSE THEY WERE PLANNING TO USE THEM THIS WEEKEND?

But… but Tegan and I were sharing a tent?! This was too much horror for one brain.

"Teeg, please explain why I'M the one blushing?"

But we both knew they'd done it – Teeg admitted it after an intense two-week investigation by Rach and me. Despite sharing every single detail of our lives, Mikey and Tegan's, er, private life was just that. She was too protective of Mikey, of all of us, to share details.

Teeg shrugged, not taking my bait. "'Cos you're terrible at dealing with normal life things like –" she grabbed an extra-large pack off the shelf and read the label "– extra endurance condoms for maximum duration and pleasssssssure." She threw them straight at me. I leapt back, like if I touched them they would somehow trigger a virgin alarm to go off. But instead of hitting me, they hit the floor and high-speed-slid into a foot. That belonged to an old man.

PLEASE NO.

He picked them up and studied them. I grabbed Tegan's hand. But what happened next was more alarming.

He smiled, put them in his basket and walked off.

Jaw. Drop.

"Maaaaan, even his OA-Peen is getting more action than me?!"

Tegan put her arm round me. We'd talked about this loads. It wasn't that Adam and I had decided we should. Or shouldn't. It was just we'd never ever talked about it either way.

And what with his brother always being at his house, and my mum not understanding the concept of a-door-being-closed-meaning-maybe-you-shouldn't-just-walk-straight-in, we'd never been in a situation where anything more than snogging *could* have happened. Until now.

My secret relief was that because Adam was performing, he was going to be in a different camping area to us, so at least I'd dodge any weird discussions about if we wanted to sleep together. In a tent sense. Or *any* sense.

"And does that bother you?"

I didn't know how to answer. Tegan thought I should take the pressure off myself. That it was no big deal (although maybe that's an easier thing to think when you've already dealt with it?). That if Adam and I weren't ready to chat about it, we probably weren't ready to do it.

"Uh, I dunno." I shrugged, weirdly awkward about the whole thing. "Guess it's probably not the right convo for here anyway."

She gave me a squeeze. "Well, we have alllll weekend. And I mean that literally, as we'll be awake practically 24/7. Those shifts start EARLY."

She wasn't wrong. And we needed to get going so we didn't miss our litter-picking crew induction.

We were meant to get the bus home, but our shopping was so heavy that I had to beg Mum to pick us up. It didn't exactly bode well for carrying it all across multiple fields later, but we'd cross that bridge (and multiple fields) when we came to it.

As soon as we got back home Mum started to get emosh. "Your first festival! Such a special time! I still remember mine…" She said it like how other parents might get sentimental at their children's first day of school. She brushed my cheek with the back of her hand. "I left some essentials on your bed." The thought of what Mum considered *essential* made me shudder. Panicked in case she went into detail, I made our excuses, and pulled Tegan upstairs. Turns out Mum's festival "essentials" consisted of a sachet of cystitis relief drink, some diarrhoea tablets and a pack of vegan jelly that went off in November 2015. Now running late, I packed up all the non-essentials (pants, hairbrush, socks, etc.) as Tegan got on her phone for last minute signature-hustling for the petition, while simultaneously shouting out the packing list she'd made to help us (I knew she meant "me" but was too nice to say).

An hour later, I was the sweaty, proud mother of a beautiful, bouncing rucksack. I announced its birth on my Insta Story. Tegan's was a neat capsule, mine was a sprawling blob, items tied to it in all directions (wellies, tote bag packed full of optimistic shower stuff, ancient sleeping bag that still had the stain from when our old dog gave birth on it, school camera Mr Lutas had let me borrow for the last time).

Adam immediately commented on my story, saying it was "so big we should probably name it". And "that name should be Dave".

Yes! We were so couply we now casually named rucksacks.

Tegan brought me back down to earth with a time check.

"Fifteen minutes till we leave." Yikes, how was it 2:45?! We needed to get to the festival by four to give us time to get our passes, put our tent up (aka, mine and Tegan's first ever tiny home!) and "let those spiritual vibes take you over" (Mum's words). "Want the final update?" But she didn't want for an answer. "OMG, BELLS." She looked completely stunned. "WE'VE DONE IT!"

She showed me the page. 2003 signatures?! Unreal!!

Mission: Stop The Session Playing At RebelRocks was on! We FaceTimed Rach. Four rings later her face popped up on the screen.

"Erm, Rach. Are you…" Tegan put her hand up to her eyes. "Are you on the loo?"

Rach's face disappeared as the picture whooshed round to the cubicle door. "Sorrrrryyy!" she was shouting from the background now. "I thought it said 'audio only'!! Lemme ring back."

Twenty seconds later she did.

And again thirty seconds after that, 'cos when we told her we'd got two-thousand signatures she promptly dropped her phone in the sink.

It was time to put the next stage of our plan into action. Our draft email was ready to be sent on my laptop. Rach's brother was studying law and had worked on it this morning to make it sound extra profesh.

"Dear RebelRocks Organisers."

Tegan began reading it out, sounding extra stern.

"Along with most of our friends, we are looking forward to an excellent weekend at RebelRocks. However, before the festival kicks off we wanted to let both you, Worcester Daily News *and Radio Shire (who you will find on copy) know the latest development in the response to The Session's recent behaviour (including but not limited to their misogynistic merchandise, and offensive video-shaming of their fans). The petition to get The Session removed from your line-up has now hit over* two thousand signatures. *That's thousands of people who think the band's behaviour is unacceptable – and even*

more unacceptable is refusing to enter into any dialogue about it. As yet there has been no apology, or admittance of wrongdoing.

"We – along with thousands of others – strongly feel they should not be a headline act of a festival, especially one which celebrates music, art and using your voice to stand up for the issues you care about. In addition, The Session's merchandise should not be sold at RebelRocks, as this further legitimizes their behaviour.

"Are you going to ignore the thousands of people who feel strongly enough to put their names to this??"

Tegan was almost shouting.

"Are you going to ignore the chance to do the right thing?? You still have four days to stop The Session playing their Sunday slot. To allow them to perform is to endorse their misogyny and bad treatment of their fans.

"We require a response before the festival starts on Friday. Yours sincerely, Tegan, Rachel and Bella."

There was a tiny fraction of silence before Rach and I both whooped.

It was *amazing*. Even if I was a tiny bit terrified Tegan had talked us into putting our names on it.

"Teeg – that sounded ace?! You guys smashed it?!" I high-fived Rach via the phone screen.

Tegan blushed. "Do you think it might work?"

Rach shouted back from the phone. "It's GOT to. The Session playing RebelRocks is naaat happening."

I put my arm round Tegan. "Not on our watch anyway."

"Shall I press send then?" asked Tegan.

"We'll count you down! In fact…" I got out my phone. "Let's do it liiiivee on the @StopTheSession account…" It had over 1.5K followers now. "Rach, you can introduce."

I clicked "Live" and held the camera up to film Rach's face.

"Hi, guys! Itsssss a-happening." I ignored her weird TV presenter voice. The viewer count rolled up to twelve. "The petition to stop the monumentally rancid Session playing RebelRocks has hit, drum roll … TWO THOUSAND signatures." Twenty-five viewers. "So you are watching THE MOMENT that we let the organizers slash the papers slash the radio slash the entire world know! Are you ready?"

A flurry of hearts started to fly up. I guess they were!

"Five…" Teeg and I joined in. "Four…" Tegan's finger hovered, ready to click send. "Three … two … one … SEND!!!"

WOOO. We cheered as Tegan ceremoniously clicked, then gave a thumbs up at the camera, always last in line for attention. Guess it was over to me to say something.

"So YEAH!!! Watch this space for all the latest on the campaign against The Session and for backstage RebelRocks action." Whoa. Did I actually sound quite cool? No one needed to know "backstage action" meant "bin emptying". "So all that's left to say is…" I pulled Tegan into shot and paused for a grand finale.

But it wasn't Tegan's voice that spoke. It was someone else's. And it was extra, EXTRA loud.

"Did you want the extreme heavy-flow tampons, Bella, or just heavy like normal?"

Oh.

My.

God.

Why did my mum think it was OK to walk into my room and shout these exact words whilst carrying a box of tampons so big it looked like it could absorb a small sea?

I wasn't even due on for THREE WEEKS. Not that the 226 viewers needed to know that.

I looked back at the screen. A flood of crying laughing emojis were not what I needed to see right now. Especially not the one from Jo.

"MUUUUUUUUUUMMMMM!"

I clicked "end" and threw the phone at Tegan as if I could distance myself from what just happened.

But it was too late.

I'd already seen the one from @HeyItsTheSessionHQ that said, "🚨🚨🚨 Tragic runs in her family 😄".

So I did the only thing I could. Threw myself into a state of denial and hoped against hope we managed to pull this petition off.

CHAPTER

TEN

The ends of my fingers were totally numb.

My right arm felt as if it would never work again.

And my left buttock was in spasm. Sp-ass-m.

BUT WHO CARED?!

'Cos after staggering across two fields, along the world's longest path, and through an actual stream (I *may* have taken a wrong turn, but all fields look the same) Tegan and I were finally here.

RebelRocks.

Where anything could happen. And probably would.

After weeks, months of dreaming, the only thing standing between us, and the most exciting thing to ever happen to us, was a big metal fence. And the fact I was so exhausted I couldn't even crawl.

"WEEEEE MADDDEEEE ITTTTTT!"

I dropped Dave to the floor, along with the Tesco bags that had twisted round my fingers. But I didn't get my arm out of the strap quick enough, and Dave took me with him, yanking me backwards like a giant beetle. Although, in this sunshine, a lie-down was just what I needed. I closed my eyes, happy, sweaty, content. Even the air smelt more exciting.

I breathed it all in, a mix of bonfire and food and possibility, and no parents and sausage and freedom.

Tegan gently put her bag down and knelt beside me.

"I can't believe how *big* it is." Even Teeg, the world's most unflappable person, was flapped. The festival site we'd been trekking towards was like nothing we'd ever seen. Beyond the fence the whole hill was covered in tents and paths, stages and flags, and people. A pop-up city full of all the very best things – music and food and places to hang – and none of the boring bits like dry-cleaners and funeral homes that you never see anyone go in or out of.

I lay as still as I could and tried to save this memory somewhere I'd be able to access for ever.

I felt weird. Light all over.

I couldn't work out what it was.

- That I had four nights and five days with my best friends stretching before me.
- That the music coming in waves from speakers would soon be real-life bands playing stages.
- That one of those bands was my boyfriend's.
- That exams were officially over and for the first time in my life I had zero homework-guilt to deal with. (Plus I'd agreed with myself I wouldn't think about results, or colleges, or anything Scary Future like that, as I didn't want to ruin my weekend).
- That I never had to go back to St Mary's again.
- That for this one weekend, who we saw, what we ate, what we wore, what we did – everything – was totally up to us.

I wasn't exactly sure what boggling was, but my mind was totally doing it.

Right here, right now, I felt free.

Untouchable.

Grown up.

In charge of my whole life.

Ready to take on anything. Including The Session.

OOF.

A trainer nudged me in the side-bum.

"Get up, beetle child. You're lying in a massive cowpat."

Oh.

My.

Daveballs.

I didn't need to open my eyes to know *exactly* who it was.

THIS COULD NOT BE HAPPENING.

I tried to sit up. I was so cross I didn't flinch at accidentally plunging my hand into the aforementioned cowpat.

"What the hell are YOU doing here????"

I was NOT going to take my sister turning up lying down. Even though that's sort of exactly what was happening, as Dave was pinning me to the ground.

Jo folded her arms, looking down at me as I scrambled around.

"As IF Mum would let you come on your own. She's crazy, but not THAT crazy."

Objection. This was a woman who used to think when people said they'd "ask Google" that Google was just a person who knew a lot. She totally WAS that crazy.

"So what?!" My chill level had plummeted to below zero. "You're here to *babysit* us?"

Jo shrugged.

"If *that's* what you want to call it."

"It's an attack on my freedom, is what I'm calling it."

"It's you overreacting again is what it is."

ARGH. I hated her. But if I shouted back I'd make her look right.

"Jo! Long time no see." Trust Tegan to try and smooth the atmosphere over, but the pleasantries didn't even make a dent in the shade Jo and I were throwing at each other.

"So I have a *cool* idea ..." I was fully engaged in eye-to-eye warfare with Jo. "... that you do one ... now?"

"But we're having so much fun already?"

I scowled so hard I felt my eyes strain. But instead of being at all bothered, she bent forward and RUFFLED MY HAIR.

ARGGGHHHHH.

Unauthorized patronizing hair touching was the straw that broke the camel's back (well, if this camel hadn't already had its back broken by the world's heaviest rucksack).

I gave up trying not to shout. I pulled my arms out of Dave and stood up.

"I'm NOT buying this, Josephine." She hated it when I called her Josephine. It wasn't actually her name which meant I loved it even more and did it as much as possible. "We both know this is NOT a Mum thing to do. And even if it was –" I crossed my arms "– which IT'S NOT – why did no one mention it to me before … say, TURNING UP RIGHT NOW TO RUIN EVERYTHING?"

If you were to look up the definition of a "scene" it would probably be a video of this moment.

Jo did a classic older sister move and blinked calmly, saying nothing. She knew full well the calmer she stayed, the more irrational I'd look. Which would make me more irrational. ARGH.

"Don't act like a moron, Bella." She looked at me like I was the pathetic one.

"Says YOU, Surprise-Turner-Upper-At-Festival-er … er." I was still shouting. And also regretting wearing my "CHOOSE PEACE" T-shirt. "In fact, I thought you were broke – how come you managed to afford a ticket?"

"A spare one came up from one of my friends. His parents have a bar here." OF COURSE THEY DID. "Mum was nice enough to pay half. Sweet after she'd forked out for yours."

My rage hit a new level.

"You … know … full … well … she … didn't…" Breathe, Bella. "Get … mine." Bella, breathe.

"WEAREWORKINGASLITTERPICKERSYOUTO-TALCOWBAG!!!"

Jo smiled sweetly, as if she'd only just remembered. "Oh *yeah*?"

AS IF parents were allowed to have such a blatant favourite child?! And as if that favourite was allowed to rub it in the non-favourite's face so much?!

"So how did you talk her into paying for yours?!"

She shrugged. "Generosity, I guess? Maybe helped by the small suggestion that you shouldn't be left on your own in a field, considering the height of your adulting skills include once setting the lounge curtains on fire when you made beans on toast." She gave Tegan a despairing look. "Don't ask."

"Erm, that was *actually* when I was being a first-class dog mother and had made Mumbles a birthday cake. But she had a slight incident when blowing out the candles."

"Oh yes." She smiled. "My mistake. That's a totally sensible thing to do."

ARGH. I swear the only thing she was learning at university was how to become even more irritating.

She was impossible to argue with. But it was clear she wasn't leaving. All I had left was Option: Guilt Trip.

"Well, don't think you're staying to keep an eye on

165

us. So go find your mates and have THE BEST time with them. And when Teeg and I are picking up bits of mangled burger at 5 a.m., you enjoy thinking about what you've done."

"I'll be asleep."

"You won't be." I dropped my voice to the level of a murderous psychopath. "'Cos I'm going to hunt you down and put the remnants in your sleeping bag." I half meant it. "With added gherkins."

She hated gherkins. Although that was as a foodstuff (OMG THANK GOODNESS I JUST CHEERED MYSELF UP REMEMBERING HOW MUCH I LOVED THE WORD "FOODSTUFF") – I'd never asked about her feelings towards them as sleeping companions, but I assumed it would be similar.

"Don't threaten me… or I'll tell Mum." Whoa. Had she really gone there?!

"Isn't there an age limit on dobbing someone in to a parent?"

"Isn't there an age limit on being all 'life's-soooo-unfair'?"

"Isn't there an age limit on *making* someone else's life soooooo unfair?"

"Nope." Jo looked at the entrance. "So how about I take a photo of us now as proof for her that we're together? Then we can head off to get our tickets. Separately. And stay out of each other's way. Until the end when she'll pick us all up and we'll tell her we all had a great time?"

Sounded simple. But also like Jo was getting everything her way.

"And if we don't take the photo?"

Jo thought. "I'll tell her I saw you telling someone you think ice cream for dogs is just a fad."

My sister was an evil genius.

Still, one photo was all it would take to get her as far away as possible.

I summoned as much of a smile as I could as Jo snapped a selfie, before sending it to our group, alongside the caption "REUNITED!"

Mum replied with three heart emojis, which almost made me feel guilty for the deceit.

But not guilty enough to stick around – with Tegan's help I hoisted Dave on to my back and headed as fast as I could in the opposite direction to my sister.

CHAPTER

ELEVEN

It was official.

RebelRocks had magical properties.

As soon as we'd headed our separate ways it was like Jo, and all her annoyingness, got trampled away by the hundreds of happy people milling about. Even the sun seemed to be brighter. And soon, I was back to being as happy as I was before the ambush. *Fam-bush*. Maybe even better as Tegan and I sashayed our way towards our own special "staff" entrance.

Now, I'm a firm believer that *stuff* doesn't make anyone special. The houses people live in. The cars they might/might not have. Whether they wear labels or charity shop finds.

However, moments after our bag check (and my

concerned, but ignored, cries of "stop tickling Dave"), my entire belief system was called into doubt.

Who even was I any more?!

Because with one click of a metal punch, I felt different. Special.

I looked down. And smiled like I'd made it.

A small piece of red fabric on my wrist that officially meant we were more important than most people. I wasn't being cocky. It officially said it. "VERY IMPORTANT PERSON". (It might also say "DUMP ACCESS" after that, but no one needed to know that.)

Tegan waggled her wrist at me. "Check *us* out?!"

"I am so here for THIS!" I waggled mine back. "Number one rule of wristband club?" I left a dramatic pause. "Don't tell anyone about wristband club…"

Tegan raised an eyebrow. "Just post it on Instagram with a suitably obvious comment?"

I dug the camera out of my bag and smiled. "You know me too well… Wrist, please!"

Teeg never liked appearing or being tagged in anyone's pics, but was fully resigned to her pivotal role as Insta-BFF so held out her arm. I snapped away (making sure the words *Dump* and *Access* were nowhere to be seen), and posted, along with the comment:

BRB. Hanging with the (wrist) band @MyFriendWhoRefusesToBeTaggedOnInstagram and soon to be @ItsRachelTBH #RebelRocks #veeeyeyyyypee #StopTheSession #HashtagBlessed

Tegan gave it a solidarity like before helping lift Dave back on to my back, she was still carrying her bag around as if it were no heavier than a feather. A really, really light feather.

"This way." She set off down a path, through the city of tents.

Walking and carrying heavy things were two of my least favourite pastimes, and my hand still smelt of cowpat, but I had a grin so wide random strangers kept smiling back. I already loved it here. And before we knew it, we were in our workers-only campsite.

Home.

It was a massive field, with only about fifteen tents already up, so we had our pick of the area. Tegan had been watching camping YouTube tutorials – tentorials – so I followed her lead as she picked a spot by the wire fence (in her words, "next to the edge of a field Rach can camp in – and close to the Portaloos, but not so close we're in the waft zone").

I'd never felt joy like the joy of taking Dave off for

the final time. It was like taking off a bra – that you'd been wearing for four years straight.

"OK. An hour and ten before we have to have our first staff meet so…" I looked at the tiny bag with our tent in. "Shall we put this up, then have an hour to get changed, de-sweat, and generally have the best time ever?"

"Heccccckkkkk yassssssss!" Teeg whooped.

It was weird. I'd never really been that interested in adventuring outdoors, sleeping in tents or enjoying nature. But as I looked at our little patch of field, I felt like I might start watching *Countryfile* or suggesting camping as a legit summer holiday.

I plopped the contents out. "I officially declare our new home. OPEN!"

Life couldn't be better.

An hour later I'd changed my mind. Lots had happened:

- I'd almost flicked out Tegan's eye with an unruly tent pole.
- In panic I'd then yanked it back so hard the pokey metal bit snagged through my shirt and got caught in the stitching of my bra, thus making a hole which drew even more attention to my major under-boob sweat.

- I'd then stepped backwards on to my variety pack of Walkers Crisps – they were effectively now Walkers Dusts.
- A tent peg had pierced right through the sole of my pump, and almost, almost into my foot (it said to wedge it into the ground! It never said human feet were not an acceptable way to do this!).

…And the tent still wasn't up.

I hated camping.

"Teeeeg. I never want to see another tent again as long as I live."

She handed me a tin of baked beans to try and help hammer in a peg that was refusing to budge. "Remind me again why just lying on the ground in a sleeping bag is a bad option?"

THWACK. The beans were actually quite a good shout. It was the most the peg had budged in five minutes.

"Potential hypothermia, extreme damp, and substantial risk of someone stepping on your head." She whacked her peg, using a bottle of Diet Coke wrapped in a sock. Despite having actual muscle in her arms, as opposed to just arm-shaped flesh like me, she was

172

also struggling. "But once we've got these last ones in we'll just need to peg the inner in, and we'll be done." I could totally see why people lived in houses. This was *exhausting*. But with immense teamwork, we eventually did it. Throwing our stuff inside, we hurried over to the big marquee – headquarters for all the crew.

A beardy man in a woolly hat (even though it was one gazillion degrees outside – *or was everything outside when you were in a tent?*) was at the far end, standing on a table, a bunch of people gathered round. We shuffled to the back as he introduced himself as Ross. After a quick welcome, he took us through the rota. We were the "Sunrise Shift", with our first shift straight after this, and then three more – Friday, Saturday and Sunday, 5 to 9 a.m. We were in teams of six, picking and sorting everything we found, from stuff on the floor through to rifling through the huge oil-drum bins. Not exactly glam, but it was my ticket here, so I wasn't going to complain (well, I was, but not when scary Ross could hear).

"So, any questions?" He'd finished the health and safety bit (*Don't do anything stupid. Don't die. And if you do, don't blame us. But you'll be dead so you can't *unhinged laugh**).

I stuck my hand up. Everyone looked round – I

smiled into the middle distance to mark myself as a friendly crew member with all of our best interests at heart. "Will we have any picker-upper thingies?"

Ross nodded. Phew.

"Yup. These." He stretched both hands out. "State of the art … hands." Everyone laughed. Thanks, guys. "So always wear gloves, 'cos you don't want to get a kebab stick impaled through 'em … or stick your fingers into something that rhymes with poo…" He looked right at me. "Oops, sorry, my mistake. I meant something that IS poo."

Cue round two of slightly alarming solo cackling. Then he handed us the last bit of our work attire – high-vis jackets – as he hissed to remember he was "Lord of the Dump". Shudder. Tegan Velcroed hers up and shimmied like there was any way on earth we could style this out.

"Neon gilet is GO!"

I knew her technique. Be extra positive because she knew I was stressed about being spotted by all the people we knew who weren't having to work – most specifically Luke and Ska. And I could add Jo to that list as well – she'd use this as laughing-at-me ammo for years. Wearing high-vis really made being low-vis so much trickier.

As we made our way round the site for the first time, it was like nothing I'd seen before. Tegan and I had to hold hands when we got our first glimpse of the main stage. It was enormous, mirrored REBELROCKS letters shimmering all the way along the top of it.

"Teeg." I was speaking slower than normal, taking it all in. "It's EVERYTHING I hoped it would be."

She pointed to the top of the stage where something was glinting.

"With an added glitter ball sheep."

We both gulped. If it was exciting enough now – with no crowds and no performers – what on earth was it going to be like tomorrow when it properly kicked off?!

I couldn't let my brain go off-leash and delve into the mental gold that was Adam playing, for fear of melting from the head down. So instead I focused on finding large bits of rubbish to make my bag look the fullest it could do on the least work. Although it really didn't feel like work when the whole place was full of the loud *thud-thud* of a soundcheck. It was like being backstage ALL THE TIME. Plus with Tegan to chat to, it was like tidying my room, just outside – and with less temptation to procrastinate by rearranging my 1975 posters.

We got waves and "hi"s from all the other workers

too. *Everyone* seemed happier than in normal life. Like we were all in some secret club, while the real world carried on somewhere else. Things peaked after the man at the printed T-shirt stall waved us over and asked if we could do a quick tidy round. Happy to help, Tegan and I got it done in under a minute. The lady running the doughnut stall next door, D'Oh Nut Stand, then asked us to do the same. Sixty seconds later not only were we the proud tidiers of her area, but also the proud owners of two free bags of freshly fried doughnut balls.

This was the life!

Teeg and I saved them till that night, when we were back at our tent. It had turned chilly, so we got in our sleeping bags and sat outside to eat them (the doughnuts not the sleeping bags), watching everything happening around us. I took some arty camera photos of the site in the moonlight, and some less arty ones of Tegan and me, seeing who could fit the most doughnut balls in our mouths. I even tried to make campsite friends, and headed over, bean can in hand, to a group who were struggling with their pegs. But as I approached they pulled out a mega hammer, and I had to do a U-turn and walk back, acting as if taking a tin of beans for a walk was a normal thing.

As I got back, Tegan threw her phone in her bag as

if I'd caught her using it when she shouldn't. I knew her too well to be fooled.

"Good day one?" Maybe she'd tell me.

She wiped some sugar off her mouth. "The BEST."

We chewed for a bit.

I knew *exactly* what she'd been looking at. Updates from the organizers. Or lack of.

"Worried about tomorrow?" Our happiness at the signatures going up was being dragged down by a total lack of response from the organizers, or any of the press. We'd said they had to respond by tomorrow but all we'd got back so far was a steady stream of hate on our @StopTheSession account from really hardcore fans of the band.

And when the organizers got on stage tomorrow to properly launch the festival at midday, if The Session were still on the line-up … well. We didn't have a Plan B.

My phone broke our worried silence by vibrating.

Maybe Adam had messaged? I reached out for it.

But it vibrated again.

And again. Like when a charging wire isn't properly plugged in.

Tegan and I looked at each other.

What was happening?

Why had her phone started to do the same?

I picked mine up. My notifications were on fire.

Forty-nine new followers?

Normally I'd feel excited. But this didn't feel good. More and more were coming through. Fifty-three. Fifty-four.

Along with posts on my previous photos.

Something was wrong.

And when I headed to my feed, I knew exactly what.

I felt physically sick.

And it wasn't from eating so many doughnut balls.

It was official.

The Session had hit a new low.

CHAPTER

TWELVE

Plip.

EURGH.

Where was I?

Why was my ear wet?

Why did I feel like an ice cube?

"Bells…" A hand shook my shoulder. "Bellsssss!" I fumbled for my phone. It lit up the room. No. Not room. *Tent*. And it was 4:50 a.m. Ahhhh … everything came rushing back.

I'd wrapped a sock around my face in the middle of the night to try and stop the onset of frostbite. And I'd clearly been dribbling into it ever since, so now my ear was wet with my own night-dribble.

My limbs slowly reconnected with my brain. I was

crumpled into a heap at the bottom of our tent, sort of like a human croissant. Guess this is why sensible people don't pitch up on a slope.

I pulled my sleeping bag back up over my head, hoping to defrost my nose (if it was indeed still attached to my face and not rattling around in my bag like an odd-shaped ice cube).

The hand wobbled my shoulder again. "C'mon. It's time."

I stuck my head out of my sleeping bag and grunted. Teeg was already fully dressed and giving me a cheery wave. Standard.

"We got another couple of hundred signatures overnight." This was amazing news, but all I could manage was a slightly different grunt back. Luckily Teeg knew my noise repertoire well enough to understand that at this time in the morning this grunt signified "that's epic news".

"Rach couldn't sleep and sent another email to the press and organizers with the update. You should read it."

I knew why Rach hadn't been able to sleep. For the same reason as us. Last night, she'd been holding back tears on the phone when we realized what was going on. What Brian had done. Not content with ridiculing our petition, he'd gone one step further. Posted the personal profile pics of Rach, Tegan and me in his feed, calling us out as leaders of #StopTheSession and tagging in our own personal handles. This was a man who had over half a million followers. Worst of all was what he'd said underneath:

Trying to 🙄 *The Session? Get a life. These are the people who are opposing free speech* 🐍🐍🐍. *Sessionites, go do your worst #StopTheSessionHaters*

All three of us had hundreds of new followers – all of them there just to watch our every move and tell us how awful we were. Rach had changed her profile to private. I'd wanted to do the same, but Tegan had talked me into being brave enough to stay public: "Stay loud," as she said.

She was probably right – but it would be a whole lot less terrifying if I could just hide.

As Teeg pulled on her boots, I snuck a quick look at my feed. Over a hundred comments since I fell asleep three hours ago. Wonderful. Tegan clocked what I was up to and pushed my bag of clothes over to me. "Oi. Get a move on. We've got litter to pick."

Getting dressed inside a tent turned out to be like

trying to complete *The Cube*. There isn't enough room to extend your arms or legs, let alone stand up into anything straighter than a crouch. How Tegan had done this whole palaver without waking me I would never know. Gymnastic training had served her well. All my rummaging meant my stuff was now spread all over the tent whereas Tegan's was still neatly packed. Sometimes we were like yin and yang. If yin was a tidy competent human, and yang was one who once wore her school skirt inside out.

"Bells? You OK in there?" Tegan was back from her wee, her torchlight silhouetting me as I scrabbled around. My jeans undone, I pushed myself out head first.

"I liiiivvve!" I whisper-wailed, staggering to my feet, my trainers clunking into place. I thanked the Gods of Temporary-Material-Based Housing that tents didn't have mirrors. I didn't need to see myself to know I looked like a jumble sale on legs.

Tegan, however, was wearing leggings, a couple of pairs of socks that were bunched above some heavy-duty boots, two jumpers and a raincoat. And she made it look ay-mazing.

"Welcome to day two!" She smiled. I tried to hug her, but had so many layers on that my arms wouldn't bend. I resembled a scarecrow attempting to engage in human interaction. "You OK?"

"Just dealing with the fact your look is so ICONIC."

"Ha! As if. It's just old gym stuff I threw on." She pointed the torch up the path. "Shall we go?"

As we walked to the meeting point, the air was so cold I was both sweating and shivering all at the same time. *Swivering*. The sun was rising, tiny campfires were still smoking and loads more tents had popped up around us. A couple of muffled voices could be heard, but it was impossible to tell where they were coming from.

This.

Was.

Amazing.

We were part of something that belonged to *us*. Unique and special and secret from the rest of the world. I put my arm through Tegan's and squeezed her.

She squeezed back, letting me know she knew all the things I was thinking and thought them too. I kept my voice down so as not to wake all the people who weren't stupid enough to be up at this time.

"I know this is cringeworthy, but … I'm so happy you're here to share this." I promptly tripped over a guy rope. Teeg yanked me back just before I totally faceplanted on to a tent. "Aaaaand I'm even more happy you're here to stop me from starting the world's earliest pile-on."

She laughed. "Any time."

But I hadn't finished.

"Ignoring the fact that Rach isn't here yet, that we're being trolled by an evil pop star, that we're freaking out about later –" I ignored Tegan's judgmental raised eyebrow, and ploughed on "– that we're about to see more mushed rubbish than I'd wish on any human ever … except maybe Luke … and that we're awake at a time only meant for small mammals and postmen and postwomen…" I paused, knowing that this was going to sound cheesy. But I didn't care. In fact, bring on the cheese. Make me a verbal stuffed-crust. I stretched my arms out and looked up at the sky symbolically. "This is kind of perfect."

Or not.

'Cos a massive blob of water hit me on the eyelid. And then another blob. And then some sort of multi-blob situation. Water blobs were falling everywhere from the sky! (I suppose the more common name for this is "rain".) It was like I'd summoned the world's heaviest downpour. Please tell me Brian hadn't got the weather to hate on us too?!

I was in a field with nowhere to shelter. And no coat.

With a quick "Wait here" Tegan sprinted back to the tent, leaping over guy ropes as she went. She was too nice to say what she was probably thinking. That maybe she had a point when she'd told me not to take my only waterproof coat out of my bag to make room for a second box of Coco Pops. Especially as I'd forgotten to pack bowls.

I was still thinking about what clothing I'd sacrifice for foodstuffs when Tegan returned, a scrunched ball of black plastic in her hand.

"Here." I took what she was holding out. A bin bag. She tore a hole in one of them.

"It's the best I could do." My face fell as I realized her plan. "Look, I'll wear one too…" She pulled it over her shoulders. "It'll be fun." "Fun" was one word for it. Another slightly more accurate one would be "mortifying". "You'll thank me in four hours when you're not soaked to the bone."

But as I pulled them on, I thanked her now. The rain was torrential. I ended up putting one on each leg and tucking them into the belt of my jeans. I was like a Victoria's Secret Angel. If Victoria's secret was that she loved wearing refuse sacks topped with a high-vis jacket.

After a regroup with our team we headed down to

the main site. There wasn't much litter to pick up from overnight and as we trudged around, the rain began to ease. As the morning wore on, the temperature rocketed to a boiling hot summer's day and my bin-bag combo made me feel like I was in a sauna for one. I'd never sweated so much in life – and I'd even once tried to do a Davina home workout with Rach and her mum.

"Almost there, Bells." Tegan looked at her watch. "Only twenty minutes left."

I smiled weakly. Not because I didn't want to smile more, but because I'd already bent down over two hundred times and my muscles were threatening to go on strike. All my spare energy was going into keeping positive about The Session. The organizers were due to make the final line-up announcement at midday, and that was only 2.5 hours away. If something was going to happen, it had to happen soon. But with every second, more and more normals (as we'd started to call the not-VIPs) were arriving, heading to pitch their tents before the music started, chatting excitedly about who they were about to see. Despite wanting to think about anything else, we kept on hearing them talk about The Session petition. The snippets of chat I caught mirrored what was being said online – people either were 100% with us, or thought we should get over it.

As the buzz grew, so did our nerves. So for the last bit of the shift, Teeg and I invented a game to pass the time; bag-sketball. Basically throwing rubbish into each other's bags basketball style. We'd managed forty-nine catches in a row, so when I spotted a half-eaten sausage I ran for it, knowing a last-minute slam-dunk would put a smile back on Tegan's face.

"She spots an opportunity..." I swooped down. "She grabs her prey!" I snatched it. "She moves like a graceful puma..." I spun back round as Tegan lifted up her bag. "And she shooooooooots." I hurled the sausage at Tegan's open bin bag. But my throw was too enthusiastic, and my glove flew off with it, sailing through the air and landing perfectly at someone's feet. Luckily that someone was facing away from us. But the sausage wanted to be part of the action too and landed slap-bang on top of the bag they were wearing. Like a cherry on a cake. But a half-chewed chipolata on a backpack.

Tegan and I looked at each other in horror. A girl sauntered over to Sausage Bag Boy, all massive hat, perfectly wavy hair, and shorts that were smaller than the pants I was wearing (and I wasn't even in my big pants). She looked disgusted.

"Babes?!" Her mouth pulled down like she'd just

smelt the Portaloos for the first time. "*Why* is that rrrevolting sausage on your back. Is it some kind of joke??"

His cry of "What?!!!" suggested not.

Oh gosh.

Please no?!

Of all the people sausage-attack could happen to, it had happened to the worst. The wurst.

Could I leave my glove on the floor and flee before they noticed the thrower was me? And I was dressed like a bin-liner?

"Fishy Balls." No I couldn't. That's the problem with high-visibility vests. They are high visibility. "Figures."

Luke kicked the poor sausage towards me. The sad little thing tumbled across the ground. Literal sausage roll. I'm sorry, sausage. I never meant for this.

What could I say?

"Oh god, it's YOU." Wavy-haired girl, aka Ska, spoke to me like I was a tiny annoying pebble in her designer shoe. She looked at me with more disgust than she did the sausage. "Any *reason* you're dressed as a rubbish dump?"

Her look – Dolce & Gabbana. Mine – health and safety.

"It was raining."

Luke was staring me down. "Which is why people have invented a thing called coats?"

I slow nodded. But he hadn't finished, a smile spreading across his face as he thought of something else to throw at me . "Or were you too distracted by your petition? Good luck with that, by the way. *Such a shame* they haven't got back to you. *Everyone's* talking about it…" He stressed "everyone" extra hard. "And I hate to be the one to tell you – but someone really should… You do know you have *zero* chance of it working, right?"

But Ska hadn't got his "make them feel even more rubbish than they look" memo.

"Oh? I'd heard the band had got booted off?" Whoa. What?! I didn't know she'd even been following it? Or even cared about anyone but herself?! "Meaning even *more* stage time for me."

Oh no. That's right. She didn't.

Luke's fists tightened, but it was too late – Tegan was all over the good news.

"Thanks for the tip-off, Ska. Just shows what people standing up for what's right can really do."

Ska looked perplexed. "What? Get my set extended?"

I looked at Luke as I replied to her. "Totally."

It was one thing being a self-obsessed douchebag. It was another to go out with one too. "Cooool. Yeah. See you guys, later." Ska lifted her model wrist and waved bye just with her fingers, like a whole hand would be too much effort for people like us.

I lowered my voice and grabbed Tegan's arm. "Hopefully in at *least* fifteen years."

But boosted by Ska's tip-off, I sass-walked off – which was actually quite tricky with a full bin bag banging against my knee and the others making a swishing sound as I flapped in the wind.

But could Ska be right? Had the reason we hadn't heard from the festival been because they were going to make it part of their official announcement? It was almost too exciting to think about.

Tegan and I hurried back to ring Rach with the news, but she didn't pick up. So I used the time to reply to some messages from Adam that he'd sent during our shift.

AARD: Good morning beef! Can't wait to see you!

He never used exclamation marks. Must be all the excitement of his gig.

AARD: DID YOU KNOW YOU'VE BEEN

SELECTED FOR A QUESTIONNAIRE? IF
YOU ANSWER CORRECTLY YOU COULD BE
ENTERED INTO A PRIZE DRAW! IS WEARING
ONE PAIR OF JEANS ALL WEEKEND:

A) #BANDLIFE, OR:

B) .
Entries must be received by midday, and will
cost the bill-payer a guaranteed massive snog.

I replied.

ME: A and B. But seeing as I forgot to bring a
hairbrush we can be together. Good luck in
your exam!!!

He got straight back. He mustn't have gone into his
exam yet.

AARD: Any update from the organisers? Tell me
if you hear! How is the fest? How is life? How is
you? How is Dave? How am I about to go into
my last exam? How How How.

I replied with the update that there was no update and got back to ripping off my bags with Tegan (which we then couldn't throw away as didn't have a bin bag for rubbish. Mind. Blown). We then had a vile wet-wipe wash and got changed. It was lame, but I was really looking forward to seeing Adam later.

PUTHHT.

Something hit our tent. Probably just a bit of mud flying up. I carried on wriggling my jeans back on.

PUTHHT.

Tegan looked at me. She'd heard it too.

PUTHHT. PUTHHT.

Was someone throwing something?

Please tell me this wasn't some kind of pro-Session ambush?

Tegan knee-shuffled her way to the front of the tent. I gave her a supportive nod. Ever so slowly she pulled back the tent flap and peered out.

I held my breath. Was it Luke again?

But unless he'd suddenly become a master of yelling "Teeeeggggggaaaaannn" in the happiest voice ever (he hadn't), I knew exactly who it was and rushed straight out after Tegan, who was already pressed against the wire fence body-press-hugging the other person I most wanted to see. Rach.

She was staggering under the weight of her backpack, every inch of her – and it – covered in glitter. A sparkly cloud showered down whenever she moved.

"I *KNEW* it was you guys!!! I've missed you!!!" It'd been approximately thirty-nine hours since our last face-to-face sighting and one hour since our last messages – so I felt the same. "Tegan's directions were perf! We're so close?!" Considering Rach wasn't allowed in the workers' field, we were only metres apart.

Tegan shrugged as if nailing everything was no big deal. "Can we give you a hand?"

Rach shook her head. "Don't think you can get in here. Encouraging shouts will have to do…"

Keen to keep the happy mood up before the drama of the announcement in just over an hour I took her hint. "GO GO, TENT MASTER!!!! QUEEN OF … err … ERECTIONS!"

Rach sniggered, and began pulling out her poles.

But she didn't need any help. Hers was one of those high-tech ones that you flick and it pops into a ready-made tent. She dragged it as near to the fence as possible and banged the guy ropes and pegs into place using our trusted tin of beans. But despite having no tents – or humans – around her, out of nowhere a guy who looked like a hipster-lumberjack-hair-product-model appeared.

"Wanna hand?" He put his hand on his hip and did some sort of hair toss. "It's all about the angle."

"Here – let me…" Another man popped up on the other side. He was so fit he made the original guy look positively ropey. (OMG, imagine if he was called Guy. Guy Ropey.) This was what happened when you looked like Rach. It was like all the fit guys in the world got a group notification when girls like her were in distress. Fit Guy Two bent down to grab one of the pegs. "Should be easy with a bit of strength."

Rach stood up. Both of them stared at her – then each other – like they were locked in silent battle.

"Thanks…" She lifted the beans back up, before whacking in the last peg. "But that should be me done. Next time I need someone to tent-splain me though, I'll know where to head."

I almost choked on my chewy fried egg. Rach threw her bags into the tent and looked at us. "So, we good to go?" Tegan and I both scrambled up. Guy Ropey and Fit Guy Two sloped off as quickly as they'd arrived. "It's time to find out if we managed to stop The Session."

Tegan looked stern. "You ready?"

I nodded.

It wasn't technically lying if I didn't use words, right?

CHAPTER

THIRTEEN

It was one thing needing an emergency wee in times of stress. It was quite another trying to achieve that at a festival. The music hadn't even started but every Portaloo had a queue at least fifteen people long. And when I finally dived into one, it had a faulty lock, so instead of being empty, it contained a semi-naked man, lunging towards me in startled panic. It was fair to say that me, and the other 50+ pairs of eyes that were staring, would never forget what we saw.

By the time I got back to the main stage to find Rach and Tegan it was unrecognizable to the place I'd left just twenty minutes earlier. There were people *everywhere*.

Rach messaged to say meet by the flag with "PUGS NOT DRUGS" on. Sadly she hadn't noticed there were at least twenty of them scattered across the crowd of thousands. I have never said so many awkward "'Scuse-me-sorry-just-trying-to-find-my-friends"s as I did in that five minutes. But I *really* needed to find them. I was petrified about the announcement, and my nerves were getting worse. Why was every person I pushed past giving me a funny look? Was it because Rach had put a massive handprint of glitter on my face? Or did they recognize me after Brian's stupid stunt?

I swerved anyone in a Session T-shirt just in case.

When the organizers came on stage, everyone's hands went up. A man in a T-shirt, baseball cap and an ironic moustache slinked towards the mic. So he was the main RebelRocks dude? The only things I could really see were the tops of people's heads and the backs of the people in front (I was desperately trying not to be squashed face first into the massive sweat patch of one guy) but I did have a good view of the huge screens that were broadcasting everything. As the man went to speak, the crowd locked in place. I had to accept reality – the chances of finding my friends was zero. I was going to have to deal with this announcement on my own.

"WELCOME TO THE FIRST EVER REBBBBBBBELROCKS!!!!!" A huge roar erupted that didn't die down for thirty seconds. All I could do was nervously clap. One of the girls next to me clambered up on to her mates' shoulders to get a better view, meaning I had an even worse one. Why thank you. I tried to lean out of the potential fall zone of this wobbling human totem pole.

"CONGRATULATIONS FOR HAVING SUCH EXCELLENT TASTE AND BEING PART OF THE INAUGURAL REBELROCKS FESTIVAL! WITH A SELL-OUT CROWD!"

Even more cheering. But I felt sick. A mixture of nerves and being part of this thousand person sandwich.

"THE MUSIC IS KICKING OFF ANY SECOND." He stepped back, enjoying the "Ooooh" from the crowd. "So, it's time to give you what you all came here for…" Please please please let this be the moment he confirmed Ska's hunch about The Session. "Stage times and final line-up!"

He gestured up to the screens and clicked his fingers. "Friday!" Phones around me started filming as the times and names for the New Bands Tent, Dance Dance Dance Tent, Speakers' Circular Corner and the Main Stage flashed up. I'd have to check for clashes later. Right now I was only concerned with Sunday. Was he going to say *anything*?

My face was on fire. I felt like everyone around me knew who I was – and what I was waiting to find out.

A message from Rach popped up – a pic of her and Teeg looking as anxious as I felt.

RACH: Here goes everything 🤖

Quickly followed by a:

RACH: AND IF YOU SEE EVIL B [That's what she now called Brian.] PERMISSION TO THROW ANYTHING YOU CAN FIND.

I looked back up just in time to see The Wet Donald Project's name on screen. Saturday at 5 p.m. An AMAZING slot?! I gave an extra-loud clap, but was too tense to yell "That's my boyfriend" like I wanted, so made do with taking a quick picture for Adam.

The organizer went through the rest of Saturday's line-up, then waited for the cheering to die down.

"Before we unveil the final day's line-up – let's talk about the elephant in the room." He took his baseball cap off and ruffled his hair before putting it back on.

WAS SOMETHING ABOUT TO HAPPEN? I wish wish wish I was with the others.

"Or should I say, petition in the field."

An icy wave of nerves shot through me.

This was actually happening.

A couple of laughs went up. Some whistles. Some general claps from people.

Please let him say we'd done it.

All those thousands of people that had signed up were counting on us.

"It's time to let you know what's been happening behind the scenes…"

An "Ooooh" went up at the same time a group of girls yelled, "Never stop The Session!!" Ouch.

"As you guys all know, RebelRocks is about standing up for what you believe in." I was fully up on my tiptoes. "To do what's right – not what is easy…"

My stomach knotted. Did this sound promising?

BLAM.

A hand slapped me on the back. "BELLS!!! WE FOUND YOU!"

Rach! I'd never been so relieved to see her face.

"He HAS to say they're off." Tegan was out of breath. "He HAS to."

She spoke loudly, her words ringing out across the uneasy silence that had settled on the crowd. Totem-pole girl turned round and smiled down at Teeg. "100%."

It would have felt good to know we had some support, but as she turned back, someone else shouted, "No chance, special snowflake!" right at her. Unbothered, she flicked them Vs.

It must be easier to feel less bothered when it wasn't your name, your face, that everyone knew was responsible.

Baseball Cap Man stepped back to the mic, giving a quick smile to the side of stage before turning back to the crowd.

"So … here's the line-up." The graphic flashed up. I scanned it as quickly as I could. But as my eyes landed on the headline slot, his voice boomed out. "Complete with The Session."

OOF.

We'd failed.

Boos and cheers rose up all around us.

I was grateful I'd borrowed Rach's spare sunglasses as tears of frustration sprang into my eyes.

Tegan was silent – trying to process what she was hearing but Rach yelled, "What the hell?!"

I wasn't sure if Baseball Cap Man had somehow heard, or just happened to be looking in our direction. "We know it's not what *some* of you want to hear, but the cheers show it's good news to a helluva lot of you. Most importantly ... we think it's the right decision. And if we can all agree one thing, it's that it's important to stand up for what you believe in."

So that was that. No explanation. Nothing from the band. Just business as normal.

Had we been completely deluded to believe we could have them kicked off?

And as Baseball Cap Man left the stage, and the music started back up, the three of us stood in silence. The crowd moved around us, even the people who'd been booing, slipping straight back into having a great time with their friends. Had this just been a bit of fun to them?

I felt like we had nowhere to go.

Rach was the first to break the silence. It was weird to see someone so covered in glitter look so sad. She showed us Brian's latest Insta Story. Him filming Baseball Cap Man from the side of stage, everyone backstage cheering as The Session's set was announced. *That's* who hat man had been smiling at. Brian had even yelled, "See all you non-losers there!"

Rach forced a smile. "At least we tried ... right?"

I needed to follow her lead. We couldn't change it now.

"Just 'cos we didn't win, doesn't mean we didn't

make them think twice. Get everyone talking about how gross they are." Even *I* knew how lame that sounded. "I mean, they had to make an official announcement about it. That's something, isn't it?"

"*Something*, but not *enough*, is it?" Tegan's voice was quiet but strong. "All those people – those names … they were counting on us."

I tried to think of something else to say but I was stumped. My brain had already done three hours' overtime by waking up so early, and it was in no mood to help.

Tegan carried on. "The festival organizers banged on about standing up for what's right, but they HAVE to know what they're doing isn't…" She sighed. Like all the fight was finally escaping her. "Why do idiots always get to win?"

"Teeg – they don't *always*." The words came out before I even thought of them. "Guess just maybe this time they did."

And if things couldn't get any worse: my sister arrived.

Just what I didn't need.

We'd agreed to pretend each other didn't exist, but she barged straight into our convo. And also straight into my shoulder, making me wonder if she was pretending

I didn't exist so much, she'd stopped physically seeing me.

Rach did a double take. I'd forgotten to tell her about yesterday's fam-bush. "Jo?! What are you doing here?"

Jo replied, "Hanging out for the weekend," as I simultaneously said, "Ruining my life."

"Riiiiight," Rach replied, trying not to take sides (although we both knew she was on mine).

This better not be Jo checking up on us.

"Did you know stalking is a criminal offence?" I folded my arms.

She looked me up and down. More specifically up. And most specifically at the topknot that was worming its way off my head. "Did you know that *hairstyle* is a criminal offence?"

Plus side. Her hair insults meant she maybe hadn't spotted that the hoodie tied round my waist was one I'd borrow-stolen from her room.

She nodded towards the stage. "Can you believe what that dude said? You guys must be *fuming*?! I know I am."

Tegan nodded unhappily. I wanted to agree too, but didn't want Jo to think I wasn't still totally mad at her. Rach replied for us.

"He's officially a Grade-A moron."

"I was *so* relieved when I saw you three still huddled here. I KNEW you wouldn't be settling for that lame excuse of a speech he gave." She looked at me. "I just spoke to Mum and she *told* me you'd be on the case." Oh, so she'd been reporting back already. "Plotting, plotting, am I right?"

None of us said anything, no one about to admit the truth.

The only thing we'd been plotting was giving up.

Although…

WAIT…

My own mother believed we wouldn't be quitting. She wouldn't have just given up with her friends. So why were we?

Jo was *right*. So was Tegan.

This didn't have to be the end.

All Baseball Cap Man had done was lay down the gauntlet. There were still two-and-a-half days until the set was happening. Wasn't this enough time to prove to RebelRocks they'd made the wrong decision? Stop The Session totally getting away with this?!

It was like I'd leant on the fast-forward button of my emotional controls. From total blankness, now I had a gazillion thoughts whizzing everywhere.

We had to act FAST. I had to get the others on board.

"Yes, Jo. Totally right. WATCH THIS SPACE."
I was even speaking double speed. Tegan and Rach
were looking at me like that time when I'd put our
refrigerated home-made face mask on, but accidentally
got it muddled up with a tub of cottage cheese. "So we
can't stand here chatting. We've got work to do."

With a wave to Jo, I strode off fiercely, willing the
others to follow.

Tegan caught up first. "Are you thinking what I'm
thinking?"

Of *course* she was.

Rach walk-jogged next to us.

"Sozzee to be late to this party, but, err, what *is* going
on?"

"We're notching things up a gear, Rach. *That's* what."

"I LIKE IT!" Rach waggled her eyebrows. "Soooo …
what exactly is the first step to this notching?"

"Well…" I began, but Rach had found the first flaw
of my plan. The only step of the plan I had so far was:

1) Make a plan.

But I didn't want to lose the confidence we were
building up.

"…Well. We're three intelligent peeps…" I

remembered my looming exam results. "Well, two, anyway. So … step one is putting our heads together."

Tegan thought for a sec. "We could add protest slogans to some of their posters on site? Or … or storm the festival radio station and tell them what's what?"

Rach's eyes had lit up. "And when they start to sell the merch we could get Mikey and Jay and Adam and make some kind of … I dunno. Slowest-moving queue so no one can ever get to the front?!"

I wasn't exactly sure what that meant, but I liked the enthusiasm. But what I liked even more was that Tegan had given me an idea. I stopped dead as it hit me.

"I think we can go even bigger… You know the saying. If we can't beat 'em – join 'em?"

Rach shook her head, glitter raining down. "You're going to have to explain…"

"The Session and RebelRocks organizers – who are *blatantly* friends – might think they've got away with it, but they might have played straight into our hands."

I rubbed my palms together like a villainous cartoon character. But who cared? I was on a mission.

"*Sure*, we might not be Brian with his gazillion followers, but we CAN fight back." My heart was pounding. Tegan nodded at me to finish. "How about we use their gig as the biggest ever platform to tell people that how they treat people is totally sexist and gross and WRONG?" A smile crept across Tegan's face, as she got it too. It was time to unleash the plan.

"How about we turn The Session's gig into the biggest protest a festival has ever seen?"

CHAPTER

FOURTEEN

The next few hours were officially some of the greatest of my life (probably joint only with the hours 9.15–11.30 p.m. last November when the freezers in our local cinema broke, and they asked us to stay behind after the film to see if we could help "dispose" of the melting Ben & Jerry's).

High off the new plan (and chomping through a burrito that was the size of a small bulldog), the three of us began to put the protest plan into action. We had to get together as many people as possible for a #StopTheSession squad to storm the crowd on Sunday and force the band to answer our questions. To do it we were going to need as much publicity as we could get, while trying to keep it below the organizers' and band's radar so they couldn't put a stop to it. Our first mission was to spread the message on site, as well as posting online in the forums of people who'd been supporting us. We set up a bunch of new profiles to try and stay under Brian and @HeyItsTheSessionHQ's radar.

"So we're agreed then?" Tegan composed herself as she chewed her last mouthful of burrito. "Head back to tents, charge phones, change clothes, then come to see Fika Party, the Action! Action! panel, Molly and the Bens and…"

"The Tomato Ketchup Conspiracy Theory." Rach finished off the careful list of bands we were going to see today with my favourite one. We'd planned with precision. "And along the way we get everyone we know to put the word out on the d-low about the protest. And speak to the stall owners to see if they can help?" Rach reckoned she could sweet talk the T-shirt printer Tegan and I had met yesterday into printing some slogan tops for us.

I nodded. "Exacto. We need as much #StopTheSession stuff for Sunday as possible."

When I'd sent Adam the picture of his set time on screen, I'd also cryptically asked him to pack some extra Sharpies and Blu-Tack for when he arrived later. As soon as he'd got out of his exam he replied to say he was on it. And that his exam had gone really well. And that he couldn't wait to see me.

S-woon. I couldn't wait to see him – and tell him what we'd planned.

First on our hit list was to stick up signs all around the festival about the protest (in places the organizers would never go, like the back of the public Portaloo doors), and work out how to make as many signs as possible to unleash on the day.

"This gig is going to be THE most talked about thing ever. They won't know what's hit them!" Tegan was 100% confident this was going to work. "Sunday, 8 p.m., you better watch out!" She said it so fiercely I almost felt sorry for The Session. *Almost.*

We made our way back before separating at the top of the hill to go either side of the fence, ready to meet up back by our tents. But as we approached ours my phone rang, so I motioned for them to carry on.

The pic on the screen gave me a familiar thud of excitement. The feeling I only ever got from Adam. Along with the instantaneous nerves about being able to come across normal over the phone.

"BEEEEEEEF."

I couldn't help but grin at hearing him so excited.

"AAAAAAAARD. Whassssup?" Although this was

a totally cringe way of saying hello, we'd agreed we'd try and reclaim it, and make it so uncool it full-circled and was acceptable again. "Other than nailing your last exam, obv?! Welcome to the other side!"

"I wouldn't say 'nailed'. But it's done!" He whooped. "I wanted to see how you were doing after earlier? I saw Brian's story. That man is a …" A car beeped at that exact moment, drowning out his word. Probably for the best.

"I told you. I'm *fine*. And I have a PLAN! BUT I'LL TELL YOU IN PERSON, OK?"

He laughed. "OK, OK!"

But I could hear something in his voice.

"There's something up, isn't there?"

He paused.

"Maaaaybe?" The way he went up at the end meant there definitely was. And it was something good.

"OI?! Don't be as annoying as *me*. TELL?!"

He laughed. His gorgeous warm laugh.

"Guess?"

"Have you found an eyeliner that can do cat-flicks evenly on both sides?!"

"I … er … don't know what that means … but I'm sure it's on a level?!"

"What? Are you here already?" I spun round. "Are you behind me or something?"

"Nah – but I will be in a couple of hours."

For the first time I noticed how busy it sounded at his end of the phone.

"Go on…"

"Are you sitting down?"

"I'm leaning on a bin?"

"That'll do…." He took a deep breath. "Bad news – I might be a bit later than I said today."

That wasn't *so* bad, I was just excited to see him. "And the good news??"

"BELLS! We just got a call from a booker! They've had a band drop out. They've bumped us … TO HEADLINERS OF THE NEW BAND TENT ON SATURDAY!!"

Woah. HEADLINERS??? This was EPIC!

"Oh. MY. GAH!!! That's AMAYYYZZZIIINNNG."

I realized I was jumping up and down on the spot.

But I was so happy for him! So proud! And beyond excited to see him on stage (where I was 100% going to loudly point out that he was my boyfriend to anyone who would listen/couldn't get away to not listen).

Unable to stop myself, I put my hand over the speaker and said to a passing stranger, "My boyfriend's headlining the New Band Tent!!" The lovely thing was they gave me an impromptu high five. The less lovely thing was realizing I was becoming my mother.

"Awesome, huh?"

"Next-level awesome."

"And you know the best thing?" I shook my head. Not *so* useful on a phone call. "Having you there to see it."

OH HELLO ALL THE FEELS.

"I wouldn't miss it for the WORLD…" It was going to be my life highlight to date.

But I wanted to say more. Tell him how he'd got it all wrong. The best thing about all of this was *him*.

"Ah, Bells. You da best. I genuinely feel a whole load less freaked about it knowing you'll be there." I grinned, basking in his loveliness. "But look. I'm going to have to go. We're squeezing in as much practice today as possible."

So *that's* what I could hear in the background. His bandmates chatting.

"Yeah – you go!"

"I'll message when we get on site!"

"Cool beans!" Oh great. My boyfriend headlined stages. I said "cool beans".

Adam paused. "You know…" His voice sounded different. Like he'd put his hand over his mouth for privacy. "I really like you Bells, right? As in … REALLY like you."

WHOA.

I wasn't expecting that. It came out of nowhere. I

was a mixture of absolutely over the moon, and totally panicked about the right thing to reply. Because the truth was: I really liked him too. More than liked him. So what could I say back?

When good stuff happened, I didn't just want to tell Tegan and Rach, I wanted to share it with him too. And when things happened at home, or my exams went wrong, or there were money worries with GADAC, it was Adam who wrapped me up in a cuddle and made me feel OK. Anything was possible when I was around him. I even tidied my room voluntarily when I knew he was coming over.

Deep down, I knew what I should say back.

I should tell him how I really felt.

Love.

Yup. I loved him.

It was a feeling that didn't seem to have a start or an end. Just an *everything*.

So could I admit it to him?

I took a deep breath. And replied.

"Me too."

As usual, I was Bella, middle name Wimp, Fisher.

CHAPTER

FiFTEEN

I was still smiling by the time I got back to our tent.

Teeg was next to the fence, sitting on some rocks and magazines she'd made into a mini stool (leaving me our one camping chair to sit on. She was The Best). Rach was the other side of the fence, chatting away, swapping into different socks and trainers.

They were as made up as me when I told them Adam's news. Rach suggested I wear my new short-sleeved polka-dot playsuit to celebrate the news. A most excellent call.

Rach's field was unrecognizable from yesterday – there was hardly any grass to be seen, just tents that were the size of Rach's garage, and bunting, camper vans, groups of friends setting up, and so many girls in short shorts (who looked like they hadn't forgotten to bring their razors and weren't on day two of leg hair regrowth like me). Where there had been space around Rach's tent, now a group of five tents had popped up in a sort of U-shape around it, each of them proudly decorated with a glittery "PARTY HQ".

"Looks like you got company!" I plonked myself down on the chair as Tegan zipped my playsuit into place.

Rach scrunched her face. "Gotta hope they're nice?! Or at least don't snore."

I raised an eyebrow. "Don't mind YOU snoring, more like?"

"Oi." She threw a sock at me over the fence. But she knew it was true. When she stayed at mine, her night noises sometimes made the neighbour's dog bark. How a face so serene could make the sound of a pneumatic drill, I had no idea. I threw the sock back, and it totally missed. As Rach went to fetch it, she peered into the new mini campsite she'd found herself in.

"Seriously, guys. These peeps are next level. They've got a full-length mirror. As in a *glass* mirror. And an actual *bucket* of glitter." Rach spotted Tegan looking at her nervously. Was it even possible to trespass when you all lived in a field? "Don't worry, they're not in."

But Rach suddenly stopped dead and dropped to the floor, her mouth hanging open. She looked like she'd seen a ghost. Which, considering it was bright daylight, and they didn't exist, was fairly unlikely. Voices were approaching – were these the mysterious campmates?

I leant as far forward as I could to get a glimpse of them. Which caused two things to happen. One very good, one very bad.

Good: Rach had struck campmate gold. Her tent buddies were people we knew very well (/knew very well from afar). The Mega Girl Crush girls!

Bad: With a sound of snapping plastic (and maybe a snapping leg bone) I spectacularly toppled off my chair.

Tegan lunged forward to save me, grabbing my foot. But all that happened was my trainer came off in her hand, and with a thump I splatted on to the ground right in front of MGC's faces, socked foot waving in the air.

Blue Hair slow clapped. "That was quite something."

Choker Girl and their mate in a retro Britney Spears T-shirt laughed. I hoped *with* me, not at me.

I waved feebly from the ground. "Er, hello." This was our chance to impress them. Befriend them. But how? Teeg helped me back up. At least one of the three of us was a competent human. Rach was still crouching behind her tent in shock – staying totally rigid as Blue Hair started stepping backwards towards her.

"Soz, mate." Blue Hair spotted Rach milliseconds before treading on her. "I'll leave you in peace." She smirked. "*Pee* being the operative word."

Rach gasped, mortified.

"I'm not *peeing*??" she shouted. "I'm just, er…" What, Rach? *Hiding behind this tent while you try and deal with the fact you're basically living with the girls we're obsessed with?* "Tying my shoe."

Impressive lie. Until I realized Blue Hair was peering at Rach's feet. Which were very much in slip-on trainers. But she didn't pull Rach up on it.

"Are they the Alexa Chung ones?"

Rach nodded. Her dad had picked them up in Japan.

"Sweet."

Rach blinked like she couldn't believe she was the one impressing Blue Hair. Maybe befriending hopes weren't lost after all?! Go shoes!

Blue Hair stuck her hand out. "I'm Marge."

"And the rest…" Britney T heckled as she walked round to check out Rach's shoes.

Marge shook her head. "Seriously? *Every* time?"

Britney T nodded.

"Fine?! I'm Marge … last name Simpson. And yes

218

– the irony of my blue hair has NOT been lost on me."

Rach was giving Marge the same look of adoration she used to give Mumbles when she was a puppy. The same look I try not to give Adam 24/7.

"I'm Rach … and these –" she pointed at Tegan and me "– are my best mates, Tegan and Bella." We both waved.

Choker Girl looked at Tegan and me as if trying to work something out.

"I know you, don't I?"

Marge flipped open a can of beer, spraying Rach's tent. "It's that girl with the loo roll from Tesco, right?"

I mean, she was technically right although I did have other descriptions I preferred. But it meant they remembered us. Remembered me!

"That's me." I waved. Again. How many times was it OK to wave at people before it became weird? Choker Girl's face suggested the sweet spot was probably one.

"So why aren't you with your mate?" Choker Girl looked at Rach like she was a lost dog. Albeit a lost dog with great shoes.

Tegan replied for us. "We can't camp together. This is as near as we can get, because we have to stay in the workers' bit." She lifted up her wristband. They looked impressed. I lifted mine up too, keen to get in on the action, but they'd moved on, so I quickly pretended to be doing a stretch instead.

"Cool," Blue Hair drawled. Sorry what?! Marge thought we were cool?! What even is my life right now?! I took a sip of water to distract my mouth muscles from the massive grin they were trying to create on my face. Marge never had to find out *exactly* what our job was. She walked over nearer to us and leant right on the fence, checking out where we were camping. Right now, I wished I'd listened to Tegan's advice that the best way of making our tent easier to find wasn't to make a flag for the top of it using a twig and a pair of enormous pants I'd bought to make her laugh. They were flapping in the breeze. "Our mate's helping out with some filming. Is that what you guys are doing?"

I stared at Tegan, channelling a "whatever you do, DO NOT SAY LITTER PICKING" beam right into her brain.

"Litter picking," she replied without missing a beat. Couldn't she have even tried to lie?!

Marge snorted. "Cool." This time she said it more like "kewl", like it really wasn't at all. "Whatever floats your boat."

I wanted to explain my boat wasn't floating at all, but it was our only way of getting a ticket, but they didn't seem like they wanted to know the details. Britney T walked over to Rach and slid an arm over her shoulder. She had gold and matt-black nail varnish. It was all too much. I swear I heard Rach whimper.

"Well, you're OK here with us." She smiled at Tegan and me. "You can consider your mate…" She looked at Rach. "What was your name again?" But Rach had lost the ability to speak, so Tegan had to answer. "Sure, Rach, yeah. Well, you can consider Rach an honorary member of the Party HQ."

OMG. Despite bad socks, not being able to sit on a chair, and having the dweebiest jobs going, we were officially befriending the MGC at a festival. Yes, it sucked having Rach in a different field, but this more than made up for it. If things went well, we could even ask them to help out on Sunday?!

So when a new message came through from Adam I felt like all the pieces for a perfect weekend had come together – but better than I could have ever imagined.

But that feeling only lasted a couple of seconds. Because as I read his message, a horror crept over me.

How could one bit of news switch everything from so good, to so unbelievably complicated?

CHAPTER

SiXTEEN

What could I tell him?

What could I tell the others?

What could I tell myself?!!

I had NO idea what to do. I looked back at my screen with a rising feeling of nausea.

> AARD: Do you want the good news or the more
> good news? Yyy

His use of yyy as our secret xxx didn't even cheer me up.

> AARD: Soz too slow. I'm going to be here earlier
> than I thought!

Which should have been great news. If it hadn't followed it with this.

AARD: And they've had a band get stuck in
America so have moved us to a new day!

AARD: 8 P.M.... On Sunday!!!!!!!!!!!!! WE'RE
HEADLINING THE FINAL NIGHT!!!!

I'd reread it twenty times already.

Adam was playing at the same time as The Session.

Which meant I had a choice.

See him.

Or go to the protest.

I'd said I wouldn't miss his gig for the world.

But now I might have to.

Otherwise I'd let my friends down. And everyone who had been counting on us to Stop The Session.

EURGH.

Why hadn't I just told Adam what we were planning to do?

"OK, lads." Britney T was scrunching her hair up. "So no one look" – aka, the one thing that most makes you want to look – "but if *you*, like us, were hoping to have THE fittest guy in the world camp next to you, it looks like our non-religious prayers might have been answered." She put her hands in the air. "HALLELUJAH HOTTIE."

I took back my earlier thought – *that* might actually be the number one thing that most makes you want to look.

Marge and Choker Girl (who we'd now discovered was actually called Lola, aka Lols – she was always making jokes, so it kind of suited her) peered in the direction Britney T was staring. Right behind us.

"Whoa." Lols fanned her face with both hands. "He is FINE. Dibs on being UT's sleeping bag bud." She raised one eyebrow. "And when I say *sleeping bag bud*, I mean 'no sleeping will happen here' bud…" She bit her lip. "And when I say bud, I mean…"

"All right, LOLS?! We get it." Marge laughed and looked at us apologetically. "UT is Lols' thing for *Ultimate Target*. Whoever she has in her sights at any given moment."

Rach laughed in a way that sounded forced, not like her at all. "Me likey."

I'd never heard those words come out of her mouth before. She was full-on friend-flirting with them. Not that I was doing much better; I'd just agreed to Britney

T trialling her new home-made glitter lipstick on me, and currently looked like a cross between a nursery art project and a "You Wouldn't Believe What Happened When My Boyfriend Did My Make-Up!" YouTube vid. Tegan was still regarding me with concern. "Remember the rule, right?" Marge was being stern with Lols. "*Wherever* we sleep, it's gals breakfast every morn?" She looked at me. "The number one rule for one-night stands. Don't you think, Bella?"

Errrr – could she not tell I'd never even had a one-night sit, let alone a one-night stand? But I didn't want them to know how out of my depth I was, so I tried to laugh with hopefully the right amount of enthusiasm to convey "hahaha, I totally get what you mean" and "hahaha, I'm laughing 'cos this topic is so not a big deal to me" and also "hahahaha, I'm pretending that question was rhetorical so I don't have to commit to actually replying". But my laugh didn't hide Tegan shifting quietly on her stool, a reminder that there was someone who knew what I was really thinking. And that we really needed to get going. We had bands to see and the protest to organize.

To stop MGC waiting for an answer, I shoved a marshmallow in my mouth and turned to see who this "Ultimate Target" was. But the hottie was hidden.

Worried she was losing him, Lols wolf-whistled so loud I swear dogs for five miles stopped in their tracks.

"You all right there?" she shouted in his direction, pushing her body up against the fence. "Want a hand?" The way she stressed the word "hand" made me think she didn't mean in the tent-erecting sense.

I could hear him walking over. Well this was awkward. I was just going to have to chew and hope it was over soon.

He cleared his throat. Was he going to be an equally as big a flirt back?

But what he said was a million times worse than anything I could have imagined.

"Yes, actually. I'm looking for my girlfriend. Don't suppose you've seen her?"

Oh, my massive tent erection.

"Apparently she's got some comedy pants on her tent."

Ultimate Target was Adam.

SEVENTEEN

I did the only thing you can do when trying to appear calm and in control in front of the boy you are in love with/girls you are trying to impress – laughed manically through the awkward silence.

"You found us then?" Tegan stood up and gave Adam a hug.

LIFESAVER.

See, brain? See, arms? This is how normal people do things.

"Total thanks to you." Undeterred by me being massively deterred, Adam bent to give me a kiss. He definitely mini-flinched at my glitter-smeared face. And then stuck to me slightly as he pulled away.

"Errr, hi." I stood up. Time to engage Super-Cool-

Festival-Girlfriend-Mode. "We thought it didn't smell so bad of the toilets here." Brain: wipe 'appearing normal' off my 'achievable list'. "They reek."

Marge snorted. "And Bella is available for weddings, parties and funerals…" Everyone laughed. Maybe too hard.

Rach walked over to the fence and threw Adam an air hug.

"TELL ALL. How did you manage to get in *there*?" She nodded at our side of the barrier. "I tried *everything* – this was the closest I could get." She lowered her voice. "I even brought in major contraband bribes … Kit Kats my dad got from Japan that taste of heaven. Well, cherry blossom and heaven, but mainly heaven."

Adam laughed. He loved Rach almost as much as we did. "Ahhh, that's your problem right there. The security guards were more interested in pasties – our Greggs stash opened up the keys to the festival."

"NOOO." She looked horrified. Adam looked even more horrified that she'd believed his terrible attempt at a joke.

"Sorry, no?! Joke?! We got these." He pushed down the sleeve of his hoodie to show off his deeply alluring forearms. Wow. I knew they were good, but even I was quietly proud they could work their magic on security guards.

"So green is for artists then?" Rach poked her fingers through and pulled at his wristband. *Wristband*. Not great forearms. *That's* what he was showing us. That made more sense.

"Bella – you didn't tell us your boyfriend was in a band?" Lols was standing up with her arms crossed. I shrugged nonchalantly and threw Adam my best "yup, I'm just an independent woman who is supportive and proud of what you've achieved but not at all defined by it" look. But Lols hadn't finished. "Oh no – *my mistake*, that's ALL you've talked about."

I nostril-flared so hard at least ten bits of glitter mainlined into my brain.

"I'm sure it's not," Adam said softly, defending my honour. "But please, please all come along, we're worried it's going to be a crowd of three situation…" Oh no oh no oh no. I still hadn't talked to Adam about the protest. Or told the others about the timing clash.

I had to steer the convo away from this until I'd figured out what to do.

"MATE!" a voice shouted up from behind our tent. Was it the God of Saving Me from Terrible Situations?

"Mate?" It shouted again, a bit more annoyed.

It was Marcus, Adam's best mate/lead singer of The Wet Donald Project/only other human who could watch the same vid of a boy snorting a crème caramel out of his nose and still be laughing on the fifteenth repeat. "Could kind of do with a hand here."

Adam's face scrunched as he mouthed, "Oops". "Coming!"

REJOICE. I'd dodged dealing with this mega-problem until our next convo.

Lols waved. "Come back and hang when you're done. Be nice to meet your bud." She winked at Adam. Marge elbowed her for being so obvious.

"What?!" Lols was all indignant. "He might need some company in that tent? They can be lonely places."

She was laughing. But I was the exact opposite of finding this funny.

If Adam was camping in the same field as us, and wasn't sharing his tent with Marcus, did that mean … he might suggest sharing with me?

Intense. Panic.

This was not the kind of conversation I could be catapulted into, unless I'd practised it at least fifty times with Tegan.

Luckily Adam was unflustered. "Don't you worry. It wouldn't be the first time we've woken up to discover Marcus has become Big Spoon… I'm kind of prepared."

Oh, thank sweet cheeses. He *was* sharing with Marcus.

"Sorry, what?" Lols looked confused. "Aren't you staying with your *girlfriend*?" I spluttered so hard I had to pretend I'd swallowed some more glitter. Did she actually say that out loud?! She hardly knew us? Why would she be assuming anything? I couldn't look at Adam. "Meaning your mate is hypothetically all alone and maybe hypothetically looking for company."

I stared at my feet (one still only in a sock) and willed a sinkhole to open up.

"Lols, you don't even know who this dude is." Marge sounded like she'd been through this many times before. "Or if he's single. Or into girls. Or, I dunno ... a murderer?"

Tegan snorted. "Reassurance: murderers don't tend to be in our inner circle."

"Or my best mates?" Adam said, sounding more than a little done with the conversation.

"Well, we *think*. Let's see how many of us are alive tomorrow." Britney T was teasing, but only her and Rach laughed. I was too busy burning up from head to toe that Adam and I had never even spoken about us staying in the same tent. And now it was a public topic of conversation, when we hadn't even managed a private one.

231

"It's not like it's possible to sleep in a tent anyway." Was Adam trying to ease the tension, or was I being paranoid? "It feels like someone's permanently four centimetres from stamping on your head."

But Lols was quick to steer the conversation back to her own agenda.

"The only thing that's *meant* to make sleeping in tents difficult is having something more fun to do in them." She winked at me. "But you guys know what I mean."

We both just stared at her.

Was she enjoying this torture?

WHY WAS SHE DOING THIS?!

"Well, I'll leave you guys to, er, chat." Adam began to walk off, trying to make a sharp exit.

Lols tossed her hair back. "Good luck making that love palace?! Bella should be along shortly."

Adam looked mortified. It wasn't me being paranoid. This was totally embarrassing. I *had* to do something.

"Just to be clear…" Oh no, my mouth had started speaking with no help from my brain. "*As Adam said*, well, sort of said, we are NOT planning on sleeping" – argh, not that word – "AS IN STAYING, together?!"

The way everyone was staring at me, Adam included, suggested that maybe I didn't need to have semi-shouted this across the campsite. This was the most in-depth convo my boyfriend and I had ever had about, er, what happened beyond snogging, and we were having it in a field, with a group of girls who didn't seem like they'd even inwardly blush at words like "moist" and "shaft".

OH GOD I JUST BLUSHED THINKING ABOUT BLUSHING AT THEM.

This would be the world's most awkward silence, if there wasn't the loud sound of Britney T trying (and failing) not to snigger.

"See ya!" Adam shouted, but he was already scurrying away. It was technically a flee.

Well, that had gone well.

Tegan stood up, looking straight at Lols. "I've never seen him leave anywhere so quickly."

So she'd picked up on his uncomfortableness too. It really had been that bad.

"No great loss," Lols said coldly. "He wasn't exactly a barrel of laughs."

"Would you be if someone was sleazing all over your mate?"

Was Teeg posing a genuine question, or politely telling Lols she'd gone too far?

Lols' body language changed, her shoulders opening up like she was ready for a fight.

"Not my fault if he can't handle being around a strong woman."

This was escalating quickly.

"And what *exactly* are you trying to imply about us then?"

In fairness, Tegan was one of the strongest women I knew. Just a shame for her I sometimes had the mental and physical endurance of a wafer.

"I don't need to imply anything, *Rubbish Girl*."

I hoped Lols meant in the litter sense.

How was this all going so wrong?

I stood up, keen to end it as soon as possible.

"C'mon Tegan, Rach. We need to head off. All that stuff to do." It sounded like a lie even though it was true.

This time it was Britney T who couldn't leave it. "Stuff? Like walk away from arguments you started but can't finish?"

I looked at Rach, trying to work out if I'd heard right, but she was also panicking at how wrong this was suddenly going.

"It's not a lie." She was almost stuttering with nerves. "We've got this protest we need to get going. Against The Session?"

I knew what the hope in her voice meant. That by

telling them about the protest we might score back some points. Calm them down.

They shot each other looks as if struck by the same realization.

Marge smiled. Softened. And she nodded at the other two, like suddenly it was OK to like us again. Phew.

"So *that's* where we really know you from – you're the Stop The Session girls?"

I nodded, relieved to have stumbled on some middle ground. "Yup. And we've got a protest we need to sort for Sunday. So when I said *stuff*, I really meant it."

Marge looked at me as if trying to work out what she thought of me. "Interesting." She pulled her phone out. "Well, look. Sorry about what just happened. Just there's nothing that winds us up more than when girls don't support girls, y'know. Had some bad experiences. We didn't realize you were the ones out there fighting the fight."

"Sure are," Tegan said, her voice still clipped. Her bag was up on her shoulder – she was ready to go.

"Look, Rach," Marge held out her phone. "Put your number in here, then I'll message you so you've got mine." Rach immediately punched it in. "If you need anything let us know. And remember, we're only ever a tent away."

Rach was smiling.

But something didn't feel right.

Marge's words were friendly. So why did they sound like a threat?

"Well, *they* were something," said Tegan as we walked down to the main festival site.

"They weren't *that* bad…" They'd lent Rach some pineapple-shaped sunglasses on her way out. In return, Rach had given them the benefit of the doubt. "Think we just got off on the wrong foot."

Tegan snorted.

I kept quiet. I agreed with Teeg, because it had really felt like Lols was enjoying every second of winding Adam and me up, but knew Rach was trying to see the positive side of them. Maybe she still believed they were as cool as we'd always thought, or perhaps it was because they'd declared her an honorary member of Party HQ. Either way, now we were heading away from them, it didn't feel like the right time to push it. Especially as I hadn't been able to find Adam, and all my messages saying that I really needed to speak to him had gone unanswered. I had to make sure stuff was OK after earlier. Which was going to be even harder as I still had my big decision to make.

His gig. Or the protest.

My boyfriend. Or my best friends.

Eurgh.

I was going to let someone down, however much I didn't want to. I was going to have to figure this one out on my own.

But lucky for me, if there was one place on earth that helped fill my head with happier thoughts, it was right here. Even the sun felt like it was shining extra hard, extra happy, although I did kind of regret my playsuit. I was sweltering.

We needed to lift our spirits, so taking a break from prepping for the protest, we squeezed our way to the front of the barrier for our first gig of the festival. Squashed at the front of the huge crowd, I almost lost my voice singing along to every word. It was awesome. We jumped around like loons for the whole thing. They should totally teach moshing instead of athletics at school. I did more exercise in that forty-five minutes than I had done all year. Best of all, every time I looked at Rach or Tegan they were smiling as much as me.

So, with happiness fully restored, as soon as it finished, we turned our attention to making sure every Session poster around the main fence had a #StopTheSession added to it. I got stomach-twisting nerves every time we pulled out a pen to write on.

But Tegan argued we had the moral high ground, and by our fifth one, our confidence had grown so much we'd also started scrawling *12 p.m. Sunday. Doughnut be late* on them. Nice Doughnut Lady – also known as Brenda – had offered use of her D'Oh Nut Stand as a meeting point to make banners and posters on the day. We figured people who wanted to turn up would go to the effort of finding out what we meant.

I stood back and pulled my camera out to take a picture of our latest bit of handiwork for the website.

"Incommmmming…"

OOF.

A heavy lump plonked on to my back. A surprisingly furry lump.

I knew exactly what – or who – it was. I turned around expecting to see Mikey – bit taller than me, dark haired, scruffy, freckly, smiley face. But instead I recoiled at the sight of a 5'11" panda with scary red eyes. And his friend, a giant crab.

"So on one of the hottest days of the year you dressed as a fluffy demon panda? How's that working out for you?"

Mikey used his broken arm to pull his animal suit even further down over his face and did a full spin. He'd accessorized with a neon bum bag. Strong.

"I think you'll find it's a ring-tailed lemur." He peeled the hood back; underneath he was a sweaty mess. "It *may* have been the last one left. And it *may* be approximately 1000°C in here."

Jay pulled his crab hood down. Could a person be that red without actually melting?

"...And they may also be the only things we've packed this weekend."

Rach looked like she might be sick. Tegan looked totally unsurprised.

"And you wonder why I said there was no way I was sleeping in a tent with you."

They both laughed. I couldn't believe they could chat about this kind of thing so casually. Must take notes.

"So what's the plan then?" Mikey sat down on the floor. I'd never seen a lemur cross-legged. But then again I'd never seen a lemur.

Jay lay flat out beside him. "Mike said you might need some help with getting things set for Sunday?"

A heckle came from a passer-by in a trilby. "Nice crabs, mate."

Mikey sat up, all indignant lemur. "It's a lobster, *mate*? Know your crustaceans?! "

Even though Jay had his eyes closed it still looked

like he was rolling them. "That's the tenth time today. And I've only had it on two hours."

Rach laid out starfished next to him. "Oh well, it's not like you have *literally nothing* else to wear." She laughed, which turned into shouts of "Oi" as he tried to flop one of his pincers in her face.

Tegan sat down next to me and got her phone out, to look at the list of what needed to be done today.

We stopped laughing, and paid attention as we remembered the task at hand. Protest planning. Mikey buffled (bum shuffled) towards her, and leant in to talk. Because of the way his lemur head was dangling, it looked a bit like she was being eaten. "Teeg, give us stuff to do, OK? We want to help."

Tegan gave him the kind of smile that if Adam gave me I'd physically be unable to not say *uhuhruhrhrrhrururururur* right in his face.

Jay heard and sat up, shrugging his lobster shoulders. "For reals. Tackling the patriarchy takes everyone, right?" I was glad Jay had his eyes obscured by a lobster antenna (or whatever those long dangly bits are), 'cos for all the years I'd known him, I'd never seen this side of him. I never knew he had so many layers?! "Plus girls fancy boys who are into feminism, right?"

He raised his two pincers in the air, giving himself

his own "holler", which was short-lived, as after a quick glance between us, Rach, Tegan and I all piled on him, arms and legs flying everywhere as we let out a war cry.

Turns out lobster suits provide excellent protection from prodding. Maybe I should get one for around the house whenever Jo's back? But we were people on a mission, and soon we'd tickled him into submission, and from a foetal position he'd apologized for the error of his ways.

Once we got our breath back – and Jay was satisfied with the protective barrier of bags he'd built between us – I went back to the plan.

"So I'm on 'trying to blag free stuff for people to wear, wave, whatever'? But –" I slurped my Capri Sun "– manage those expectations 'cos my blagging skills are as good as my bowling skills."

Mikey looked puzzled. "I don't remember you being bad at bowling, Bells?"

"You don't remember it 'cos I've refused to do it ever since I broke two fingers and caused the 'first-ever ambulance to visit GameCity in its fifty-year history'." Yes, I air-quoted. "Their words, not mine."

"I see." Luckily he hadn't. It was a disaster. I'd fallen forwards with the ball and had flown seven metres down the bowling lane. "So what else can we do?"

Rach sat up. "I'm going to post as much in the forums and on the hashtag as possible. You could help with that? I updated the blog too. Talking of which, can I get some photos of the graffitied posters, Bells?" I nodded, happy to be of use, and flicked the wifi button on my camera to send them to my phone. "We're already getting loads of comments on Insta."

Tegan's eyes lit up. "Lots of people down to turn up?"

"Not yet…" Rach sounded as positive as she could. "But I'm sure there will be. We've still got today and all of Saturday to get people on board."

We all made noises of agreement – I hoped none of them had the same nagging feeling we were setting ourselves up for just another failure. But this time, instead of being able to hide behind the internet, we'd be there in real life, in the middle of a crowd of die-hard Session fans, who, according to a post last night, "wanted to shove our heads where the sun didn't shine" (I could only hope they meant Alaska in the winter).

Eurgh.

Why was it so scary standing up for what you believed in? Why couldn't it all be about having a nice-comfy-sit-down for what you believed in instead?

But Tegan wasn't going to let our spirits drop again.

"I'll start digging into who runs the festival radio, and

Lemur, Crab – argh, sorry, Lobster – if you've got any ideas about how to drum up support here that would be hay-mazing."

Mikey narrowed his eyes, as if he could spy an idea creeping over the horizon.

"I miiiight have something…" He picked up his phone and started typing. "Can you give me a couple of hours?"

"Sure thing…" Tegan sounded intrigued. "So how about we head to the stalls and get stuff started. Meet back here at seven for The Tomato Ketchup Conspiracy Theory?"

They were one of my fave punk-pop bands and I didn't want to miss them. Adam and I both knew every word to every song – he sometimes played along when I was round at his house. He really wanted to watch them tonight, so I was hoping he'd be there too.

With time ticking, the five of us headed off, making a beeline (although bees tend to go in lots of loops, and ours was a lot more straight) to the market area. You could buy *everything* here. Animal tails to pin on to clothes, postcards to send back home, a picture of your face made out of lentils. One queue was so long it snaked round the back of the Portaloos. Being British, we were magnetically drawn to it. We walked past all the people who had clearly been there for ages, overhearing one lad telling his mate it was "worth it 'cos they were going to sell out by the end of the day" because "it's the kind of stuff you could clean up with on eBay". But when we got to the front of the van, to see what it was for, it couldn't have been worse. It was the queue for The Session's sexist merchandise.

"I can't believe it," Tegan hissed with rage, turning her back on it. "Do people have zero taste?"

I almost didn't want to show her the handwritten sign next to the display. *See what the fuss is about. Get your hands on the most talked about merch of the festival!*

"Do you …" A dark thought hit me, and I couldn't hold it in. "… reckon it's so popular because of us trying to stop it?"

The girls underwear saying "Property of The Session" had already sold out. Most pants news ever.

Teeg rubbed her hands over her face. "Yuh-huh."

"Well, *this* has backfired." Rach had a knack for saying what we were all thinking. "Anyone got any ideas?"

I didn't have an idea. But I did have something.

A call coming through from Adam. It was decision time.

And after what I'd just seen, I had to choose the protest. Didn't I?

He'd understand. Wouldn't he?

"Hiyer, Beef." Hearing his voice flooded the fear straight back.

"Hiyer, Aard." I didn't sound like myself.

The problem with phones is there's no getting round an awkward silence.

And we were officially in one.

"Er…" Adam was first to break it. "I can't be long as we're carting more kit from the van, but you … you said you wanted to speak?"

"I could have helped?" Skilful diversion technique, me.

"S'OK. You seemed busy."

I thought back to when I last saw him. When Lols made him flee. Cringe.

"So, er, you going to tell me what's up then?"

The words were on the tip of my tongue. It was now or never.

"I, er, just wanted to say…"

I swallowed. I could do this.

"Sorry about that girl earlier." Or not.

"Oh?" He sighed into the phone. Was it relief? "Her? No probs."

"She's, er…" *What, Bells?* A lame excuse of something you can talk about to buy more time?

Luckily Adam finished my thought for me. "Intense?"

Phew. At least we were on the same wavelength about one thing. "Intense about tents."

He laughed too. "But that's not your fault. I thought you were going to say something really bad... Like you couldn't make our gig or something?!"

ACTUAL STOMACH LURCH.

He chuckled like this was the funniest thing he could have thought of. I did the only thing I could think of: laugh as if I wasn't the worst girlfriend in the world.

"As if." It was one of those unhinged laughs that could all too easily turn into a cry if I was left unattended. Rach saw and gave me a thumbs up to ask if I was OK. I shook my head and stumbled through the next bit of conversation as we agreed to meet after he'd finished unloading the kit and I'd promised to take pictures of The Tomato Ketchup Conspiracy Theory if he missed them. Then we said bye and I was left staring at my phone, wishing I could fast-forward my life by three days.

"Whadup?" Rach headed straight over, Tegan right behind her. Mikey and Jay had disappeared, which is actually quite an achievement when one of you has claws that flap above your head.

I wasn't sure whether to tell them what was going on. Which would mean admitting that I'd deliberately avoided telling them about Adam's set change, because I didn't know what to do.

But I was freaking out. And they were my best friends – and soon I'd told them every single detail, including the dilemma I was in.

When I stopped there was silence. *Please* let them not be mad.

Tegan spoke first.

"You know what I'm going to say, don't you, Bells?"

And from the way she was looking at me, I did.

"That sometimes there isn't a best thing to do?"

She nodded. "Yup." It was something she said all the time. "So sometimes you just have to do what you *think* is best."

But that was my problem. Sometimes it felt like my head and heart bickered more than me and Jo.

"Wouldn't it be, like, totally zero-cool to ditch my mates for my boyfriend though?" I cringed at how I was casually trying to pretend I wasn't asking for advice, while hoping they'd reassure me I'd made the right decision.

Tegan put her arm through mine. "You know my motto – girls support girls."

Rach lifted her hands in the air and mouthed, "Preach!"

"So if you did want to go support someone who's given *you* loads of support, like your boyfriend, that's not ditching us, that's just having a rubbish choice to make, right, Rach?"

Their support made me feel like it could all be OK after all. I felt weirdly emotional – more so than when I finished the last doughnut.

But as I went to reply, the music stopped and the loudest boo went up.

The stalls lights had gone out.

The people behind the counter were all running about.

Oh My Doughnut Balls.

Was it our first bit of good luck?

The merchandise stand had totally lost power. The card machines were all out, and the tills wouldn't open. No one could buy anything!

The crowd around us was starting to get angry, but one face was smiling in the middle of it. Tegan.

"Our time to leave?"

She didn't need to ask twice. We made a sharp exit, but after trying the festival paper printer, two T-shirt stalls and one flag printer, it was already time to meet back up with Mikey and Jay. And we'd had no luck. But as we explained to them the little progress we'd made, Mikey couldn't stand still, his animal head bobbing around as we spoke. Was he having a lemur-based breakdown? He didn't seem at all bothered by our lack of progress, and jumped in as soon as Rach had finished.

"Sooo, do you want some more bad news?" He didn't give us time to answer. "'COS IF YOU DO THEN I'M SORRY BUT THE LEEMSTER –" which is what he'd started referring to the Lemur and Lobster duo as "– CAN'T HELP."

He unzipped his bum bag. "Tell me giving up your Saturday night to babysit your child of hell next-door neighbour doesn't have its benefits?!" He pulled out a wodge of postcard-sized bits of paper.

WHOA.

Flyers. Printed with the time and date of the protest. And almost word for word what Tegan had said earlier when she was explaining it to Jay.

If you want to show the true spirit of RebelRocks, then head to the main stage at 7.45 p.m. Sunday. Let's show everyone the power of people is bigger than any band. It's time to STOP THE SESSION. Bring whatever you can – signs, flags,

> voices. If you care about equality it's
> time to demand respect – and get The
> Session to admit what they're doing is
> NOT OK.

It even had our social handles on.

> All support appreciated. Meet @ the D'Oh
> Nut Stand 12 p.m. Sunday if you want to
> get crafty and make banners in advance.

Yes the Leemster!!

The three of us threw our arms around Mikey. It was like cuddling a giant teddy bear (that was a bit muddy and smelt slightly of mould).

"First ever GOAT lemur!" I said into what I think was his neck, but could have been armpit (if lemurs have arms? Or do they just have four legpits?).

He made a muffled "Ah, shucks", but I knew he was loving it. Despite having a permanent vacant lemur look he really had been paying attention.

"My neighbour was heading down, and owed me a favour." He was grinning like someone who knew they'd struck gold. "I can explain to my dad why his printer is near dead another time."

Tegan flung her arms around him again. "So your brother was in on this too?"

"Uh-huh. He printed them out. You know he loves you almost more than I do."

He said it causally, but we all knew he'd loved her since before they were even together. Rach grabbed a bunch to put in her tote bag.

"OK if I hand these out tomorrow morning when Teeg and Bells are working? Catch everyone early?" Sounded like a perfect plan. Mikey had given us the boost we needed.

"Oh and one more thing." Jay had a naughty look in his eye. "You've got to ask yourselves why if all the power goes off for a stand, none of them think to check the generator?" He pulled something tiny out of his pocket. Was it a fuse? "Top tip, walk confidently dressed as a lobster and you get in *anywhere*."

Sorry what?! Jay and Mikey had cut the power to the merch stand?!

"You evil, furry geniuses?!" I high-fived his claw.

"So next time you see Ms Ashley, please tell her that even if I fail physics abysmally at least I definitely learnt how to unwire a plug." I'd been scared writing on a poster. These two must have lemur/lobster balls of steel. Well, fluff and steel. "Sure they'll figure it out soon.

Kinda their fault for assuming that two people looking like us are so obvious we can't be up to something bad. Hiding in per-lain sight."

BOOOM.

A drumbeat thudded out from the main stage speakers. The opening chords of The Tomato Ketchup Conspiracy Theory. Without another word, the five of us ran full speed towards it. And fired up on Mikey and Jay's amazing news, we leapt around to the whole Tommy K set, arms round each other in a big, bouncy mosh circle. I even filmed the whole performance of "Rascalifornian" for Adam.

I felt on top of the world.

Which was just as well. As in less than half an hour, I was going to feel right at the very bottom.

CHAPTER

EIGHTEEN

"See you back here in ten," were the last words I said to the others.

That was over an hour ago.

Back when I didn't know sixty of the most traumatic minutes of my life were about to unfold.

I stared up at the ceiling of the St John's Ambulance tent, trying to understand how I managed to end up here, and how I'd achieved my own shame-fest.

Flashing an entire field of people.

Creating – and wearing – an adult romper made entirely out of loo roll.

Being stretchered out of a Portaloo.

Speaking to a man who may or may not have been a toilet-fume-based hallucination.

It had started so well. All I needed was a wee. And the queue for the Portaloos hadn't been that long.

When one became free, despite it smelling of a mixture of warm death and the alley near my house, I ran towards it. Come to me, you tiny box of dreams!

Sweet relief was finally here!

Or not.

Because as I slammed the door shut I remembered I was wearing the ultimate enemy to bladders everywhere. A playsuit. A brand-new playsuit. A brand-new zip-up playsuit.

Why hadn't I foreseen this disaster?!

I contorted my arms behind my head but couldn't feel anything.

I tried going up behind my back instead.

Still nothing. It was all made harder by the fact that every surface in this Portaloo looked like one touch and you'd die of a terrible disease.

This is why girls always go in twos. Because, yes we can invent popcorn that tastes of birthday cake, but who needs clothes that mean you can go to the loo on your own AS A GROWN ADULT?!

This was torture.

I. Needed. A. Wee. So. Bad.

To think, I'd been so excited when Tegan had helped

me put this on earlier – why hadn't the penny dropped about spending a penny? Who cares about washing instructions, they should sew in a "Need to Know" list for when you first wear stuff.

C'mon, Bella. Don't panic.

What would Jo do?

Wear sensible clothes and never be in this situation? That didn't help. Even imaginary Jo was annoying.

I thought through options.

What was the etiquette of popping my head out and asking a stranger? *Oh, hello – I don't know you, but could you step into this confined space and undress me?* Nope, that was a lawsuit waiting to happen.

There was nothing for it. I was just going to have to ring one of the others and wait for them to come and help. But that would take a while. And judging by the way I felt, I didn't have a while.

Unless … what if there was someone outside I knew? I hoisted myself up, balancing my feet on the flat bit either side of the seat, and peered out through the vents.

All I could see was a man dressed as a giant corn on the cob, wobbling as he went into the cubicle next to me.

Within seconds he was whistling and weeing. In

what unjust world was a playsuit less practical than a giant vegetable costume?

I sighed. And dialled Rach.

Surely she could be here within five minutes? I could hold on for five minutes. Couldn't I?

But when she answered she was way too near loud music to hear anything I was trying to tell her.

Our conversation consisted entirely of her shouting, "Bella, are you OK?"

And me shouting back, "No, PLEASE COME TO THE LOOS IMMEDIATELY I'M BEING HELD HOSTAGE BY MY PLAYSUIT." To which she'd reply, "Bella, are you OK?"

It was like déjà vu. Déjà loo.

Even my emergency plan was not going to plan.

I hung up and went to message her instead. But a noise stopped me.

"Baba?" A man's voice echoed around my cubicle. It felt eerie and omnipresent like when God speaks to people in films. Except in my case I think it was the drunk corn on the cob shouting from next door.

"Are you –" there was no other way of saying it "– the corn on the cob?"

He must have heard me shouting at Rach.

"Sure am." He chuckled to himself. "You all right there?"

"Oh, you know. Just busting for a wee and can't undo my zip."

He made a comforting sympathetic noise. For a worrying moment I thought he was going to offer to help.

"Do not you worry." That's the thing about festivals. Everyone was nice to each other, even complete strangers. I could be a *right* weirdo for all he knew. Although I wondered what exactly his definition of weirdo was. Person not dressed as salad item? He carried on cheerily. "I've got *just* the tip. Works for me every time."

"Every time you wear a playsuit?"

"Nah, when I wear these costumes."

So this was a regular thing for him. Of course.

"You see that toilet paper dispenser?"

"Uh-huh." It wasn't hard to spot, what with it being the only thing in here.

"See the key?" There was one poking out at the side.

"Oh yeah."

"Well, easy does it, but if you turn your back to it and bend down, it works as the perfect hook." Wow, he was about 6 foot. He must be super flexible. "Trust me. Years of practice." My silence suggested I was unconvinced. "I'll wait while you give it a go if you want?"

I looked down at the floor. It was very … wet. And brown. To the left of the holder was the door. To the right was the loo. There was nowhere to put my hands down for balance. I prodded my thighs. They'd have to squat like they'd never squatted before.

And there was no way I could risk dropping my phone down the pit of doom. So I pulled out some sheets of loo roll, put them on the floor in the corner and laid my phone on top of them.

With a three-two-one, he counted me down.

I turned my back, squatted down (keeping my eyes firmly up as I didn't want a closer view of *anything* in this Portaloo) and wriggled about.

And … he was right. The thin, jagged key hooked straight in.

I stood up and my zip pulled down easy-peasy. I was seriously impressed.

"You're a genius!"

"Why, thanking you." His door swung shut, his work done. I scrambled my arms out and pulled down my tights. "Enjoy the weeeeeee!"

And I did. It was magical. If this were a Disney movie, small birds would be flying around the top of the cubicle chirping a happy tune as a rainbow appeared in the sky. But it wasn't, and all I heard was someone nearby farting in tiny instalments.

When I'd finished, all I had to do was zip back up and head out. I *had* this. I was a pro.

But as I turned my back, bent down, and attempted to re-hook the key back in, I must have moved too quickly. The zip got stuck. Properly, not moving, stuck.

I fished behind me to unhook it. It must have caught in some material. I could probably sort it out with my hands. I did that move where you put your hands behind your back and make it look like someone is snogging you. I was worryingly good at it. But the zip was a couple of millimetres too far up my back to reach. Wriggling down, I took my right arm out of the sleeve to give me a bit more room to move.

It hurt, but if … if I … twisted to the right I could just about reach.

But as my hand felt round, I realized it wasn't the zip that was stuck. It was the whole thing. With all my wriggling the material had got twisted round the key.

I was attached. By my back. To the loo roll holder. With my arm and half a Minions bra sticking out.

But the more I struggled, the more I wedged myself in. I needed help.

Feebly I yelled out, "Corn on the cob man?" Unsurprisingly nothing came back.

People could probably see the shaking cubicle and were avoiding it at all costs.

Panic crept in.

What if I got stuck here all day?

What if I *died* here?! Before I ever got to find out if One Direction's hiatus really was temporary?

They wouldn't even need to splash out on a coffin. I could be the first person to be buried in a Portaloo.

No. Calm down, Bella. Mum would never let that happen.

There was no was she'd bury me in non-recyclable plastic.

So how could I escape?

I looked at my phone in the corner of the cubicle. Maybe if I could reach it I could ring Rach again.

I leant out as far as I could whilst my back was still attached to the wall. But no matter how much I stretched, I ... just ... couldn't reach. Maybe I could pull it over with my foot?

Sweat dripped on to my nose. Eurgh. This was like getting stuck in the world's tightest dress in a sauna changing room, but with added exposure-to-poo-particles jeopardy.

I HAD to reach my phone. But if my foot was going to have any chance of making contact with it, I had to liberate it from being stuck in this stupid playsuit. It was all or nothing. I pulled off my trainer. My right foot now couldn't touch the floor or my tights would absorb the toxic toilet-floor juice. Balancing on my other foot, I squatted down and stood up. I pushed, I pulled. And after a few minutes I'd managed to roll the playsuit down to my left knee.

I was doing this!!

I gave myself a short break to get my breath back. And wished I hadn't, as every time I inhaled I remembered how much it stank in here. Was oxygen *really* that important? All around me people were carrying on, as if the greatest ever test of physical endurance wasn't happening metres from them. But with one last push I did it. I liberated my entire right side from the playsuit.

When most people say they're half-dressed they mean in a more traditional way. Top or bottom. Not me.

My body looked like it had a personality disorder. The left side was fully clothed, trainer on, standard human. The right side was sweaty, red, wearing only a Minions bra, flesh-coloured tights and some bright neon-pink boy pants.

But I'd hit the jackpot!! I could reach my phone!

I dragged it towards me with my toe. But as my hand finally wrapped around it my fingers came into contact with the slimy, cold back of it. Eurgh! Floor juice! I laid it down on to the top of the loo roll holder so I could dry it off.

Well, that's what I meant to do. But what I actually did was put it not quite all the way on the flat metal surface. And as I reached for the loo roll I clipped the side of it.

My phone flipped up and flew through the air, landing straight into the loo with an alarming *plop*.

My only hope of escape had disappeared into a hole that I couldn't bring myself to look down.

If anyone ever wanted to see a Portaloo shaking as it emitted a bellowing "Nooooo", then they were in luck.

I actually wailed.

I was stuck. Right-side-naked. Phoneless. Friendless.

There was now only one means of escape. The absolute last resort.

I was going to have to open the door.

Expose my situation – and myself – to the world.

I looked down.

Could I really do that?

I don't know if it was the fumes, lack of sleep, or sheer desperation, but I had an idea. As quickly as I could I pulled out as much loo roll as possible to wrap around me. I stuffed it into my bra, wrapped it around my leg, poked it into the top of my tights, anything to cover my nakedness. And around a hundred sheets later I looked half human (left side), half mummy (right).

Loo-uis Vuitton it wasn't. Desperation it was.

Before I could change my mind, I lifted my right foot, balanced it on top of the latch and pushed down.

The door didn't move.

"Help."

Nothing.

I was sweating so much some of the sheets had already turned to sludge.

I tried again, louder.

"HELP."

Still nothing.

With a deep breath, I leant back, and with as much force as I could, kicked at the door.

It flew open.

To reveal a miraculously empty field, so luckily no one ever saw me in this state.

No, my mistake, it revealed a massive crowd of people already gathered round the door, peering at the weird shaking thing inside (aka me). Some were filming, some just watching, but all were looking totally horrified at the half person, half absorbent-tissue creature they found crouching before them.

I waved, now in a full ball-like squat trying to save any dignity.

"Hi."

The piece of paper covering my right bra strap floated down to the ground. Even it could no longer bring itself to be associated with me.

At least I didn't know any of these people.

At least they didn't know my name.

"Bella Fisher!!" A perfect human clad in a unitard (with no zips, I feverishly noted) pushed herself forward, loudly confirming to the world exactly who I was. Thanks, Ska. Just who I didn't want to see. My first thought should have been: *End this ordeal*, but it was actually: *How has she found time to re-contour her make-up, while I haven't even managed to fully brush my hair?!* "Why are you covered in loo roll?"

"Because it looks great?" Deadpan jokes were harder to carry off when you were eye level with people's groins, looking like you were at a fancy dress party for one.

"It really doesn't," she answered, with honesty that I could have done without.

"I was joking."

She looked genuinely surprised at this news.

"So, can you help me?" I looked round. There were a *lot* of people. "Can anyone help me?" I gestured behind me. "I'm stuck."

It finally dawned on Ska that I was here by necessity, not through choice, and she strolled off to get help.

After what felt like for ever, a kindly face appeared. A St John's Ambulance lady.

"You OK, love?" I smiled at her, relieved. Ska was peering over her shoulder, looking way more concerned than I knew she really was: she was loving being part of the drama.

"Well, despite being totally stuck and looking like I'm partway through being embalmed? Yes, I'm great." I smiled so she knew I was just laughing at myself before anyone else could.

"This lovely young lady –" she smiled at Ska "– said you'd hit your head?"

"No."

"Right you are." The nice lady peered at my back. "So how did you end up like this?"

"A corn on the cob told me it would be OK."

She softly stoked my hair like I was a dog about to be put down and turned to Ska. "You were right, dear, she's very confused."

Then she leant over and looked at where my playsuit

was caught up. "Oh, dearie me, you look like you're stuck good and proper."

I nodded, happy someone could finally see my predicament. How were they were going to get me out. Cutting my clothes? Would they require specialist machinery?

"Will … will I be OK?" I asked, sounding frightened.

"Well, we might have to get the fire brigade in," she said. "Or just do this."

She pressed a little red button underneath the loo roll holder and the whole thing sprang open. The key fell out and my playsuit unravelled itself.

I was frozen with disbelief.

That was my dramatic rescue?!

How had I not seen that button?!

But at least the ordeal was over.

I said, "Thank you," more embarrassed than relieved. Finally I was free to get dressed and run away as fast as I could, no more public humiliation.

Or so I thought. Because the nice lady put a firm hand on me and told me to stay totally still as I wasn't going anywhere, until I'd "been checked for a head injury as I was talking gibberish".

I probably shouldn't have told her my festival highlight so far was The Tomato Ketchup Conspiracy

Theory. Or that I'd taken bad advice from a corn on the cob.

Which is why I ended up being stretchered across the site to the St John's Ambulance tent, head in a neck brace, phone alongside me in a latex glove, after she'd very kindly fished it out of the toilet. Miraculously, it was still working, so after some intense wet-wiping of it, I alerted the others, and they soon arrived, concerned. But more importantly, with a spare pair of leggings and a new T-shirt.

It was time to get changed, and get on with the festival.

CHAPTER

NINETEEN

They'd been really worried and had searched everywhere for me. I felt terrible for stressing them out And for putting their fun, and protest prep, on hold.

Mikey and Jay had been speechless when I'd told them what happened, which didn't reassure me that Tegan had been telling me the truth when she said it wasn't that bad.

I wanted to make it up to them all. Especially as the good news about the protest had taken a turn. While my phone was in the loo, @HeyItsTheSessionHQ had posted picture upon picture of Session fans in the merchandise they'd bought today, along with direct comments addressed to Rachel, Tegan and me. It meant whoever ran the account was here. And they were not letting their hatred of us drop.

Which is why, as we headed to the New Bands Tent, I came up with my worst idea yet.

I'd never really paid attention to it before, but in the middle of the main route between the stages was a round, open-air stage set up with microphone, speakers and a massive sign that stretched round the roof of it, saying "SPEAKERS' CIRCULAR CORNER".

Speakers wanted, it said.

Five-minute slots, it said.

No experience necessary, it said.

And somehow, I found myself about to go up on stage.

It had felt like a good idea seconds earlier, but as my foot stepped on stage, it took every inch of resolve not to run off screaming, "There's been a terrible mistake!"

Hundreds of people stretched out before me.

Girls, guys, a long-haired man I kind of recognized, a couple of faces I knew from school, loads more I didn't.

And they were all looking. At me.

Plus side: at least I was fully dressed, and not trapped in a toilet.

Not so plus side: my palms were sweating, my heart was pounding, and I'd forgotten how to … speak.

What had I been thinking?!

Maybe I did have a head injury after all?

I looked at the floor. Jo always says to look at your feet to remember everything is normal and going to be OK. But my legs were wobbling so much I looked like a Strictly dancer doing one of those weird standing-on-the-spot dances.

Had anyone ever crumpled from nerves before?

A man in a Glastonbury '99 T-shirt plucked the mic out of the stand.

"Please welcome…" Whoa, his voice was loud. He looked at me, so I could remind him of my name. "Bella," I whispered, my voice cracking. He smiled reassuringly. "Belly" – oh well – "who's going to be talking about…"

He pushed the mic into my hands. This was it. All I wanted to do was bail, but instead I looked at Rach and Tegan.

"I'm going to be talking about why it's so important we…" Deep breath. "Stop The Session."

I waited for silence. Worse, for the boos.

But all I got was a cheer. And despite being a bag of nerves, and smelling more than any person should do of toilets, I began.

I started slowly at first, my voice wobbling. But with every word I said about The Session, about how it was not OK to exploit their fans, that girls weren't objects, that they should be using their position for change, not to make things worse, I got more and more fired up. And so did the crowd – I even got spontaneous whoops.

All day we'd been surrounded by Session fans, but right now there were real people on our side. And not just my friends.

The only time I lost my words totally was when I realized one of the whoops was from … Ross?!

People *really* cared. Even him?!

And every time I looked to the side of the stage, Rach and Teeg were grinning, arms round each other.

Was I making them proud? A bit of me wished Jo was here to witness it. Mum would never believe that I was up here, doing this. I mean, *I couldn't*, and I was me.

But I had to do what I came here for: get as many people to turn up on Sunday as possible. With a reassuring thumbs up from Tegan and Rach, I launched into the end section that we'd practised as I was waiting to go up. It was borrowed from a talk we'd seen earlier about "not expecting to see change unless we make the change for it to happen". When I said it, it got the biggest cheer yet. But I was running out of time. I had to be clear, be quick, and NAIL IT.

"So who's with me?"

A big swelling "Wooyyyeaaaahhh" rose up.

"WHO CAN I COUNT ON TO COME AND HELP STOP THE SESSION?" Another massive roar. "OK. So listen up. Here's the stuff you need to know…" The cheering dropped. They really *were* paying attention. "Anyone who wants to make banners and flags – and they really will make a BIG difference 'cos we need to be a visible as possible – meet midday Sunday at the D'Oh Nut Stand over by –" I pointed "– the bottom of the helter-skelter." I paused. "Full disclosure, best ever doughnut balls I've eaten. Brenda is a GODDESS." Blank faces stared at me. "If you're coming on Sunday, hit us up on @StopTheSession, so we can make sure we've got enough for everyone."

A hand shot up. Ross. "I'll bring high-vis vests! Make us really stand out!"

He was smiling at me?! This was *weird*. I was smiling about wearing one of his skanky yellow vests. This was *weirder*.

"Awesome … if anyone else has, er, ideas, bring them along." I sounded dead authoritative! "We're all in this together!" Or not. I gulped, pretending I hadn't just turned to vintage *High School Musical* at a time of political importance.

"I've got an idea!" shouted a girl. I saw her hair before

I saw her face. It was Marge, with Britney T and Lols alongside her. Had they seen it on our social and come to support? "How about we save ourselves the effort? It's not going to work."

People actually gasped. One of those people was me. Mikey full-on booed.

"Well, erm, I guess that's your opinion," I started. Why hadn't she said something earlier, rather than wait till I was up here?

"Not just mine – it's what most people think." Marge rolled her eyes at the people next to her who were giving her serious evils (although they were nowhere near as bad as the one Tegan was doing from the side of the stage). "And you can stop giving me those looks. I'm all about –" she pointed at her T-shirt, and read it out "– *Girls Supporting Girls*" (she was hiding it well) "which is why I think we should put our efforts into something that could *really* work…"

"Like?" Tegan heckled back, unable to stop herself.

Marge shrugged. What was she trying to achieve?! 'Cos if it was putting me off, she was doing a great job.

"ONE MINUTE, BELLY!" the man who introduced me yelled.

Great.

I had to get Marge out of my head. I had to focus on what I was here to do.

"Well if you look around, I think we have a really good chance of making this work?!" I sounded quite convincing. "The main thing is we ALL HAVE TO TURN UP if we are going to show The Session that we mean business." Finally I got a big cheer. The crowd were back on side. "To show them they can't get away with what they're doing." Even bigger cheer! "That we're standing up for what we believe in. That we're being true to ourselves, even when it feels scary!"

They were loving it!

"But we have ALL of us here, so even if it's hard, we have to give it a go!" More applause. I was connecting with them! "I mean, long story short, earlier on I was being stretchered across the festival after getting kidnapped by a Portaloo, and it can't be worse than that?" This time I only got confused applause and sympathetic smiles. I should probably stick to the important details – when and where the protest was going to be.

But that's when I saw another face I wasn't expecting to see.

And this one made my mouth dry up.

Adam. Adam, who I hadn't told about the protest yet.

And my last few seconds were ticking away.

I glanced at Rach, and Tegan next to her, who was almost jumping with excitement.

I HAD to say what I needed to.

I HAD to finish.

But how could I when it meant telling Adam I was going to miss his gig?

In front of hundreds of people.

"So meet me…" My voice wobbled. I pointed at Rach and Tegan. "And these two masterminds, by the sound stage… Together … we'll take on The Session."

Hands went up in the air. Shouts of "YESSS". Adam yelled, "Go, Bells!"

"Be there." I knew I had to say it. Deliver the killer blow. I couldn't look Adam in the eye. "7.45 p.m., Sunday."

I had to hold my voice together for one final sentence.

"Protest starts at 8, when I'll wave my sign by the tree at the main stage."

The crowd cheered but I felt hollow. I looked to see Adam's reaction.

But he was gone.

Waving bye, I jumped off stage, gestured to Rach and Tegan to wait for me where they were, and ran as fast as I could to find him.

CHAPTER

TWENTY

I yelled Adam's name but he didn't stop. I'd never seen him walk so fast.

"AARD!!"

Could he hear me over the noise, or was he avoiding me at all costs?

I felt sick. If I thought stepping up on that stage was terrifying, it was nothing compared to how I felt now. Had I ruined everything?

It was getting dark, but it was still light enough for me to push my way through the crowd towards him. I managed to catch him up.

"Hey! Adam." He stopped. We were standing next to each other but I felt far away from him. "I…" I searched for any clue to how he was feeling. "I'm sorry. I should have told you."

He dropped his eye-contact. People were swarming around us, laughing, chatting, and in the middle of it, I might be about to be dumped.

"I'm an idiot. A complete idiot."

"Bells…" He looked up; his normally happy face serious. Worse than serious. *Sad.* "Why didn't you just tell me?" He smiled in that empty way that means there's zero joy in it. *"To be true to ourselves, even when it feels scary* – that's what you said, right?"

"I…" but I didn't have an excuse. "I just didn't want to let you down. To let *anyone* down."

"Letting me down? Is that what you think this is?" He looked me dead in the eye. I should really explain why I smelt of loo and air freshener, but now probably wasn't the time. He was about to say something *big*. And I could guess what.

We were metres away from the rubbish dump. And I was going to get dumped. It was almost poetic – if it wasn't the worst thing that had ever happened in my life.

My right eye prickled.

No, eye! Not now! Don't cry!

THINK HAPPY THOUGHTS.

Mumbles' face when she eats spaghetti! Rach doing interpretative dance in her giraffe onesie! Percy Pigs!

"You don't get it, do you?"

He pushed his fingers across his forehead.

"Get what?"

This was the moment. I braced myself.

And Adam … laughed. How could he laugh? "Bells. It may come as a shock to you, but despite your terrible approach to telling me what on earth goes on in your head sometimes, I'm … well…" He looked a bit nervous. "I'm dead proud of you."

So he wasn't dumping me?

He was being nice to me?! Was I having a post-Portaloo fume hallucination?

"So … so you weren't storming off?"

He eyes widened, realizing what I'd thought. "No! I'm just massively late to meet Marcus. I stopped when I saw you on stage and told him I'd catch him up."

All I could do was stare.

And blink.

And maybe breathe. My emotions were so all over the place I couldn't be 100% sure there was even any oxygen left in my body.

AND THEN HE HUGGED ME.

I was so shocked I couldn't even contribute to it, so just looked a bit like a human lollipop – rigid, confused, slightly melting.

"So you don't hate me?"

He stepped back. "*Hate* you? Of course I don't." My entire body flooded with relief, like the feeling your head gets when you take out a ponytail that's been too tight. I didn't realize how tense every muscle had been. "Not after all those Tommy K pics you sent – not to mention you're doing the coolest thing at the festival! Taking on The Session! And yes…" He grinned. "I follow @StopTheSession so I figured it out earlier." Whoa. I hadn't thought about that. Lying really wasn't my forte. His smile dropped a bit, and his voice slowed. "I just wish I could be there too…" So did I. "And of course I wish you could come see our set."

I jumped in before I could stop myself.

"SAME?! Like a million times the same."

He would never know *how* much I wanted to see him play. And see him so happy. And watch his sexy drumming arms in action. And face. And knees. And feet.

"But whatever happens, Bells…" Oh yes. Real life. I snapped back into looking at his actual sexy arms. And face. And knees. "*Whatever* happens, please, please, can we just be honest from now on? No matter what?"

"No secrets." I smiled, feeling like happiness was coming out of my very core, even though I already knew it was a lie.

Because there was one thing I was still too scared to say.

How hard can telling someone you love them be?

CHAPTER

TWENTY-ONE

Tegan was buzzing when I got back to Speakers' Circular Corner.

"Bells. Guess what?"

"Zayn and Gigi are back together?" She shook her head. She knew their break-up had hit me hard.

"Nope. Better." She started to wait for another guess, but was too excited and blurted it out. "We've had twenty new sign-ups for the protest!" I'd only been gone ten minutes; this was incredible! "And eight of them are going to join us on Sunday at midday to make some flags!"

This *was* awesome news!

Rach held her hand out for a high five. "You are officially A QUEEN!"

High on the good news, we headed off to enjoy the evening. I already knew it, but Rach, Tegan and I were a perfect team. Tegan made us put on the extra socks she'd secretly brought (how could two small pieces of clothing do such a good job against hypothermia?!), Rach splodged glow-in-the-dark glitter on our faces and I handed out the Chupa Chups I'd brought for energy. Bear Grylls, eat your heart out (although he probably would in a survival situation).

But lollies weren't enough and our first stop was food. After a tip-off from Mikey, we ate a burger so delicious we had to lie on the ground, staring silently into the stars to contemplate what had just happened. Some people spend their lives working towards a career, or happy loving relationships, but all I wanted from my future was to experience another gherkin like that one.

Once we'd managed to drag ourselves out of our food comas, we met up with Adam and Marcus, and together with Mikey and Jay, ended up dancing along with a mobile silent disco.

And once we'd started to dance we didn't stop. As soon as one thing finished, we'd hear the roar of the crowd from another part of the festival and ran to join in. Who knew we were going to be part of a fifty-person conga to a kazoo rendition of "New Rules"? Or take part in field-wide power ballad singalong yoga? The whole evening was a blur of laughing, hugging, running, shouting and knowing I had the best friends in the world. As the final light of the day disappeared, I'd started to forget what a world with parental nagging and revision and stress felt like.

We even managed to get right to the front of the crowd for the main stage headliners. It may have helped that a giant lemur with a broken arm in the air led the way through the endless groups of people. The massive screens at the side of the stage showed just how huge the crowd was behind us. This was the stage The Session were going to be playing on Sunday and the size of this crowd brought home how big our challenge was to make sure anyone would take any notice of us. But I could worry about that tomorrow. Molly and the Bens had come on stage and it was like they'd switched an on button for everyone here. Bouncing along, I got hit in the head by trainers as people crowd-surfed, my ribs got squashed as a mosh-pit formed beside us, and dubious liquid splatted all down my head as the people behind us threw cups (please please please let it be warm beer and not any other yellow liquid). And I loved every second.

When it had finished, we headed off to explore what secret things were happening around the site, which is why at midnight I found myself in my first ever public karaoke situation. Karaoke was something I normally limited to three places – in my room, in my sister's car, in the shower. My singing was *that* bad. In junior school I actually got asked to mime in the school nativity. But here I was, getting up on a tiny stage, in a packed tent, alongside Rach and Teeg, a lemur and lobster as our backing dancers, Adam and Marcus beatboxing (which they couldn't do, so it was just them going, "Boom da da boom") with hundreds of people cheering us on.

As the first note of "Man's Not Hot" boomed out, Rach threw her hands in the air, the crowd did the same, and we launched into a word-perfect rendition. I have *never* seen a lobster and a lemur dance with so much enthusiasm in my life.

Rach mainly added random "never hot"s, but as Adam, Marcus and I finished the last chorus, Tegan got a funny look in her eye, and without any warning, flung herself into a one-handed handstand, in a sort of gymnastic break-dance hybrid. She spun and leapt about, arms and legs flying – and the crowd went wild. We were cheered off like heroes. Mikey and Jay then stayed on to do a full rendition of "Bang Bang" by Ariana Grande, Jessie J and Nicki Minaj, and I laughed so hard I cried tear trails that cut through my glitter. Ariana may have the vocal range of a goddess, but I'm pretty sure she's never attempted to do the caterpillar whilst dressed as a Madagascan primate.

Then we headed to the dance tent, where the DJ was playing massive tunes mixed in with retro pop. The whole group of us shuffled right into the middle.

"Beefy! Finally!" Adam grabbed my hands and we attempted a sort of couple dance. Which we stopped quickly, as were both so terrible it mainly involved treading on each other. "I feel like I've hardly seen you properly since I got here."

I smiled. "Well, here I am," I said, and gave him a quick kiss, before stepping back and joining in with his latest dance move – interpretive dancing of dealing cards.

I loved how I felt around him.

I loved how he always wanted to make life fun.

I loved the way he was a worse dancer than me (actually quite remarkable).

So why was I too scared to tell him how I felt? Was it because if he didn't feel the same, a tiny part of me might break, and never get put back together?

"So –" Adam put his hands around my waist "– you were going to tell me about what happened earlier?"

I shuddered, picturing Ska's face all over again. I

leant in to tell him the whole story. But he mistook my leaning in for something else. And suddenly we were that gross couple snogging in the middle of the dance floor. And quite frankly this seemed way more fun than telling him about my toilet trauma.

"ENOUGH." Lols was right up in our faces. "Just get back to your tent already?!"

What was *she* doing here? Why was she so obsessed with our tent life?

Adam gave her a half-smile and turned his back on her throwing himself back into our dancing. For solidarity I pulled out the "ordering a burrito" scenario, which was a multi-person routine, involving both a customer and at least two people making the imaginary burrito, meaning I could rope in Tegan for support.

I tried to get Rach in on the act too, but Marge had nabbed her and was shouting into her ear. When I tried to shimmy over to give her an escape, Rach just smiled and carried on talking.

I didn't understand those girls. They acted like they hated us – well, Tegan and me anyway – but always seemed to turn up like they thought we were friends.

At least I knew one thing about them. After today's performance at the campsite, followed by Marge's heckling at my speech, I no longer cared about impressing them. I was more bothered about avoiding them.

I tuned back to fake-dance-eat-nachos with Adam and Marcus, but Adam was standing still, staring at the girls who'd jumped up on stage, to dance in their rainbow catsuits and matching wigs. They were like something off a bad music video. Maybe even an exercise video. Were they doing spotty dogs as an actual move?! I gave Adam what I hoped was an appropriate "whoa, they're really going for it" look. But Adam shook his head and pointed. A lot.

Oh. My. Days.

Without meaning to, I grabbed the nearest thing to me. Tegan.

"LOOK!!!!" I said it so loud everyone heard and turned to see.

They'd started what looked like an interpretation of the running man. I needed evidence. I took my phone out and started filming.

Marcus leant over. "Do you know them?"

I shouted back. "More than know them. The left one's my sister."

I'd never seen anything like it.

Was Jo having an out of body experience? Had she been possessed by someone different? Someone fun? I waved at Rach to come over, she would *love* this. But she was too engrossed in her convo with Marge.

I edged forward to get a better view. But as much as I waved and shouted, Jo was lost in her own world. She was touching her toes. Now, galloping with an arm lassoing in the air? Were they really attempting a leapfrog on that tiny space? I held my breath. Yes, they were. Although her friend may have just got her leg stuck across Jo's neck, but they were too busy enjoying themselves to care.

What *had* happened to my sister?!

This was the best thing I'd seen all festival. It. Was. Phenomenal.

I did what any loving sister would do. And sent a pic through on our family group.

ME: Jo can certainly let her 🌈 hair down. 😄

An hour later she was still dancing, my message had had no response and it was almost 1.30 a.m. I was yawning almost as much as I was dancing so Tegan and I decided to head back, which started a ripple effect. Adam and Marcus headed off with Mikey and Jay to get some food (apparently post-midnight pizza tastes way better than daytime pizza). Although it meant less Adam time, I was secretly relieved as it meant no awkward goodbye around the tents when we got back.

Needing my sleep, I interrupted Rach and Marge's chat. Marge looked seriously unimpressed, like I was taking her property.

"Rach, you fancy heading back?" We were happy to stay out a while longer if she wanted to. Never leave a man standing.

She nodded. "Sure. Give me a sec to say my byes."

"But Rach?!" Marge pouted. "The night's just getting started?!"

Rach shrugged. "But these guys are going to bed. And I've got flyering to do in the morning."

Marge laughed and shook her head; she'd heard the uncertainty in Rach's voice too. "Don't be lame." She shimmied. "This is when festivals really get going."

Tegan stepped forward. "We *could* stay out for a bit longer?" She didn't want to leave Rach with MGC (who I needed to urgently rebrand into GWWANAACOAM. Girls Who We Are Not At All Crushing On Any More).

Britney T stopped showing some guys the tiny tattoo on her collarbone that said "You Are Too Close" (she told us it was to stop people perving, but I only ever saw her make randomers get closer to read it) and joined in.

"Just ditch that shift. It's super tragic. It's not like they can take your tickets off you."

Good to know she thought we were "super tragic".

"We don't mind, do we, Teeg?" I mean, I *really* minded, and would rather do anything than get up in less than four hours to pick up containers of Chinese noodle leftovers, but binning off the binning didn't feel right. Plus, Ross terrified me.

Marge looped her arm through Rach's and tugged on it. "You can stay with us, babes." She rolled her eyes at Tegan and me like we were her keepers. "She can stay with us." She said it extra slow, like we were being unreasonable wanting to make sure Rach was OK. I was struggling to understand why Rach would even *want* to spend time with them. "Honorary member of Party HQ, right? And don't worry, Rubbish Girls, we wouldn't do anything you wouldn't do."

Marge winked.

We looked at Rach.

But she stayed silent. And by not saying anything, she told us her choice.

So for the first time ever, Tegan and I headed home without Rach.

Neither of us were in a hurry to say the obvious.

Was this just what jealousy feels like?

CHAPTER

TWENTY-TWO

EURGH.

Why was waking up always so awful?!

Why couldn't someone invent something to make it more fun?! Or could we just agree to scrap mornings as a thing? Like daylight saving time, but Horrific Waking Up Avoidance.

I fumbled for my phone. Please, *please* tell me it's 3:30 a.m. *4:30 LATEST*. I *HAVE* to have a least another hour's sleep ahead of me. But my eyes refused to open. I emergency-prised them open with my fingers.

PURE HORROR. It was 4:49. My alarm was due to go off in sixty seconds. Or less (I always set it a couple of minutes early so I can lie semi-asleep thinking how much I hate waking up.)

HAD I EVEN SLEPT AT ALL OR JUST DONE A LONG BLINK?!

It felt like someone had stuck a hoover in my ear overnight and sucked out all signs of life, just leaving a big thumping pile of dust where my brain used to be.

"Ten mins, Bells." HOW WAS TEGAN ALREADY DRESSED?! "Need a hand with anything?" HOW WAS SHE SMILING?!

"Everything," I tried to reply, but all that came out was a sound similar to when our blender broke. Tegan laughed.

BEEEEP BEEEP BEEEP.

Argh. Even my alarm sounded like it was ringing extra cheerfully just to wind me up.

"And *that* – " Tegan prodded me in the side " – is what midnight hip-hop karaoke does for you." But I wasn't listening. I'd discovered an even greater horror lurking on my phone.

Mum had replied to my picture of Jo dancing last night.

MUM: Love u darlingdaughters! So proud to see uu enjoying yours elves. SMEL.

(She was trying to make "So Much Everlasting Love" happen. It wasn't.)

MUM: SORry I couldnt reply sooner. Had a man aboutthe house if you knowhat Imean.

Hello, message NO ONE ever wanted to receive from their own mother. Why did she have a "man about the house" in the middle of the night? Or worse. *Overnight*.

I full-body shuddered so hard Tegan had to nudge me to check my sleeping bag hadn't gone into spasm.

To stop her worrying, I dragged myself up, using my phone torch to find any clothes. I'd already given up any sort of filing system. Well, not strictly true. My filing system now was just empty it all out and whatever I found was what I'd go with.

This was what I'd planned:

DAY TWO OF FESTIVAL LOOK: 90s indie with a twist of glitter.

ACTUAL LOOK: whatever was warm enough and I could reach.

I was about as close to a zombie as a human can be.

If the first two shifts had been a breeze, this one was a hurricane. A hurricane of sticky cups, manky food containers that all involved at least two types of primary-coloured sauce, and bits of clothing that had been discarded. Who *were* these people who didn't notice they were missing a sock?! The only good thing about feeling so near death was that even the discovery of a pair of pants shaped like an alligator with half a cucumber in didn't alarm me. All I thought was *non-recyclable*.

Two hours in and a follow-up from Mum came through. Sleep-deprived, hangry, and scarred from earlier, I opened with caution.

MUM: PS HAd a great last nightcant wait to tell you all about it!!

NO. BRAIN. COULD NOT. DEAL.

I bleurghed out loud.

"You all right, Bells?" Tegan threw a cup into my bin bag, as I stood emitting weird noises, like I was malfunctioning. Should I just throw my phone in with it to protect my sanity from more Mum updates? Nah – it was way too useful. (Not for emergency calls but properly good things – like Adam messages or the filter that puts a tiny dancing panda on your head.)

Jo replied with a smiley face. Classic.

So she was up? That meant a perfect opportunity for getting back to the much safer agenda of more footage from last night.

ME: We had a great time too.

I posted some video of Jo playing air guitar. And what looked like air flute.

MUM: SO PROUD OF MY BABIES.

And also:

MUM: YOU GO GRILLS!

I think she meant girls, unless Jo had developed a weird nickname I didn't know about.

"Bells, seriously. You OK?" Tegan looked genuinely worried.

"Just wondering if just 'cos I came out of her vageen, I really am definitely related to my mother." I buried my phone back in my pocket. "So, the usual."

Tegan laughed. But that's because her mum is normal and doesn't do things like turn up to school in a

Santa hat in summer because she's decided to throw a surprise Half-Christmas party on June 25th.

I messaged back a thumbs up, and as Jo wasn't taking the bait, a couple of the most arty shots of the festival I'd taken on the camera. Mum was really impressed with the one of the morning mist all seeping up around our campsite. I switched my phone off as I couldn't cope with any more drama this early in the morning. I'm so thankful Mum was old when the internet was invented. The thought of what horrors would lie one life-changing Google search away if she'd had an iPhone when we were younger, made my mind boggle.

But things were looking up, as we'd arrived at Brenda's D'Oh Nut Stand, and she gave us another bag of doughnut balls and a cup of tea each.

I sat on the bench by Tegan, happy for a quick break, and sipped my tea. I wasn't sure if water could technically get hotter than boiling, but if by some scientific anomaly it could, it was happening right here in this polystyrene cup.

"Not … good … mornings." I was really struggling today. "Need. Sleep."

Tegan nodded. Our friendship meant joining words were sometimes an unnecessary waste of energy. It also meant she didn't judge me for eating five doughnut balls in a row. But the sugar helped, and after betting on how many flyers Rach would have handed out this morning (I went for 70, Tegan went for an on-brand optimistic 105), Ross arrived to ruin our fun.

"OK, guys, no messing about. We're off to the backstage area, and if I find ANY of you have gone off wandering on solo missions, expect to find yourself ejected from the festival quicker than you can say, 'your face is covered in sugar'."

Well, at least that's what I think he said. As soon as I heard the words "backstage area" I zoned right out and into a world of A-list celeb spotting and gossip for days. This was SO exciting.

But when we got there, instead of feeling like I was roaming the corridors of Radio 1, it was like we'd been let loose in a coach station. A coach station in a field, full of buses with blacked-out windows and giant wing mirrors.

"Well, this is…" I looked around.

Tegan finished off my thought. "Disappointing."

"Exactamundo." I peered at the one nearest us, standing up on my toes, Tegan doing the same. The outside of the coach gave zero clues as to what – or who – was inside. "Litter-picking crew, who dis?" I said to the massive expanse of black glass.

But as I did a thought hit me, and I elbowed Teeg. "Do you … do you reckon one of these could be The Session's?"

Tegan raised her eyebrows, unimpressed at the idea. "Who knows? Who *cares*?!"

"They could be in there. Doing band stuff." I nodded towards the inside of the bus.

Tegan shrugged. "Yeah. Probably eating Shreddies and writing more tweets about how lame we are…?"

We stared at the windows for any sign of life, but there was nothing.

"Well, on the tiny off chance it's them in there, this is what I'd say to them…" I put my hands on my hips. And tried to think of something profound.

My mind went blank.

So instead I leapt around on the spot, waving my arms and whisper-screaming the most threatening-yet-low-volume *arggggh* I could. I channelled Jo's wild moves from last night.

Tegan smiled. "Nailed it."

Ross shot us a look, so we smiled sweetly and scurried back to work. Half an hour later we'd cleaned the whole area. It was dullsville – the only exciting discovery was that backstage Portaloos had mirrors on the back of the door (obvs I made Tegan wait just outside the door. That was the new rule). Seeing my first full-length reflection was my most traumatic moment of the festival so far. I really didn't need confirmation of how ridic my bin-bag high-vis combo looked, especially as Tegan's super simple mac and neon vest made her look like she was in a retro indie band at a rave.

As we walked through the metal five-bar gate, out of the area, Tegan shuffled closer so we could chat without Ross busting us.

"Shame Adam didn't get to stay here – *imagine* the goss."

"Imagine him telling us what The Session *really* get up to?" We'd have ammunition for weeks.

"He could tell Brian where to go."

"Yes, please?! And imagine all the convos we *wouldn't* have to have had with Lols about us camping together."

Tegan winced. "Yeah, I meant to speak to you about that yesterday. You looked kind of…"

"Freaked out?"

"I wouldn't have said that."

"Yeah – 'cos you're too nice." I swung the rubbish bag up on my shoulder as we trudged along. "It's just not the convo I want to be having right now."

Tegan nodded slowly. "Bells, you know if you're not ready to talk about it, you're certainly not ready to do anything about it, if you know what I mean?"

I did. But I had no idea how *he* felt. And I still had two more nights sleeping five metres away from him with Lols' mouth worryingly near to say whatever it wanted.

When we got back to our tent, Rach was nowhere to be found, but Adam was sitting outside his tent on a box of Red Bull cans. He was flicking water out of his wet hair where he'd just been washing it with a bottle of water. Yup, my boyf was officially a sexy perfume advert. It almost hurt to watch he looked so fit. Whereas I hadn't even brushed my teeth today, let alone hair. Maybe I could duck into my tent to sort myself out before he saw me?

"Beeeefy!" Too late. But his face lit up when he saw me. If I didn't have at least five different food sauces splashed down my front bin bag I'd totally go in for a hug. "The celebs return."

Well, that was one way to describe our karaoke efforts.

"Er, not quite celebs, but yup, we have returned." I pulled off my bags and threw my rucksack into the tent.

When I came back out Marcus was standing up brushing his teeth with his finger. Did a toothbrush really take up too much bag space?! "You guys crack me up."

I looked at Tegan. She looked at me.

I looked at Adam. He looked at me.

What was going on?

"Did…" Adam's smile had vanished. "Did you guys not have your phones on you?"

Hello, least reassuring words in the English language.

Instead of a reply, I dived back into my tent and turned my phone on. I'd missed a group message from Rach from about 1:40 a.m. Apparently, The Session had done another interview taking the mick out of our petition. And they'd accused us of sabotaging the merchandise stand. How did they know?! But Marcus wouldn't find that funny. Would he?

But a millisecond later, when I opened Instagram, I didn't need any more explanation.

The technical term for the noise that came out of my mouth was "howl". "Teeeeeeeeeeeeeeeeeeeg."

Turns out when I'd been goofing around outside the tour bus, there *was* someone in it. The Tomato Ketchup Conspiracy Theory, who had filmed me and posted the clip.

Which was pretty awful.

But nowhere near as bad at the fact @HeyItsTheSessionHQ had somehow found it, figured out it was me and reposted it on their account, tagging me in along with this lovely comment.

Urban dictionary called. They saw this vid of Bella Fisher and said there had been a new definition of waste of air #NotThePropertyOfTheSessionPlease #SomeoneStopHer #StopTheSessionHaters

Which Brian had then reposted, video and all, adding his own comment. Weren't lead singers meant to sleep in until the afternoon, not wake up early to unleash a bitchy comments on a sixteen-year-old girl?

"Embarrassing. And if anyone's thinking of turning up to their lame-ass protest at our gig, think again. Session fans mean war."

So he knew about the protest? We'd lost the element of surprise. Now all we had was the element of making sure loads of people turned up. Which was proving to be a very hard element.

The hate on his post was unreal.

We always thought the grief they were giving us was a joke, now we know they are too.

Bella should probably give up on life now.

#TheSessionWontBeStopped

Oh look, it's a dancing slug #IWouldn't
#NotEvenWithYours

Crawl back under your rock, bin bag girl.

I passed the phone to Tegan. Could I stay in this tent for ever?! I had two John West tuna snack pots, some marshmallows and 1.5 packs of chewing gum. I could survive on that. Cows just eat grass and they always seem happy.

"*Ah,*" was all Tegan said. Followed by, "Nice of Brian to tag and repost. A real quality guy."

"Knock knock." Oh good. Just what I needed – Adam putting his head into our tent and witnessing me having a minor-to-quite-substantial breakdown, surrounded by at least four pairs of pants that were strewn over my sleeping bag. I threw two behind me and flopped back with my arms stuck out to try and obscure the others.

"Come in?" His head poked in. Luckily he was too distracted by Tegan staring at my phone to see my pant disaster. "You hadn't seen the Tommy K post then?"

Tegan looked across at me in a star shape across the tent floor. "Whatever gave you that impression?"

I wasn't even sure which bit I was freaking out about.

The whole world seeing me as an unhinged dancing human litter bin? Or the hate I was getting for it?

"Did you know Brian had posted it too?" Adam's face dropped, meaning he definitely didn't. Tegan scrunched her nose. "It's not exactly the world's *most* positive comments section to read."

"Bells…" Adam crouched down, concerned. "You OK?" I'm guessing the fact I'd stopped being able to blink answered that. "If it helps, I thought you looked awesome…"

C'mon, me. Be the Bella you want to be. Breezy, confident, cool. Try and laugh this off.

I sat up robotically. "Yeah, yeah. No big deal." Aka, the British for "my life is ending but let's not make a scene".

Tegan was jabbing her finger towards my shoulder. I felt across with my hands. There was something there. I pulled it off.

Oh, excellent, I'd accidentally given myself a shoulder pad of My Little Pony pants. And now I was holding them out like they were a piece of scientific evidence.

I HAD TO GET ADAM OUT IMMEDIATELY BEFORE I DID SOMETHING EVEN WEIRDER LIKE DISCOVER I'M WEARING A TAMPON AS A

TINY HAT. "I'll come find you in a bit." I was officially gabbling. "I just need a moment."

"If you're sure?" He didn't sound convinced. More sort of concerned. "Still want to meet later?"

I nodded, but in the absence of me being able to think straight, Tegan made an arrangement to meet in a couple of hours and Adam cleared the area. When he left she shuffled over and put her arm round me. "You know this will be OK, right?"

But I couldn't lie to her. "I'm not so sure."

"Well, I am." She stood up as best she could in a tent that was only rib-high. "So let's go find Rach and help get SO many people to the protest that Brian decides to go and live in a hole for the rest of his life … while campaigning for equal rights around the world." She lolled her head from side to side. "His hole will have good internet, OK?"

But after half an hour of looking round the campsite, Rach's phone was still going to voicemail, and there was no sign of her. We had a new biggest worry.

We should never have left her with Marge and co.

TWENTY-THREE

By the time we'd done a lap of the festival looking for Rach, it was half ten. When we arrived back at our tent, on the other side of the fence the only sign of life was Marge, flicking through photos on her phone. When she saw us she walked over to the fence.

"Hey, viral sensation." Great, Marge knew about the video already. "You guys missed a mad one last night..." She turned her phone round, showing us a video of what looked like Rach standing on her shoulders, being supported either side by Britney T and a man dressed as a giant pencil.

There really was nothing we could say except, "Whoa." Tegan glanced towards Rach's tent, only one thing on her mind.

"Did Rach get home OK?"

"She …" Marge bit her lip. "… definitely got home OK." Well that was a massive relief. "Though it miiight have been slightly later than planned. Like … maybe just before you guys headed out?" She slapped her hand over her mouth like she'd let a secret slip. "We saw her this morning when she went for a wee and told her you wouldn't mind…" She held her hands up. "Don't shoot the messenger!"

"As long as she's OK." Tegan's reply had a coolness that was so subtle maybe only I picked up on it.

I tried to ease the tension.

"She's probably out now, which is why there's no sign of her."

Suddenly there was the noise of what sounded like a giant hedgehog rustling in the undergrowth.

"I AM SOOOOO SORRYYYYY!!!!" Rach's tent wailed. After all that she was here all along?! "I fell back asleep?!"

A mass of red hair – more of a knot than a style – poked out of the tent, followed by the blinking and bleary face of Rachel. She stumbled towards us, still in last night's clothes. "I have failed us."

"Morning, Rach." Tegan walked towards the fence. "Am I right in thinking this means you haven't started handing out the flyers yet?"

Rach wrinkled her nose. "Sorry. You know what I'm like..." We did. She was a girl who once fell asleep having a filling. So why had she stayed out so late if she knew she had important stuff to do for the protest? Didn't she care any more? I needed to fill her in on the latest development.

"Well, Brian's been a complete twonk today, so I'm completely fuming." I sounded as annoyed as I felt. "Slash totally mortified. While we were looking for you, people kept shouting 'bin-bag girl' at me."

Rach's face softened. "You've been looking for me?"

Tegan raised her eyebrows and nodded. "Just a bit."

Rach put her hand over her face. "I'm so sorry, guys. Won't happen again." Marge coughed as if she didn't believe her. We all ignored her. "Bells, do you mean the video? I can't believe Brian did that." So she'd seen it too. "I mean, fair enough, I laughed when Tommy K originally posted it."

Marge sniggered. "To be fair, we all did when Rach showed us..."

Rach had passed the video around? Great. I knew we didn't have sides, but if we did, I'd wonder whose she was on.

Rach carried on, unaware of how much that had stung. "But they were being sweet about you. Brian reposting was a douche move. I meant to message to check you were OK." She cringed again. "But I must have drifted off."

"Yeah. You must have done," Tegan muttered.

This conversation wasn't going anywhere nice. I tried to move it on.

"Good night though?"

Rach's trademark massive smile came back. "One of the best." She laughed to herself. "Seriously, Bells, who knew Jo had it in her? She was wiiild."

It was deeply satisfying to have found something Jo was truly terrible at.

"I would *never* have guessed that was your sister. You *could* have warned us you were related to the world's worst dancer." Marge flung her arms and head about all out of sync. It was actually quite accurate. Marge and Rach cracked up at the impression, but I had to force my laugh. It was one thing me thinking mean thoughts about my sister – after sixteen years of being tortured by her, and always having to sit in the back seat of any car journey, and her turning up here, I'd earned it – but somehow it didn't feel as funny when it came from someone else.

Rach caught her breath. "We did some more filming after you'd gone. Absolute classic. Remind me to show you later."

But did I want to see it? Or watch any more of them laughing at my sister?

Gah. It wasn't even eleven and already today was too full of confusing things.

"And guess what, Bells." Marge bit her lip like she'd made the most exciting discovery. "Rach was saying we might be college mates?"

Was it just me, or did that sound less of a friendly offering and more of a threat? I looked at her, trying to work her out, but Rach jumped in to explain. "Not *quite* what I said. I just meant if we end up going to separate places."

So she'd told them I'd messed up my exams.

Marge smiled sweetly. "Yeah, we're going in to our final year at Shire Sixth Form."

I smiled back. "Great."

I had a feeling neither of us thought that was true.

I couldn't deal with any more of this convo so made an excuse to duck out and see Adam. There was a *phutt-*

phutt-pad-a-phutt coming from outside his tent. He was sitting on the grass in front of it, deep in concentration, humming to himself and drumming on some cans.

I walked right up to him before he noticed. He stopped with a start.

"Pretend you did *not* hear that?!" He looked mortified.

"Practising? Your drumming sounded ace."

"Stop flattering me." He fanned his face, smiling. "NO! IN FACT DO NOT! …Never stop?!"

I grinned and ran through all the compliments I *could* give him. Wondrous forearms. Weirdly cute way of hiccupping. Excellent taste in pizza toppings. All totally appropriate to think *about* him, but probably not to say to him. I needed something less weird. "…Nice tune?" TUNE?! Who says tune?!! Was I suddenly a forty-year-old piano teacher?!

"You kidding?" Adam stuck his tongue out. "Somehow Dad's got the stupid Session in my head, and now I keep finding myself humming it." He shook his head, disgusted. "PLEASE KICK ME NOW."

"I TAKE IT BACK THAT SONG WAS AWFUL. But … I will not be kicking you." I poked him hard in the head. "A disappointed prod is all you're getting."

"Not the disappointed prod?!" he fake protested, but

I did it again as it was a nice excuse to touch him, and then sat down next to him. He put his arm round me.

I rested my head on his shoulder. This was pretty perfect. We sat quietly for a couple of seconds, before I spoke.

"How are you feeling about tomorrow?"

"Oh, Bells. I'm BRICKING IT. I mean, practice was great, but the stage and stuff, it's just so … big."

I smiled, gutted yet again that I couldn't be there.

"Adam, you'll be great. Just go out there and do what you do best." I gave him a kiss on the cheek, and my most confident smile.

But I had my own worries too.

The Session and their fans were out for us.

Was this protest really going to make any difference? Or just make me even more of a target than I already was?

TWENTY-FOUR

Reunited, Rachel, Tegan and I went on a mission handing out protest flyers in every campsite we could get into without the security guards chucking us out. Tegan had stopped being in a mood with Rach, and Rach was being extra helpful to make up for this morning. The only blip was when she quietly asked if we were *sure* the protest was a good idea, and if there *was* a better way to make the band listen, but Tegan shot her straight down, telling her not to listen to Marge. It sounded like a direct quote from her. But after Rach had said it, she didn't mention it again, and threw herself into handing out the most flyers out of all of us. She even blagged some material and pens to make flags on Sunday.

And by the time we'd dropped them off at the tent, eaten some crumpets (Rachel's treat), jumped around to five bands, and seen two amazing talks, things felt back to normal. I felt loads better. Especially as we'd had another twelve people say they'd be at the protest, and three were going to come and make posters with us first. The crowd was going to be thousands strong, so we needed a lot more people to make a difference, but at least we knew some people were on our side.

I always took Polaroids of extra-special moments, and the three of us here lying in the afternoon sun felt like a moment I wanted to have on my wall for ever. My camera whirred, and after a few seconds the picture of Tegan, Rach and me squashed together, doing peace signs, a mixture of pouting (Rach), tongue out (me) and ginormous smile (Teeg) slid out and started to develop.

"ICONIC!" Rach grabbed it out of my hand and kissed it. It was ace. I stuffed it in my bra for safekeeping. Fingers crossed it'd be sweat proof.

"Oh, hiyer, guys." A voice that wasn't one I expected came from above our heads. I looked up. "Or should I say bin bag girl?"

Oh, hello, person I least want to see. Is what I wanted to reply. What I actually said was, "Oh, hi."

I congratulated myself on my restraint. Had Luke just come over to gloat?

"Loved that vid this morning, Bells. You're hilaire." Yup, he'd just come over to gloat. "First loo roll, then bin bags. You really are a quality bird."

I tried not to gag at the "bird" bit. He'd done that just to wind me up, so I ignored it.

"Got to give the fans what they're after." I fake laughed, *flaughed*, as best I could.

"Reassuring to know you've got a future in litter picking though, Fishy. You know. *If college doesn't work out.*"

He was such a barrel scraper.

"Oh, it will." Tegan was straight in there to stick up for me. I looked at the ground, not sharing her confidence but not wanting to give it away. "And even better – 'cos Bells will be with us, *you* won't need to obsess over her any longer."

But he didn't have time to insult me any more as Adam, Marcus, Mikey and Jay arrived, chomping their way through what I think was their second pizza each of the day. We'd last seen Mikey heading towards the food stands, on a passionate rant about why "brunch"

315

was acceptable, and how he was going to make lunch/
dinner – *linner* – happen.

"Nice panda suit." Luke sneered at Mikey.

"Nice face," Mikey shot back.

"Well, I'll leave you guys to it." He looked at us all
as if we wasting his time, rather than him coming over
to us. "And if you want to listen to some *proper* music
–" he looked at Adam " – not like the Damp Donald
Problem..." He knew *exactly* what their band was
called. "Ska is on stage in thirty. It's going to be the set
of the festival." I couldn't think of anything worse. But
at least it meant Luke headed off. I shuffled next to
Adam and lay down with my head resting on his shins,
the sun beating down on my face. Give or take Brian's
attempt to ruin things, we were having a perfect day
together. Hanging out with everyone, seeing bands,
laughing at all the fancy dress outfits which had seen
better days.

Marcus cleared his throat and wiggled his eyebrows.
"So, shall we do it then?"

No one knew what he meant.

"Explain," Adam demanded.

Marcus shrugged as if it was obvious. "Go see Ska?"

I gagged (quite hard when lying down). Marcus
threw a plastic fork at my head. He meant it to bounce

316

off, but 'cos I hadn't brushed my hair in ages, it speared my hair and just sort of stayed there.

"Sounds like one of your worst ideas to be fair." Mikey put his arm around Tegan and planted a massive kiss on her head.

"You might wanna wash that, Teeg." One of Marcus's favourite pastimes was teasing Mikey. "He's been what? Almost forty-eight hours straight in that panda suit?"

"IT'S A LEEEEEMURRRRR." Mikey leapt over and bundled Marcus under him, Jay following in with his pincers. I pulled my proper camera out. Silhouetted, they looked sort of epic and gladiatorial – if gladiators had worn fluffy animal suits and one of them had half an uneaten pizza slice stuck to one foot.

But Marcus hadn't been joking, and with nothing better to do, we found ourselves pushing and shoving into the middle of the crowd at the New Bands Tent to see Ska.

Even though it was her, I was still excited. There's nothing better than being in the middle of a crowd you can't see the edges of, everyone waiting to hear the first booming note play out, looking for clues something might be about to happen on stage. Luke had already posted a thousand pics of "how his baby girl had the biggest crowd yet". She didn't, but his pics did make it look like she had. He'd ended up standing near to us. Probably to strategically gloat. Well, this was going to be fun, aka, not at all fun.

And as soon as Ska came out, I knew I was right.

She was in a gold reflective unitard.

Her hair looked like something Selena Gomez would class as a good day.

She didn't even walk – she was carried on by a group of guys, all dressed in black, literally standing on their shoulders. Was that even possible? Sometimes I fell over just standing on the floor.

She looked like a goddess.

I, however, was wearing a white T-shirt I'd just dropped mozzarella on, had third-degree sunburn on my chin, and when I'd just blown my nose, glitter had come out. I wouldn't say I was at peak #SelfLove right now.

Luke leant over to his mate, transfixed by Ska. "Soooo fit, mate. I mean. Seriously." He said it loud enough for me/most of the crowd to hear. I picked a bit of cheese stain off my top self-consciously.

Ska's man-platform slinked to the front of the stage and stood still. Ska eyeballed the crowd.

Luke snapped his fingers in the air and hollered, "THAT'S MY BIRD!" Tegan shouted back "people aren't property", but the crowd was too loud for him to hear.

Everyone was whooping and clapping, desperate for the set to start.

There had been a buzz about Ska and the Lets all weekend. Until a few days ago, nobody had really heard of her or her music, but this weekend she'd got all her #ModelSquad to post about her, and in just seventy-two hours she'd basically made herself a bona fide celeb. The sides of the stage were packed with people I recognized from other bands, as well as smartly dressed groups of people all whispering behind their hands, like they might be from record labels. Luke hadn't been exaggerating about the interest in her.

Could I *definitely* bear to watch this? It couldn't be nice for Adam either – I knew how worried he was about no one turning up for his gig. That if tomorrow didn't go well, this could be his first – and last – time playing a proper stage. *Why* did I agree to come?

But I'd left it too late to leave. The crowd fell silent (give or take a few wolf whistles) as Ska slowly dismounted her human pyramid. Luke turned and gave me a double thumbs up. I mustered what dwindling spirit I had to smile back. He was *loving* this.

Ska walked up to the microphone. I closed my eyes, wishing I was *anywhere* else. Even sitting my exams again.

But … nothing happened. I reopened them.

Ska was … doing a handstand. Had I missed something?

I sideways glanced at Adam. He had his head tilted, also trying to figure out what on earth was happening.

Someone shouted "sing something" at the front of the stage. Was the mood shifting?

BOOM.

The first note played out. A band marched out. And just like that, the crowd were back on side, cheering wildly. Ska stood up from her handstand. Bleeping started. Was she some kind of modern-day Lady Gaga?

BOOM.

BEEP.

BOOM.

It sounded a little like when Mum's smoke alarm starts to run out of batteries.

Ska strode up to the mic. But instead of singing, she … did a forward roll??

I put my hand on Adam's shoulder to push myself up to see more. What was happening? Why was noise playing and not a song? Hadn't they soundchecked? Or was this it?

Ska was now flat on the floor.

Was she OK?

AAAAAEEEEEEEWWWWWAAAAAEEEEE-HHHHHAAAAAAHHHH.

A blood-curdling scream rang out. The man in front of me ducked a bit and put a finger in his right ear.

She wasn't OK?! She was in pain.

People looked worried.

Was someone going to help her?

I turned to Luke, concerned – he looked as freaked out as everyone else.

But no. Ska stood up. One arm in the air. She was OK!

Phew.

The crowd cheered as she lifted the mic to her mouth – she must be about to explain what was happening.

She took a deep breath and … made the wail again.

Oh. My. Unitards.

It was her *singing*.

The band launched into a mess of beeps and bangs and chords as Ska sprinted around the stage like her life depended on it, singing and wailing. *Sailing? Winging?* I had no idea.

And she was dancing. Like really dancing. Although limb flinging would be a better description – it was like what I do when I'm alone in my bedroom, but more – so much more. Jo had *nothing* on her. It was mesmerizing, but I'm not sure if it was in the way she intended.

UHOHOOOO ICCCCHHHHH EIIIIICHHHHH BBOOOOOONNN

Were they words, or just noises? Wait … was it German?

I'd never seen such a large crowd look so … confused.

"Bella." Adam's mouth was right up to my ear, whispering straight into it. It actually felt kind of hot – was someone talking into your ear meant to feel nice?! Argh. *Brain*. Not the point. "What. *Is*. Going. On?"

OK. So, the world's most understanding person was also having a problem understanding. That was reassuring. I looked at Luke. He wasn't smiling any more and his mates were all nudging each other.

Ska was now doing jumping jacks. Nope, now she was hopping.

The song stopped abruptly. Most people were too surprised to manage to clap.

"REBBBEELLLLL ROCCCKKKKSSS," Ska purred into the microphone. "THANK YOU FOR HAVING ME!"

OK, maybe *this* was the bit where it got normal.

She dropped into a crab. Or not.

"She's into crabs like you," someone yelled at Jay.

"I'm a LOBSTER," Jay shouted back like a man/lobster on the edge.

Ska stood back up.

"ARE YOU FEELING GOOOOOOD?" The crowd were so confused that instead of making generic cheers back, they actually answered (I heard an "I'm a little hungry", and an "It's quite cold"). Ska was unfazed. "ARE YOU READY TO FEEL … EVEN BETTER?"

Luke yelled a "Hell yeah" back. The only one.

Ska flung her head forward, tucking her mic up and under the curtain of her hanging hair. She looked like a big hairy talking lamp.

"OK. LET'S FEEL THIS LET'S DO THIS LET'S BE AS ONE LET'S TAKE WHAT WE'RE GIVEN LET'S BE THE CREATURES WE ARE LET'S LET IT OUT LET'S BE BRAVE LET'S BE UNFILTERED BE WILD BE CAGED BE TAMED BE YOU YOU GET ME?"

I totally didn't. Was she possessed? Normally she just banged on about how hot her own wrists were.

Luke looked alarmed but shouted encouragement anyway. "BABES, YOU'RE KILLING IT!"

"She's certainly killing *something*," Crab Heckler shouted straight back.

"I WANT TO GIVE YOU WHAT YOU WANT,"

Ska shouted, her arm wrapped around her head holding her own chin. I think what we all wanted was someone to explain what on earth was going on. The band were staring forward. Maybe they were robots? Nothing would surprise me any more. "TONIGHT ISN'T ABOUT ME IT'S ABOUT US IT'S ABOUT BEING FREE."

Luke was right. I *was* glad I caught this gig. "SO FOR MY SECOND SONG –" OK, so that *had* been a song "– I WANT TO COVER AN EQUALLY STRONG POWERFUL WOMAN."

Ska then launched into a version of "Runnin'" by Beyoncé (Tegan had to physically restrain Rach when she twigged Ska had just compared herself to Bey). However, when Ska got to the first chorus, instead of singing the word "runnin'" she pulled out a golden glittery recorder from her unitard leg and played one long note on it. Which she then repeated every time she should have be singing the word "runnin'".

It. Was. Jaw. Dropping.

When it finally finished Luke said words like "avant garde" and "experimental" and "current trend" as loudly as he could. Weirdly he didn't also say "my girlfriend has totally lost the plot".

Rach thrust her phone in front of me. It was the hashtag result for #SkaAndTheLets – post after post of pictures of Ska from the side of the stage and from the crowd. The main three letters being posted alongside them being W T and F. When the next song finished – well, I *think* it was the same song, but it went on for ten minutes so it was hard to tell – Ska threw her recorder into the crowd. Instead of catching it, people parted, letting it fall to the ground (note to self: look for that on our last litter-picking shift tomorrow – it might be worth something if she goes viral). Ska didn't notice, still looking smug, truly believing she was pushing the boundaries of art, rather than eardrums.

A tiny, tiny bit of me felt sorry for her … but it was buried under a year of her being the Queen of Mean to me so I didn't pay too much attention to it.

As Ska lifted the mic to speak again, Adam tightened his grip on my hand like we were in a scary bit of a movie and were genuinely afraid of what might come next.

"THANK YOU, MY FELLOW HUMANS… THANK YOU FOR EXPERIENCING THIS WITH ME." She turned to the back of the stage and crouched into a tiny ball. "TONIGHT WE ARE ONE." She leapt up. Please let her Lycra seams hold. "TONIGHT YOU ARE INSIDE ME."

Mikey belly-laughed so hard his lemur hood fell right over his face – and he wasn't alone. Half the crowd were in full-on hysterics. The only reason I wasn't is because Adam was next to me and I was pretending to be a nicer person than I am.

Luke was staring at the stage – even he knew how bad this was. The only person who seemed to have no concept of how much people were enjoying it for all the wrong reasons was Ska.

"TONIGHT WE ARE MOVED BY LOVE. WHO IS IT THAT FEELS ME?"

Seeing an opportunity to win some points back, Luke put his hands to his mouth and yelled.

"I FEEL YOU. FEEL YOU *ALL OVER*." He then did this weird slow, satisfied nod to make sure we all knew they were together – in *every* sense. "LOVE YOU, BABES."

But Ska didn't hear him – or if she did she didn't acknowledge it, sitting down and dangling her legs off the side of the stage.

The words "LOVE. REAL. LIFE. YOU. ME." were projected in big white letters behind her. Luke's voice was the only thing we could hear. "This is the bit I was telling you about. She said I was her *muse*." Ska stood and tiptoed to the back of the stage.

Luke raised his voice to an absolute shout. "THAT ARSE. I mean?! So fit, mate. SO FREAKIN FIT."

Ska stopped still. Before jumping three times on the spot and whipping back round to the audience.

"LOVE IS A CONCEPT," she was shouting double speed, "BUT WE ARE PEOPLE NOT CONCEPTS WE ARE FREE AND WE ARE BEINGS AND LOVE IS FOR EVERYONE."

Luke's smile had frozen.

"WE ARE BODIES WE ARE FEELING WE ARE ME WE ARE YOU AND WE MUST DO."

Ska slowly walked up to the keyboard player and … was she whispering to him?

Nope.

No she was not.

She was full-on snogging him.

Luke turned to me, as if checking whether I'd seen. Like it was possible to miss. The cameras had zoomed right in and you could see every detail on both of the huge screens. Too much detail. Even a spit string between them. I smiled sweetly and gave him a thumbs up. He mouthed something about "art".

But the kiss was still happening. The only noise coming from the speakers was a slurping that sounded a bit like when Mumbles drinks water.

Luke cheered. "Love it, yeah, all part of the plan." He was talking to absolutely nobody. He then shouted at the stage. "Meet me backstage, yeah?"

As he waited for an answer that was never going to come, Ska slinked over to the guitar player, took her face in her hands and went in for an even longer kiss. They only stopped when the four men dressed in black from the start returned. Everyone breathed a collective sigh of relief it was ending.

Then re-inhaled that sigh when Ska went up to the tallest one, put her hands through his hair, and went in from the most graphic snog yet.

Breathless, she broke away.

"THANK YOU GOODBYE GOODNIGHT I DIDN'T KNOW WHEN IT WOULD BE TIME BUT THE TIME IS NOW AND THE ENERGY HAS BEEN AMAZING AND YOUR TIME IS NOW AND NOW IS MY TIME. TIME TO BE ALONE. ALONE WITH DEREK."

And making out with Derek, she got carried off whilst clamped to him like a limpet.

I've never seen a crowd of people so still. It was like a mass game of musical statues. Everyone was entirely motionless, mouths open, trying to figure out what they'd just seen. Or if we were all having a mass hallucination from some sort of burger poisoning.

Well, all except one. Because Luke was marching as far away as he could get from the stage, his face like absolute thunder.

Adam leant over and grinned.

"I guess at least my gig can't be any worse than *that*?"

CHAPTER

TWENTY-FIVE

After that unforgettable gig, there were still three more bands we wanted to see, and the seven of us stayed and leapt around to all of them. But even though Mikey and Jay – spurred on by the chanting of "GO PANDA, GO PANDA, GO PANDA" – crowd-surfed during the headliners, attempted to clamber on stage, and got wrestled into submission by four security guards (with actual tail fluff flying up in the air – I caught it all on camera), when Tegan and I were back in out tent, Ska's performance was still the only thing we were talking about.

"I'm wondering if I should get her number to chat about joining the gymnastics team." Tegan's muffled voice came from her sleeping bag. The night was so cold it was already a bag-over-face-to-survive-the-cold situation. "I've *never* seen someone bend that way." Coming from a girl who could get her leg behind her head, that was a big claim.

I poked a straw through the tiny gap in Adam's hoodie and swigged my third Capri Sun of the night. I'd pulled the toggles so tight around my face I only had a 50p-sized opening exposed to the freezing temperatures. I buried back down into my bag to check that I'd set my phone alarm for our final shift tomorrow. 4:48. BLEURGH.

All my battery chargers were dead, so this evening my phone was strictly on an emergency-use-only basis (i.e., taking pics of Tegan looking like a mole in her sleeping bag). Tegan was using her phone to do the other important stuff – stay in touch with Rach who was out with MGC, and keep an eye on numbers for tomorrow.

"Any good news before we go to sleep?"

Tegan shuffled around – buying time for an answer.

"Lots of comments – so *sure* that means there'll be loads there tomorrow…" Which meant we hadn't had any more people get in touch to say they were definites. Even though no one could see, I grimaced. Hard. Tegan was already starting on the "it'll be OK – we tried our best" chat, which was a million miles away from the "we've got this!" of yesterday. I just had to *hope* beyond *hope* that when we got together tomorrow at midday to start making the banners there would be plenty of people there to help us.

I lay in the dark and cold, listening as people headed back to our tents around us.

But it wasn't noise keeping me awake; it was worry.

Tomorrow was a big day.

The protest.

Adam's gig.

And all around us were a lot of Session fans who wanted us to fail.

CHAPTER

TWENTY-SIX

I woke up what felt like seconds later, only one thing on my mind.

SWEET CHEESES I NEEDED A WEE.

Despite it being so cold I thought I would open my tent to find a snowy wilderness, I wriggled out of sleeping bag to make the dash.

Fact. There is nothing less dignified than being in public, wearing pyjamas, double socks and flip-flops, rocking face creases from sleeping on a rolled-up jumper, and running across a field clutching a wad of loo roll in one hand, phone torch in the other, while bursting for a wee. But that's what had to happen.

And it was worth it. I headed back to the tent a new person. As I got nearer, I spotted a light moving around in Adam's tent. Was he awake too? I'd got up before my alarm, and had time to spare, so took a detour. He was awake – and he was muttering to himself. It was kind of adorable.

Marcus must still be out. Crouching down I prodded the fabric of the tent door and whispered, "Knock knock."

The shuffling stopped, then came towards the front of the tent.

"Beefy?"

"Uh-huh…" The zip went up. "G—" A sleepy, ruffled, extra-gorgeous Adam face appeared. All humans slept, so why did seeing him all soft round the edges make my thought processes stutter? Get yourself together, Bella! "—uten morgen."

He grinned up at me. "Well, this is a nice first thing to see in the morning." He must be in that waking-up stage where you can't really see detail. I let it slide. He rubbed his face with his hands. "I could. Not. Sleep… How cold was it?!"

"New levels."

"Plus, today's the day." He mouthed an eek, then pointed up at me. "Ahhh – I'd forgotten that's where it went." I still had his hoodie on. Was that why he'd been freezing?

I started to take if off, but he stopped me. "Bells – keep it!"

He took my hands in his, taking away my choice. His hands felt all toasty. And he smelt of warm, and cuddle, and him. And suddenly, despite neither of us having brushed our teeth and me not having woken up all my limbs yet, we were kissing. And it was incredible. As in *seriously* incredible. So incredible I tried to push through the thigh-squat-pain barrier to keep it going as long as possible. But, as I have the balance of a newborn foal (and due to my razor crisis, the exact same amount of leg hair too) it wasn't long before I ended up toppling over, and into his tent. And on top of him.

Which just meant we did even more kissing. I wriggled out of his hoodie, knowing he needed it but would never take it back. But who cared about hypothermia? This kiss was worth it. His hands were in my hair (I really hoped I'd removed that fork), my hands were up and under his T-shirt (his skin was soft and warm and felt both really out of bounds and totally mine all at the same time) and all of us seemed to be pressing up against each other. It didn't feel awkward, or weird, or clunky – just amazing. I was totally lost in it. I never wanted this to end.

But my phone had other ideas.

And chose this exact moment for my alarm to go off (technically, I'd chosen this time, but *still*).

Things I hated right now:

- My alarm
- My phone
- The concept of alarms
- The concept of time

The noise made us pull apart, the self-consciousness that had disappeared instantly reappearing and slapping us both around the face. I searched around for my phone, but I'd dropped it outside the tent. ARGH.

"Talk about timing." Adam laughed under his breath. I had no option but to fully disentangle from him. I crawled out and grabbed my phone, hitting snooze, before heading back in. "Sorry – but I …" Eurgh. I so didn't want to finish the sentence. I didn't want to have to go.

He nodded. "I know – you gotta go. But—" He reached over to the scrunched-up hoodie I'd tried to leave behind. "Don't think I didn't see this. Have it back. Don't want you freezing out there." Truth was, I loved wearing his stuff. It was like getting a secret cuddle the whole time.

"Thank you." I took it from him.

He looked me dead in the eye. "It's not entirely unselfish. Cos if you freeze, we wouldn't get to do this again." MAJOR STOMACH LURCH. He wanted round two as much as me?!

I crawled back out of his tent, dazed and drawing a total blank of how to reply (that didn't involve me doing a happy dance). As I stood up he waved with both hands from down on the floor.

"Seeya, Bells. And thanks… That was…" He grinned. "A nice way to start the morning."

I pulled his hoodie on. "Sure was."

To put it lightly. He propped his head up on his elbows.

"I'll try and be there at 12 – but we've got 'on stage walkthrough rehearsal' whatever that is, so if not I'll be there in spirit." He'd already explained he couldn't make the prep session for the protest, but it was lovely that he'd even think about trying to with all his stuff going on. He waved again and blew a kiss. I blew one back. Turns out we're both super cheesy before 5 in the morning. With potentially my biggest grin to date I headed back to my tent. It was not normal to be awake at 4:51 a.m., to be about to pick rubbish for four hours, and to be *this* happy. But I wasn't the only one smiling.

'Cos Lols was on the other side of the fence, staring straight at me. She blew me a kiss, taking the mick out of the one I'd just given Adam.

I pretended not to see her, even though we both knew I had, and ducked into my tent to get ready. Seven minutes later Tegan and I were out of our field and walking down to do our final shift. People were still returning from the fun of last night. And one of those people was running towards us.

"I *thought* it was you guys!" A smudgy, happy-looking Rach stopped in front of us. I'd never known her have so much stamina. Sometimes she fell asleep during *The One Show*.

I twirled and pulled on my top. "Y'know, I'm starting to like Uncle Vest-a." That was my new name for it/him. "You just getting back?"

Rach got the concern in my voice and pointed behind her. "Marge is with me. I *may* have just had an hour's kip while they danced." She cricked her neck. "Turns out floors can be *surprisingly* comfortable."

Tegan did a mini eye-roll; she wasn't even pretending to like them any more. Rach totally saw. "C'mon, Teeg, they're not that bad."

"Let's agree to disagree on that one." Tegan had admitted to me last night that she thought they were trying to turn Rach against us, although she had no idea why. I wouldn't go that far, but as much as Rach got on with them, they did always made me feel on edge.

"Well, they've been great to *me*." It was as close to annoyed as I'd ever heard Rach. "And get this, while you two were sleeping, we ended up sharing a hot dog with –" she scrolled through her photos "– and Bells, brace yourself." She turned her screen around. "Ruby from Tommy K?!"

Whoa. In front of me was a massive, grinning group selfie of the four of them with the lead singer – the kind that would have totally gone on my wall, if I'd been in it. Or anywhere near it. Not sleeping miles away.

But something about it made me look twice. And I didn't know what.

I felt uneasy. Why was I trying to catch Rach out?

"Awesome…" I tried to sound impressed, but I saw a flinch on Rach's face. Did she hear the jealousy I was trying to pretend wasn't there? Marge sauntered up and put her arm round Rach.

"Big day today…" She knew we didn't need reminding.

"Too right." Teeg looked down the path towards where Ross was gathering our group. "But first … we recycle."

I thumbed my vest out. "Putting the cool into re-cy-cool since the year '18." No one laughed. "So, er ... we'd better be off."

And with nothing more to say, we headed off, not even trying to repair the weird atmosphere between us. Which is why, when we finished our final shift and handed in our jackets for the very last time, I had no idea why Lols, Britney T, Marge and Rach were all on their feet clapping as we walked towards our tent.

What had I missed?

Lols was holding a can of Fanta in the air. And staring right at me. Rach was doing raise-the-roof hands.

What was going on?

Tegan and I stopped next to our tent and stared.

"Lads of Party HQ – I propose a toast." Lols put two fingers to her mouth and whistled.

Were they actually as happy as us that we'd finally finished our shifts. Or... My heart fluttered as an idea popped into my head. Did they know something about our sign-ups that we didn't?!

"Guys, come on over!" Lols beckoned Tegan and me to the fence. We walked towards it slowly, cautiously. What was this? I looked at Rach, eager for a clue, but she'd turned to Lols. I couldn't quite hear what she said, but it sounded something like, "Are you *sure* this is a good idea?"

Lols looked at her like she was crazy. "'*Course*. It's a *monumental* occasion. So..." She raised her voice up again so we could all hear. "Please be upstanding to celebrate this joyous news."

Britney T whooped. I glanced at Tegan, but she was as quiet as me.

Why had Lols clambered on to her chair?

"Cans in the air," Lols was shouting. People walking behind her had turned to stare. "C'mon guys, let's see those hands up?!" I looked at Tegan, and together we lifted our arms nervously. "And let's go wild, let's go crazy for..." For what?! "Bella *finally* losing her V plates to her absolute stone-cold hottie of a boyfriend last night."

What?! What was happening?! Was this a joke? But I didn't have a moment to take it in as Rach was whooping. Britney T was yelling "Get it, girl!" and Marge had run up to high-five me through the fence.

I couldn't move a muscle. What was going on?

"And there I was thinking you were a lost cause." Marge air-clinked her bottle of Diet Coke towards my hand, which was still dangling in the air, confused. "College is going to be a BLAST."

Lols turned towards me. "Anything you want to say, Bella?"

And I don't know if it was the shock.

341

Or the fact Rachel looked so happy for me.

Or the fact I was already worried about how bad my life at college would be with these girls around, but only one word came out.

"Thanks."

CHAPTER

TWENTY-SEVEN

The D'Oh Nut Stand was only two minutes' walk away.

Which meant less than 120 seconds till we found out if anyone had turned up to prepare for the protest.

The dream was we'd turn the corner and see a crowd already gathered. But today was already not working out at all as planned. And whenever I tried to concentrate on the protest, the drama from earlier thought-photobombed it.

But how could it not? Rach was being off with me. And the look Tegan had given me at the time had been the worst – she was disappointed I hadn't been strong enough to tell them the truth.

I *had* tried to go back on myself, tell Marge, Britney T and Lols they'd got it wrong, but they wouldn't let me get a word in, too busy speculating on all the details. It was like they enjoyed seeing me flustered. Enjoyed me finding out that it was Rach who had told them I was a virgin.

Her sharing my secrets with them hurt. Why was it even their business?

Eurgh. I couldn't stop myself being mad about it. Mad at myself. How stupid had I been sticking the Polaroid of us in my bra for good luck vibes today?

I was too grumpy to talk and judging by our silent walk down the hill, Rach felt the same. I was cross she didn't seem convinced it was me telling the truth that nothing had happened. And she was cross I kept asking where they'd got the info from, refusing to drop it. I think she felt I wasn't being honest with her about last night. I said they were weirdly obsessed with my love life. She said they were just being friendly and it was me who had the problem.

EURGH. I had no idea what was going on with them.

At least this time tomorrow they'd be out of my life,

hopefully for ever, but at worst until college. All I had to do now was stop them making any more trouble. Which was hard, as Rach had already let slip that on their first night out together, Lols had tried to talk her out of the protest, because they thought it was a "lame idea that would never work".

I was fuming. Mainly at them, but also a bit at her. Why couldn't she see straight through them? That the only thing they seemed to care about was causing trouble – mainly at my expense.

But was this it now, or did they have anything else up their sleeve? After this morning, I had to keep them away from Adam at all costs. I just didn't trust them.

"Guys." Tegan had her gymnastics-teaching voice on. "I'm not sure what was going on back there, but is there *any* way we could all agree that we're tired and there's been a mix-up? We can *absolutely* come back to it and sort it out properly, but for now we HAVE to deal with what's happening. Meeting all the people for the protest. To work together to stop The Session. Remember?" She rubbed her face with both hands as if this was all a bad dream she could wake up from. "It's the three of us ... we can do anything."

Normally her team talks worked a treat, but this time all she got were grunts.

345

But this semi-truce would have to do, because it was time to turn the corner to the D'Oh Nut Stand.

Find out if anyone had turned up to prepare for the protest.

Pessimistic me decided not to look in case there was no one there.

Optimistic me thought I'd spotted a group of people already gathered.

Realistic me decided I needed to know one way or the other. So, with my heart thudding so hard it made my breath wobble, I scanned the area.

And...

Couldn't see anyone.

"Maybe they're round the back?" My voice was all high. "Or the side?"

But as we walked nearer, one thing became clear. Our supporters weren't at the back. Or the side.

They just weren't here. The only person who was here was Brenda, who had traffic-cone cordoned off an area for us. A big empty area. And the only people that were walking towards it were ones who were trying to get round it to buy doughnuts.

After all this, nobody was coming.

Fifteen minutes of sitting on our own later, and Tegan had run out of terrible excuses (*we'd forgotten to put all of our clocks forward for BST and had only just realized/there was a second doughnut stand we didn't know about where loads of people were probably waiting for us/ The Session had already pulled out and there was no need for a protest*).

"I might have *one* idea." Rach was looking at her phone. "You know everyone who commented to say they were coming?" There had been at least twenty. "Some dude has spent the morning messaging them saying the prep session was cancelled."

I checked over her shoulder – she was right. We'd been so busy bickering we hadn't been checking our accounts, or keeping everyone updated as normal.

It was a low move by someone, but it was our fault for dropping the ball when we should have been on it the most. I looked around. All the boxes of stuff we'd collected around us. All the effort we'd put in.

All for nothing.

Should we pack up and put this whole plan out of its misery?

As soon as I thought of it, I knew the answer. Failing sucked. But failing because we'd stopped working together sucked even more.

I had to do something.

I stood up and picked up a box of the pens, card and

flags we'd collected over the last few days. "Right then."
I plonked it on top of the picnic bench between us. "We
haven't got all day." Rachel and Tegan looked at me,
confused. Failing was one thing. To not see it through
would be even worse. "Let's get making. I for one am not
going to let The Session get away with all those sexist
slogans. And what they said about Rach and all their
fans." It was my subtle attempt at clearing the air. "It's
not like a there's a minimum number for a protest, right?"
I mean, there was a minimum number for a *successful*
protest, but the goalposts had changed. They were now
wider than a pitch, and I was not going to let one stupid
argument be bigger than the three of us.

Rach lifted another box and opened it up. "Resistance
takes persistence, that's what you always say, Tegan?"

Tegan nodded, and with a quiet determination the
three of us opened everything up, getting out everything
we'd collected, a team again. With Rach at one end, I
started to unroll the massive plain fabric banner she'd
blagged. But as I did, a black-and-white furry paw
grabbed the end.

"Sorry we're late!" Mikey doubled over the bench,
totally out of breath. "Jay got his pincer stuck in a cash
machine. Four people had to help yank him out. It was
not pretty."

The Leemster didn't seem to have noticed that the three of us were very much on our own. Or if they did, they weren't making a thing out of it.

"So what's first?" Mikey peered at the boxes. "Banners, flags, what?"

And he didn't know it, but single-handedly he'd just made everything seem less hopeless. A protest of five didn't seem so bad. Sure, it wasn't going to be enough to stop The Session – or even make them notice we were there – but at least we could finish what we'd started.

I weighted down the ends of the banner.

"So for this we decided to go with 'Stages Aren't for Sexists' right?"

Everyone nodded except Mikey.

"I still vote for 'Make Music, not Spew-sic' but I've been outvoted."

I ignored him. He ignored me ignoring him. "And for the flags we've got 'The Session Need a Lesson', 'People = Equal' 'Girls Aren't Up for Grabs' and 'People Aren't Property'."

Someone flicked my ear. "I could do a killer design for those if you wanted?"

My sister.

"*You're* here?" Which, considering I could see her, was a weird thing to say.

"I've seen your art coursework, Bells – I couldn't let the family name get tarnished." Jo put her hand out. "You've got glitter on your chin, by the way." She licked her finger and rubbed it off. "Now show me where the pens are and I'll get started."

If there's one thing I'd say about my sister, it's that she's really annoying. But if there were two, I'd add that she's amazing at design, and was more than happy to have her skills right now. We might not have quantity of items, but we were going to have quality.

I handed the pens to her, saying a massive thank you. Well, I was going to, but didn't want to sound too cheesy, so actually said, "Don't mess it up."

"Oh, and I brought some help too ... if that's OK?" A group of six people standing at the edge of the area all waved. (One of them I totally recognized as her dancing friend, although she looked very different when standing still and not doing a chicken impersonation.) Our protest had officially hit double figures!

"Nice one, you guys!" Tegan beckoned them over. "Grab a seat. More pens and card and stuff are there. Help yourself to whatever you need."

Brenda shouted from behind the counter. "And include drinks and doughnuts in that too." She raised her fist. "What you lot are doing is bloomin' brilliant.

Talking of which..." She nodded behind my right shoulder. I turned around – it was the T-shirt printing man from next door who had told us he couldn't help.

"Brenda told me what you lot are up to and turns out I had some spare stock after all..." He stumbled on his words as he noticed a lemur and lobster slaving over some lettering. "So if you, er, wanna head round here, I might be able to help."

Rach picked up the paper with the slogans on. "I've got this." She walked over to T-shirt man. "Let's go raise hell!" He looked alarmed. "Aka print some T-shirts."

Rach winked at Teeg and me before swishing her long hair over her shoulder and striding off with him. I loved that this was happening. But, even more, I loved that we were beginning to feel like us again. Jo stood up. "I'll go help with the Photoshop, get them started. Back in a sec."

And that's when our first bunch of complete strangers turned up. They'd overslept but rushed over with a cry of, "Better late than never." Apparently, they'd had some friends who were going to come along too, but after seeing all the abuse Brian had given me, Rach and Tegan, they'd decided to stay away.

I couldn't hate him more. And while we might not be able to stop him, I knew one thing. Our protest *wasn't* a disaster. Whatever happened now, we'd proved that putting an idea out there could bring people together. And soon we had three picnic tables full of people all working away. Some I recognized from our litter-picking crew, some from my talk yesterday, and some were people who'd been in touch on social and had been wise enough to ignore the lies about it being cancelled.

Out of all the things they could be doing at the festival right now, they'd all chosen to be here, doing this.

It was awesome.

I got my camera out and took photos of everyone in action. As I snapped an arm went round my waist, a voice whispering in my ear.

"Well, THIS is pretty amazing."

What was Adam doing here?!

"Aren't you meant to be at that walkthrough thingy?"

"I maaaaay have played at least one song double speed." He shrugged innocently. "A drummer's got to do what a drummer's got to do. But I *had* to come and say good luck!"

He was in black jeans rolled up at the ankle, white classic Adidas, and an oversized plain black T-shirt. He called it his "band look". I called it his "intensely extra-fit look that made me do a silent gulp it was so overwhelmingly hot" (I only called it that inside my own head/once on Messenger to my sister but that was an accident 'cos I thought she was Rach).

I gave him the biggest hug. "You know you're officially the best, right?" Getting an up-close smell of his hair, his neck, made me feel all wobbly on the inside. He was like a human bacon sandwich.

He leant back, luckily unaware I was comparing him to a breakfast item. "Says the person who's made all *this* happen."

"It was a group effort," I corrected him. Right now Tegan was with Mikey, showing a group of strangers the list of slogans we'd written up on Brenda's chalkboard, and Rach was next door with my sister at the printer.

"And Beefy, you are *in* that group! So what can I do? I've got …" He looked at his watch. "… about five minutes before they officially notice that I've disappeared, so use me wisely."

Well, that was a phrase he should never utter around me and expect a coherent response back.

I picked up some paper to buy time to stop my mind thinking things not appropriate for this time of the day.

"First up, you can tell me how this walkthrough thing went."

He wrinkled his nose.

"Two words. Imposter syndrome. And that's when no one was watching, they were just walking past eating baguettes. Can't imagine what it will feel like tonight when people are actually watching? Well, when I *hope* they're watching…"

"Shush, you. 'Course they will. And I've asked one of my litter-picking buddies to film every second, so I can recreate the entire thing when we get home. Although don't tell Mum, as she'll probably join in and tell us some horrif story of her 'wild festival days'. Actual shudder."

Adam grinned. It was dazzling. He'd had his braces off a couple of months ago, and now his teeth were Netflix teen drama perfect. "Talking of shudder, guess who I saw backstage?"

"Ska?"

"Worse."

"Mrs Hitchman." Adam rolled his eyes in despair.

"Not sure what your old headmistress would be doing here, but no."

Then it hit me.

"The Session?"

"I can't be sure, but it looked like Brian deliberately threw a coffee down one of his assistants." He nodded slowly as I took it in. "I know, right?"

"So he's not just a massive sexist idiot, he's also an all-round bad human?"

"From what I saw, the actual worst. Wish I'd managed to get pics. Have some proof. The rest of the band were sitting around, letting it all happen, playing some quiz game on one of their phones."

"Shattering my backstage rock-and-roll illusions there."

"Maybe they were just trying to hide their nerves 'cos they know you're up to something?!" I laughed, appreciating his blatant optimism. "Soooo, what can I do?"

I looked around to see what quick job could work. But without warning, my blood ran cold.

Because three people were striding right towards us. Three people I was hoping to never see again. Marge, Britney T and Lols.

What were they doing here?

And more importantly, how could I get them to leave? Immediately.

"Hi, Bella." Lols waved with just her fingers. I gave her a weak smile back as I tried to get Tegan's attention to help, but she was too engrossed cutting out letters.

"Wow." Marge looked at everyone working. She slow clapped and spoke extra loudly. "Seventeen people." Rach wasn't around so they weren't bothering pretending to be nice any more. "Soooo great that you're still going ahead with this protest, despite the fact NO ONE is going to see it."

Could she *be* more patronizing? Yes, they might have cool hair, and great tattoos, and know anyone who's anyone, but it was time I stood up to them.

I couldn't let them come here just to make everyone feel like giving up.

I smiled as reassuringly as I could at the people making the posters. "Ignore them. They're just going."

Lols stepped forward. I could tell from the smirk on her face I'd just effectively declared war.

"Awww, don't be like that." She flicked some glitter off my top, like she cared. "We just wanted to say good luck –" she looked at Adam "– to both of you – for your big days." I held my breath, hoping she'd stop there. "Seeing as you both had such a big night."

So, she was going there.

She didn't move her eyes off me, enjoying watching me squirm on the impact of her conversation bomb.

Adam laughed. "It *was* a late one, but today is 100% all about the gig." He squeezed my hand. "And supporting this one."

He had no idea what was going on. I had to get him out of here. I could explain later.

Lols clocked me looking for an excuse, and made sure she spoke first. "Ahh, you two lovebirds." I felt like the ground was rotating beneath my feet. Why was she doing this? What had I done to deserve this? "Aaaaall over each other after last night. No wonder Bella was celebrating this morning."

Adam's hand tightened on mine. "Sorry, Lols. You've lost me."

This couldn't be happening.

"I wasn't celebrating." I yanked his hand. "We should go."

But Adam stood firm, not wanting to give in to Lols. "What are you trying to get at?" His voice was prickly.

Lols blinked all innocently. "Bella can explain."

I was shaking my head in disbelief. What was she playing at?!

"There's nothing to explain."

"C'mon, guys, it's not even a big deal." Lols shook her hair out and scraped it into a high ponytail, overly casual, like she wasn't deliberately winding this whole situation up. Adam studied my face as if I could help him understand. I looked back at him, wishing I could but not knowing how. All I knew was I had to stop this conversation before it got worse. "It's only sex."

Too late.

Adam shot me a look. I felt sick. Was he going to think I'd said something?!

"Well, what happens in tents, stays in tents, right, Bells?" He squeezed my hand – a secret signal that he was dealing with it. That he knew Lols was just being her usual self. That although this was awkward and embarrassing, we could style it out together,

Relief rushed through every inch of my body. Even my hair felt less stressed.

I squeezed his hand right back.

"Agreed."

But Lols wasn't bothered. She just laughed. "That's not what you were saying this morning though, were you, Bella?"

Adam dropped my hand. And turned back to me, confused. "Bells?"

I'd promised him no more lies. Did I have time to explain?

"There was just a mix-up." I tried – and failed – to laugh it off.

"The kind of mix-up where you stand around celebrating that you've lost your virginity? That's *quite* a mix-up?!" Marge was pretending to be completely baffled. I couldn't look at Adam.

"C'mon, Marge, that's not how it was." I didn't know

if I was telling her, or pleading with her.

She cocked her head. "But it was?! In fact, it was SUCH a sweet moment, I filmed the whole thing."

She held out her phone, playing the moment Lols was up in the chair giving the toast. It looked bad. They'd totally set this whole thing up. But why?

"C'mon, Marge! That's enough." I reached for her phone. But I was too late, the screen was filled with me, hand in the air, saying "thanks".

It looked like I really *was* celebrating.

Behind me came the sound of a metallic crunch of a can being stamped on. Adam was walking away. I felt like all the oxygen had been sucked out of the air. What had I done?

I didn't know whether to run after him, or stay and sort this out once and for all.

My phone buzzed.

AARD: Do me a favour and leave me alone.

Well, that was my decision made.

"Why'd you have to do that?" My voice, which had previously disappeared, was suddenly back. Loud, clear and furious. Tegan realized something was up and ran straight over.

Lols shrugged. "Why are you pretending, Bells? I saw you leave his tent. There's nothing wrong with the fact you had sex." She winked, just like she had this morning. It was clear that all this time she'd known *full* well nothing had happened. So why pretend to everyone it had?

"Having *what*?" Oh joy of joys. My sister had chosen this exact moment to reappear. And she did not look happy.

"Jo – can you give us some space?!"

She plonked down the pile of T-shirts she was carrying. Guess that meant "no". I did *not* need this lecture right now. But when Jo looked up, it was Lols she was glaring at. "Is there a reason you think it's OK to shout your mouth off about my little sister's –" *please don't say sex please don't say sex* "– sex –" oh she did "– life?"

To think – I'd been so worried about the protest, but now I was going to die of humiliation before it even started.

Marge stepped forward, quick to defend her friend. "Says the girl who thinks it's OK to act the fool on a podium?"

My sister stepped even closer, not afraid of anyone. "I'm not a *girl*, I'm a woman."

"Calm down, dear," Britney T said with a snigger. "Anyway, we should be saying thanks; Bella's video of you embarrassing yourself on that stage was the highlight of the weekend."

I felt a flush of regret that I'd ever taken it. Jo had only been having a good time. Considering we were all here making "Girls Support Girls" banners, I could sometimes be spectacularly bad at practising what we preached.

Jo shook her head at me. "Nice to know where your loyalties lie, sis." And just like Adam, she stormed off.

"Everything OK?" Rach arrived back from next door, doing a double take as Jo marched past her. She had no idea what she was walking into.

"Not really." Was the only answer I could give. None of it made sense. "These guys – " I pointed at Marge and the others "– were just leaving."

"But they just texted me to say there were coming to help." She looked around at some of the empty benches. "Don't we need all the hands on deck we can?"

Tegan had my back. "Not from these, Rach. Honestly, helping is the last thing they want to do."

Marge raised her eyebrows at Rach. "Told you they had a problem with us." I couldn't believe what I was hearing.

Rach looked from me to Marge to Tegan to Lols like she didn't know who to believe.

"As if?!" I turned to Rach. "Seriously, Rach, you need to stay well away from them. They're *obsessed* with ruining everything." I could fill her in later about what had just happened.

"Errr," Lols butted in, "don't tell her what to do?! You're the ones that have abandoned her every night to hang out with your boyfriends."

My mouth proper goldfished. Lucky Tegan managed words.

"We had to get back so we could get up for work." Each word came out staccato.

Marge shrugged. "Sounds hella convenient to me. At least we were there for her to have fun with."

I looked at Rach to see if she was going to say something, but she was keeping quiet. I had more than a niggling feeling she might be believing them.

"It's not convenient?! It's the truth." I had to make Rach see who it was that was being honest. "As is the fact – NEWSFLASH – I'm a virgin." I said it so loudly even Jay who was three benches away gawped at this weird TMI outburst. May have misjudged the volume slightly. "Which you completely know already. Which I'd appreciate you telling Rachel." I shook my head trying to keep calm. "Seriously, what *is* your problem?!"

Britney T's mouth dropped open. "What's our problem? *Our* problem? We're not the ones trying to get The Session kicked out of RebelRocks?!"

Marge and Lols shot her a look. But it was too late. I'd seen and knew *exactly* what it meant.

She'd said too much. Just enough for me to work it out. As least I understood now.

They were the ones who had caused issues between the three of us.

They were the ones who had made sure Rach stayed out, stopping her doing her flyering.

They were the ones who had heckled my speech, trying to put me off.

They were the ones who had thrown the whole of today's prep off with this made-up drama about Adam and me.

And as the pieces slotted together I realized what it was that had bothered me about that Tommy K group selfie Rachel had shown me.

"Rach. I know this is the worst timing, but could you just show me that picture of you and Ruby again?"

There was no reply. I turned to see where she was. And my heart sank. She was nowhere to be seen. I'd been so busy shouting I hadn't notice her leave. What kind of a friend was I?!

But I didn't need to see the selfie again to know. It was what the girls had been wearing in it that had bothered me. Underneath their hoodies. It was just a flash, but it was enough.

The three of them had The Session T-shirts on underneath.

"It's you, isn't it?" I asked, suddenly calm. They were almost impressive. "You're @HeyItsTheSessionHQ, aren't you?"

Finally, Marge smiled her first genuine smile at me. "Bingo."

CHAPTER

TWENTY-EIGHT

It all made sense.

How @HeyItsTheSessionHQ had always been one step ahead of us. Knowing there was a video of me dancing that could be shared to humiliate me and put me off, knowing about the prep session so they could set up an account to sabotage it. Once they'd realized who we were they'd deliberately got close to us just so they could use our information against us. It was cruel, mean and everything we should really expect from people who loved The Session so much.

The only silver lining had been watching them get

removed from the area by Brenda and a furious lemur.

After they'd been chucked out, luckily everyone else stayed to carry on with the protest prep. But I had to go. Because as serious as the protest was, Rach was more important. Tegan and I agreed to divide and conquer. She'd stay here, and I'd look for Rach.

As for Adam, I knew he needed to focus on his gig, so as scary as it was, if I really cared about him, I had to do what he said and give him space. So I focused on finding Rach. But after ringing on repeat, and looking in every tent, stand and stall, I couldn't find her. I slumped down on to a bench and pulled out a packet of emergency Wotsits. The rage I'd felt an hour ago had hardened into a painful ball of sadness.

My phone flashed with a message giving me a flicker of hope.

JO: FOR FUTURE REF DON'T TELL ME TO
GET LOST EVER AGAIN.

I didn't need this, not now.

ME: I THINK YOU'LL FIND I SAID "GIVE ME
SPACE".

That's the thing with sisters, you know you're going to be seeing them at Christmas in eighty years' time whether you like it or not, so there's no hurry to sort stuff out. I'd just avoid her till tomorrow, then sort it out back home – 'cos when Mum was around she couldn't yell at me.

JO: ALSO I'M BEHIND YOU.

I turned around and almost slapped my face into a white paper bag she was carrying.

She passed it to me and sat down. "Got you these."

If this was pick and mix then maybe I could reconsider how badly today was going. I peeked inside.

Nope. Today was definitely the Worst Day Ever.

It was pick and mix in a *way*. But this particular mix was about fifty silver square-foiled condoms. Which would be 0.00001% less awful if I needed them in any way, and wasn't about to get dumped.

I scrunched the bag shut, shielding my eyes. Might as well just say it.

"You know I haven't had sex, right?"

I should just record that on my phone so I could press play. It felt like it was becoming my catchphrase of the day.

"Always good to be prepared." She was as bad as Mum.

"I'm about to get dumped, Jo – so unless you mean preparing for a mass water-balloon fight, have them back."

"Oi. Don't be ungrateful. I went to the festival pharmacy for them. They give out free condoms, y'know." She sounded way too casual. Like she was always popping around town for condoms. Like she was always getting through her supply of condoms. Like she was always USING CONDOMS.

PLEASE SOMEONE STOP THESE MENTAL IMAGES!!!! I'd suffered enough today.

"Can you not use that word, please?"

"What, free?"

I huffed at her.

"Oh … connnndommmm?" I swear she said it extra slow. And loud. "Would … sheath be better?"

"You know full well it would not."

"Although, wait. So why were those girls saying you and Adam hooked up last night?"

I shrugged. "'Cos they put two and two together and made five just to ruin my life, and now Adam hates me and so does Rach and now I've ballsed everything up."

"Oh, Bells." She put an arm round me. And as

annoying and prophylactic-pushing as she was, it felt nice to know she was on my side. "So what happened?"

And those three small words opened the floodgates of me spilling out everything. About the girls, about me originally being jealous of them and Rach, about how they put pressure on me to stay with Adam, about how I was worried the protest was going to be one big embarrassing disaster, about college. Everything.

"This'll cheer you up –" she got out her phone "– at least you're not on the receiving end of these." She opened up a thread between her and Mum. Whoa. They chatted – a lot. Jo laughed at my shock. "We do have conversations without you, if your fragile ego can handle that?"

She stopped on one from a couple of days ago. "Like, how was I meant to reply to this?"

MUM: o🐙 o🐙 o🐙 o🐙 o🐙 😁 😁 Just had the longest session yet with my new man!

"Oh, Jo, I'm so sorry. No one should *ever* see that."

I laughed, wanting to show her I appreciated her trying to cheer me up, but actually I was covering up what I was really doing. Reading the earlier messages above it.

MUM: My darling Jo-Jo HaNGin there. Itll all
be worth it Just remember to look after yourself
even with all that exr=tar work love you oodles
and poodles xx 🍜🍜🍜🍜 (noodles!!

Jo hadn't mentioned anything was up, so why was
Mum telling her to hang in there? What extra work?
Was her uni stuff all OK? Had I been so caught up in
my own stuff, I'd missed everyone else's? It was followed
by:

MUM: PS Full MOON tonight would be great for
some meditation help you destress FML SMEL
XXX

I paused, trying to find something to say. Other
than; *why won't Mum stop ploughing on with FML to
mean "Feel My Love"?*

"You know I'm here for you to talk to as well?"

Jo smiled. "Any time I need advice on how to survive
on a diet of crisps alone, I know where to come."

I did an indignant "Oi" which would have had more
impact if Jo didn't clock me shoving two empty crisp
packets under my leg as I said it. But I'd seen another
message. One from Mum thanking Jo for coming to the

festival to make sure I was OK. Jo had been telling the truth after all.

"I saw that." I pointed at her screen.

She smiled and shrugged. "Yeah. Mum panicked after she said yes to you going, and was going to come herself to 'keep an eye on you'. I thought this was your better option."

It 100% was. "Guess I owe you a thanks then?"

"One of these will do." She plucked a Wotsit out. "So what's your plan. Other than emergency crisps." She knew me too well.

"Find Rach. Explain what those girls were up to."

Jo raised an eyebrow. "That's it?"

I scrunched my mouth to one side, knowing that wasn't good enough. Because as much as Rach had walked out, it wasn't like I'd given her load of reasons to want to stay. I should never have made her feel like she had a choice to make. "And say a massive sorry too. For making her feel caught in the middle... Oh, and then apologize to Adam and brace for a dumping. Basically all the fun things."

Jo nodded. "Sounds good…" but she trailed off, something else on her mind. "You know, people always have their own stuff going on too, Bells. Remember that. But," she gave me a hug, "I know you've got this.

371

And if you're honest with Adam, hopefully he'll forgive you too." Even she didn't sound convinced.

"But what if he says he never wants to see me again?" I couldn't image what life would be like if he said that. I'd have to cancel summer.

Jo tucked a piece of hair behind my ear. "It sucks, but all you can do is tell him the truth. And if you need me, ring."

I nodded, taking all the resolve I had not to dissolve into the flood of tears that were desperate to come out. "Fanks, sis."

She smiled, and without needing to say the plan out loud, we leant our heads together and sent Mum a photo of us hanging out. Being sisters. Looking out for each other.

But this time, it was real.

CHAPTER

TWENTY-NINE

There must have been over a hundred Portaloos on site. And I'd already tried eighty-six of them.

Knock knock.

Nothing.

Ignoring the annoyed shouts from the long queue, I carried on making my way along them. It was the only place Rach could be.

Until one didn't answer. It just sniffed.

Could this be it?!

I cleared my throat. And talked to the blue door.

"Rach! It's me. Bella. I've been a massive idiot. I want to say sorry. And promise you that if the man snake ever did enter the lady cave you'd be first to know. But for now, I'm a great big virgin. So ... can you let me in?"

An old man's voice replied. "What's a lady cave?"

Oops. The sniffing was actually coming from the next loo along.

I shouted sorry, moved along and tried again. And this time when I finished I heard a snuffle that I *knew* was Rach.

"Rach, *please*?" Another sniff. "I'm sorry. It must have been rubbish for you. I should have realized you felt caught between everyone." It didn't feel the right time to tell her everything we'd found out. The apology had to be made first. "I just got annoyed that sometimes I thought you wanted to hang out with them more than us."

I snuck a glance behind me, confirming that about a hundred people in the queue were watching me pouring my heart out to a cubicle door. I must look ludicrous. Loo-dicrous.

"It was hardly a choice when you two were never around. And I was stuck on my own in another field."

Ouch. Her voice sounded small, hurt – couldn't she see we'd had no option?

"We were working, Rach – it's not like we wanted to?"

"But that's the thing. You had work. I didn't have anything. But you seemed to resent me making friends."

"I guess…" I had to be honest. With her and myself. "Maybe I did. And I'm sorry about that. So sorry."

All this time we'd been going on and on about people not being property, yet here I'd been, being possessive over Rach. But she had more she needed to say.

"And when you weren't working, the only thing that seemed to matter was the protest…" Her voice dropped. "Did you never realize how hard it was for me when that video came out?"

I thought back; I'd been so cross I just assumed she'd felt the same. Never imagined some of it was a brave face. It must have been so hard to go from being a band's biggest fan to being on the receiving end of their hate. And I'd never stopped to check she was OK. "I always felt like you thought I wasn't pulling my weight, but…" Her voice broke again. "I really was."

"That's not true, Rach – you've been amazing. We'd never have got this far without you! Why do you think I've spent all afternoon looking for you, only to end up on my knees in literally the most nasally challenging place possible? The fumes are honestly giving me Portaloo PTSD from yesterday."

I couldn't tell if she laugh-sniffed or sniff-sniffed. I hated hearing her like this.

I wished I could show her how much she meant to

me and Tegan, even if we'd been really bad at showing it. Which reminded me. I fired off a quick message to let Tegan know that I'd found Rach so she could stop worrying. But because I was crouching it was hard to push my phone back into my jeans pocket, so I stuffed it in my bra. And found exactly what I needed. The Polaroid of us three from yesterday. I fished my Sharpie out and wrote on it. *Best friends support best friends. For ever* and pushed it underneath.

Silence.

But after a few seconds, with a waft of perfume, the door opened.

A watery-eyed Rach was standing above me, mascara smeared down her face and glitter smooshed all around her cheeks. She had the picture in her hand. I looked up at her. She looked down at me, did a final mega sniff, and spoke.

"What are you doing down there, Bells? Haven't we got a protest to get to?"

CHAPTER

THIRTY

We raced as fast as we could across the site. It was 7:55 p.m. but Rach and I were ten minutes away from the main stage. We couldn't even stop as we ran past the tent where The Wet Donald Project had started playing.

I didn't need to explain to Rach what I'd found out about ex-MGC. Sitting in the Portaloo, looking at her picture from the other day, she'd worked it out. And hated them for trying to sabotage everything. Including us.

We got to edge of the main stage field, sweaty and breathless. And stopped dead. There was no denying what we could hear. Filing up the whole site was the sound of the Main Stage speakers booming into life.

And even worse. The roar of a crowd.

"HELLO, REBELROCKS! WE ARE ... THE SESSION! AND WE ARE VERRRRRY HAPPY TO BE HERE!"

We were too late. I looked at my watch. 8:02 p.m. Two minutes after the protest was meant to start.

We hadn't even got to The Session, let alone stopped them. The ex-MGC had won after all.

With the cheers of their fans ringing out as the band made a joke about how they "couldn't be stopped". The Session launched into their first song. Every note they played felt like a slap in the face. A two fingers up to everyone who had tried to stop them, tried to make them say sorry. They were even wearing their "Never Ask. Never Apologize." T-shirts. Bet Marge was loving this.

Rach and I trudged the final bit of the way to the others, our spirits crushed. It didn't help that we had to squeeze past Luke and Ska, who gave us the world's most unwanted "sorry that it turned out our protest was a massive failure" commiseration hugs. But they were right. I'd hoped we'd at least see one or two banners. Maybe some flags. A couple of Ross's high-vis vests, trying to defy them. But all we saw was one sign, held by Tegan, standing on a pile of boxes by the tree where we were meant to start the protest. A furry lemur and lobster at her feet, holding a banner you could hardly read, my sister and her friends next to them waving flags that blended in with all the other generic ones around them. Other than that … there was no one.

My eyes prickled.

DO NOT CRY. I forbid you!!!

I pushed at them, pretending to wipe some dust off my face, as if the tears might think there was a roadblock, do a three-point turn and head back to wherever they came from.

When Tegan spotted us she waved with both arms and Rach blew kisses back, mending all the damage from twenty metres away. The protest might have flopped, but at least we'd achieved one thing.

Following Rach's lead, we weaved through the last bit of the crowd, to be greeted by hugs all round (Mikey's was slightly traumatic due to the fact he smelt a bit like a compost heap). I let Tegan and Rach have some space, as they launched into a mixture of sorrys/hugs/happy be to be back together.

"So no one came then?" I had to shout over the music for Tegan to hear me. The band were on their second song. She shrugged.

"I dunno – I mean, I got up here at quarter to, like we said? But… Nothing. Nothing happened."

After all that, no one had come. Well, no one who wasn't a friend, blood relation or friend of a blood relation. Maybe Brian had scared them all off? Or maybe no one had been that bothered after all. Everyone else around us were just Session fans, enjoying the last gig of the festival.

Jo leant over and butted in. "Don't you think that could be the problem?"

I shook my head. I didn't understand.

"*Tegan* got up there. And although you lot know she was joint co-organizer, anyone who saw that talk might be expecting Bella."

Hmmm. I hadn't considered that. "So … you think there's a chance someone did turn up, but are waiting for a, I dunno … signal from me or something?"

Jo nodded. "Worth a try?"

Yes – when a plan fails, there's nothing like standing up on some boxes in the middle of a field to reconfirm it in front of everyone. Brian might even see. Have one last opportunity to laugh at me.

But what had I got to lose? So, when the band seemed to be coming to the end of a song, I reached into the box of high-vis jackets to pull one on. Loads had gone missing so I added Ross yelling at me to my growing list of things to look forward to, along with (in chronological order):

1) looking like a high-vis loser on a box
2) being dumped
3) hearing graphic details about my mum's love life when I got home
4) failing my exams
5) ruining the rest of my life.

The song stopped – it was now or never. I stepped on the boxes, pulled on my high-vis and lifted my "STOP THE SESSION" placard as high as it would go (quite high, as despite my short legs, I have surprisingly long arms). On the ground Teeg and Rach grabbed the poles of our banner. Jo and her mates hoisted up their "PEOPLE AREN'T PROPERTY" flags. And Mikey got on Jay's back (it felt surprisingly reassuring to have a lemur-lobster totem pole beside me). They waved their own creation, a sign that said "BRIAN IS A GIBLET".

My face felt on fire, switching from human colour to tomato.

My arm twitched from reaching up a bit more than it could handle.

I closed my eyes, willing something to happen.

But nothing did.

Completely nothing.

And when I opened my eyes to check if it was time for me to step down, I saw something I hadn't expected.

All around me, like a carpet rolling out towards the stage, a sea of neon yellow had emerged. Flags popping up all over the places. STOP THE SESSION banners everywhere. Umbrellas that had been made into 3D stop signs. Even a customized STOP lollipop sign had been lifted up, the words "The Session" added on.

People had come.

People wanted to Stop The Session.

I didn't know who was more shocked. Me or the band.

Brian was frozen to the spot, his mouth hanging open, looking like he'd seen a ghost.

Cries of "Stop The Session" had started up.

I looked down, in shock, and realized that the others didn't have a clue what I could see. What was happening.

"Get up here." I yanked Tegan and Rach up next to me, loving their faces as they saw supporters all through the crowd. And even more, as they saw Marge's blue hair stuck in a mass of the most vocal Stop The Session protestors. There was no way the band could even try and play now. The chanting was too loud.

They had no idea what to do. And even less when Brenda's loudhailer got pushed into my hand by Mikey.

But I also had no idea what to do next. In all of our planning, we'd never thought beyond this moment.

Erm.

I looked up at the stage.

Gulp.

The whole band were staring at me. And the chant was beginning to slow so I could say something.

I should feel empowered. But I felt terrified.

I lifted the speaker to my mouth and pressed the button.

Which turned out to be a siren. Which not only made the whole field think there was an emergency, but also meant any eyes that weren't on me now were.

"We're right here," Rach breathed into my ear.

There was only one thing for it. With a gulp I pressed the other button and began to speak.

THiRTY-ONE

Well, I *tried* to speak.

Nervous hand sweat made me press the button too quickly so all that rang out was the world's loudest gulp.

Jo rubbed my back – I hoped in support and not because she thought I needed burping.

Words. Where are you?! Come to me!

I thought back to my speech from yesterday. To why we were all here. And took a deep breath. My voice boomed out.

"We're here today to STOP THE SESSION!"

There was a pause.

Then the crowd cheered.

"MUSIC SHOULD BE FOR EVERYBODY. SEXISM HAS NO PLACE IN SOCIETY!!"

Another roar of agreement. I looked up at the stage. The band were standing together at the front of it, Brian shouting something I couldn't hear. Had someone turned his mic down?!

"WE DEMAND YOU RESPECT YOUR FANS! AND EXPLAIN WHY YOU THINK IT'S OK TO MAKE A PROFIT FROM CLOTHES THAT ENCOURAGE PEOPLE TO SEE EACH OTHER AS UNEQUAL!" A cheer went up. But was that even a word?!

"AS IN NOT EQUAL. DID EVERYONE GET THAT?"

I think they'd got it.

"WORDS *AREN'T* JUST WORDS. YOU CAN TELL BY EVERYONE WHO IS HERE TO STOP YOU. AND WE'RE NOT GOING ANYWHERE UNTIL…"

The big speakers crackled around me. Uh-oh. I might only have seconds left before the music started again. I had to say what I needed to say and quickly.

But what did I need to say?!

I turned to Tegan – and she did exactly what I hoped. Mouthed "apology" while tugging at her top. Just what I needed. I raised my voice even louder than before.

"...UNTIL YOU STOP THE SALE OF YOUR CREEPY MERCHANDISE AND APOLOGIZE!"

And at that exact moment, the speakers came back into life and the whole field was full of the sound of one thing only.

The most massive swear from the lead singer.

THiRTY-TWO

"That wasn't live, was it?"

Brian asked nobody in particular. I'd forgotten the gig was being played out live on radio. Or – more accurately – his short, sharp expletive had.

All around us people had their hands in the air, pointing to the side of the stage as they yelled, "Off! Off! Off!" Over half the crowd was on our side. And those who weren't had started to leave, not liking the band enough to stay.

Brian was striding around the stage, his finger up to his in-ear talkback system, trying to listen to someone telling him what to do. But he was struggling to hear.

Looking lost, he stepped back towards the mic stand and pushed his hair behind his ears.

"OK, OK. We get it." Brian turned on what he thought was his most charming grin. "Some of you little lot have got your knickers in a twist." He squinted hard in my direction, and at some of the other people holding flags and banners. "And surprise, surprise, the ones doing all the moaning are the ugly ones." He expected a laugh. He got an angry "Oooh". He flapped his arm up and down. "Calm down, guys." He tried to laugh it off. He failed.

"Like we say –" he pointed to the big sign behind him "– *It's Only Words*. So if you can't handle a joke, then isn't the joke on you?" This time he got a sharp intake of breath from people shocked at how little he got it. Even people who'd started off not that bothered were quickly realizing what an idiot he was.

"So how about we do what we came here for? Playing some music and having some fun." He turned his back to the crowd and nodded his head to count the drummer in.

Did he really think all these people had gone to all this effort just so he could make some small talk and get back to his gig?

He could think again.

I picked up the loudhailer and jammed my finger

down on the button. Before I could stop myself, I shouted as loud as I could.

"WHAT DO WE WANT? *AN APOLOGY!* WHEN DO WE WANT IT? *NOW!!!!!!*"

I was so stunned I'd done it I accidentally stopped, in total shock.

But Rach didn't miss a beat, and leant over, pressed the button, and shouted it for me. Then Tegan joined in. And they shouted it again. And again. Until Jo and Tegan and Rach and Mikey and Jay and I were all repeating it, more determined than ever. We were not going to be silenced. And with our arms around each other, the words took on a life of their own, belonging to all the voices that joined in across the field. All of us speaking as one.

It was deafening. And Brian was livid. The band looked like they had no clue what to do. He seemed to have gone from yelling at us to yelling at them.

Brian picked up his mic.

"ENOUGH!!!!" he shouted, spitting with rage. "There will be NO APOLOGY. THE SESSION ARE A ROCK-AND-ROLL BAND, SO IF YOU CAN'T HANDLE THAT, THE EXIT'S THAT WAY."

He pointed to a gap in the hedge. No one moved.

"I suggest whoever has a problem with a T-shirt, or

whatever it is that's bothering you, DON'T BUY ONE, and the rest of us can get back to what we're here for. A session from The Session!" He punched the air.

But he wasn't met with applause.

He was met with the loudest boo yet. And no matter how much he stomped around, smiled at the camera, put his finger to his lips, it didn't get any quieter.

Rach tugged at my sleeve and showed me her phone. Pictures of me?! The words that I'd said minutes earlier, typed up and shared. One person had even made an inspirational quote graphic. The protest was all over Twitter. It wasn't just everyone here watching, it was people round the world.

"RIGHT, GUYS." Brian shouted so loud he almost didn't need a microphone. "WHO'S READY TO GET STARTED? IN THREE-TWO-ONE…"

And in the middle of all the boos, they started to play, Brian flinging himself around like he was playing to an adoring crowd.

But the boos didn't stop.

Brian jumped, leapt, stood on the drum kit.

And the boos didn't stop.

But something did happen. Something I didn't start. Something that someone I never met thought of. And we all followed suit.

We all sat down.

Like an inverse Mexican wave.

And as the band tried harder and harder, the crowd around them sat politely on the ground. I had a great view from sitting up on the tree.

The remaining Session fans did one of two things. Gave up and sat down. Or got left awkwardly standing, not knowing what to do with themselves.

With her blue hair, Marge was easy to spot, standing next to Lols. It was less easy to spot Britney T, because much to their fury, she'd decided to sit down. Guess she must have changed her mind.

The band had never seen anything like it. Nor had I.

I looked out at the sea of calm, strong protesters, loving whoever thought to start it off. One person's idea, supported by hundreds of others, really could change things. Guess that summed up the whole spirit of this protest. We didn't always know what we doing, but we always believed that together we stood a chance.

And it was working.

Because slowly, one by one, each member of The Session stopped playing.

Until all that was left was Brian struggling to sing his way through a song with the music grinding to a halt.

And eventually, even the most stubborn man in

the world had to stop. He gathered his bandmates and brought them to the front of the stage.

Was he finally going to apologize?

He picked up the mic.

"Well then. Guess there's only one thing for it." Whistles went up. He took a deep breath in, and sighed. "I would like to say The Session are massively sorry." Finally he got a roar of approval. He smiled. "FOR EVER COMING TO THIS GODAWFUL FESTIVAL. BIGGEST MISTAKE OF OUR LIVES." He grabbed his guitar. "SO SEE YOU LATER, LOSERS. AND WHEN YOU GO TO SLEEP IN YOUR CRAPPY HOMES, WITH YOUR CRAPPY LIVES, JUST REMEMBER WE'LL BE ON A PRIVATE JET NOT GIVING A CRAP WHAT YOU THINK."

And with that the band stormed off.

And even though the stage was empty, it got the biggest cheer of the festival so far.

THĬRTY-THREE

The stage lights swept over the crowd, like these people were the real stars. Total strangers were hugging each other and dancing in circles. It was awesome. But as much as I wanted to see what happened next, I wanted to see Adam more. My work here was done.

PE teachers yelling at me.

The last bus home about to leave.

Being chased by a strangely aggressive cat.

All things that hadn't ever motivated me enough to run.

But the thought of getting to see Adam in action unleashed a whole new Olympic sprinting side to me. I positively hurdled a group of people who were having a power nap on the ground. But it was worth it. Because by the time I got to the entrance to the New Bands Tent he was still on stage, playing the song they always finished with. A really fast, really loud love song – "Chicken Nugget Blues".

My heart almost popped with happiness at how huge their crowd was. And how much they were loving them. I even spotted corn on the cob man crowd-surfing.

Marcus was strutting away like he always did, secretly/not-so-secretly thinking everyone loved him. And Adam. Adam was doing what he always did on stage – eyes closed, arms flying around, putting everything he had into his drumming.

I didn't know whether to laugh or cry. I'd never seen him look happier. Or fitter. He was doing exactly what he wanted to do, and I loved it.

Shame I'd messed stuff up so badly that he was still only my boyfriend on a technicality. As heart-breaking as it was, I knew I was just waiting for him to tell me it was over.

My tears returned. And standing alone in the crowd, this time I let them roll down my face.

A boy next to me totally judged me for getting emotional about a song about chicken nuggets.

I *wish* I had the others here to see this with me. And

like some telepathic friendlepathy, my phone buzzed with a message from them.

A selfie of them pulling sad faces.

RACH: Tommy K were going to get on stage to replace The Session. YAY. But half the band's gone missing. NOT YAY.

She sent another picture of her biting her nails in fear.

RACH: People are naaaaat taking it well?!

TEGAN: Aka a near riot.

But there was only one thing I could message back with. With adrenalin rushing through me so hard that my fingers were shaking, I sent back six words:

ME: I think I have a plan.

THIRTY-FOUR

It was bold.

It was almost impossible to pull off.

And it probably wouldn't work.

But after the weekend I'd had, why should that stop me?

I needed to get backstage. Now. And I knew just how to do it.

And minutes later, just as I asked, Jay met me by the helter-skelter to help. Throwing caution – and hygiene – to the wind, we did it. Which is why a tall rugby-playing man ended up wearing a quite short person's leggings and a stripy top, and I ended up in an oversized lobster costume that smelt as bad as the bag of spare gym kit at school. Jay was genuinely excited when I found an uneaten, if not heavily flattened, falafel ball in one of the feet.

"Remember, Bells. Do what I did. Head back, claws up. Confidence and no one will stop you." Jay gave me a big hug, and wished me good luck as I waddled towards the gate. I swear he looked weirdly emotional and muttered something about "the apprentice becoming the master".

But I had to focus. And get the sight of Jay in such tight trousers out of my mind. Channelling the most confident lobster I know (obvs Sebastian from *The Little Mermaid*) I scuttled towards the gate.

And it worked like a dream. Without checking any passes, I was backstage.

But now what?! I could hear Marcus singing "Dip dip dip dip, mayonnaise dip dip dip", so knew I only had half a song left before they finished.

I looked around for where to go, where to stand. And that's when I saw her. Ruby from The Tomato Ketchup Conspiracy Theory. She was even more cool in real life. A high-res fittie. She had no idea I was gawping at her as she typed into her phone, watching the backstage monitor of The Wet Donald Project. Next to her was the guitarist, and they were both tapping their feet along; Ruby even filmed a bit of the screen. Were they Wet Donald fans?

Without waiting to think of all the reasons I was about to embarrass myself, I strode over.

"Excuse me?"

Ruby turned round. I think it's fair to say she didn't expect to see a lobster so close to her. "Are you Ruby?"

She nodded. "Yup. Are you –" she looked me up and down "– a crab?"

"Sort of. Some people call me Bella, but I answer to Acrab too." OMG, she laughed at my mum joke. OMG, I was meeting one of my idols dressed as a lobster.

But something about having pincers flapping around my face made me feel so uncool that I felt braver than normal. Forget wearing power lipstick, oversized crustacean costumes were turning out to be my ultimate confidence boost.

But what could I say next? Luckily Wet Donald had started playing an encore of "Various Things Are the Best", buying me more time. It was one of my favourites, as Adam had written it about an amazing Saturday we once had, where we ended up guests of honour at an OAPs' boules tournament 'cos we helped them chase away a swan that kept stealing their biscuits.

I smiled to myself, not sure if the memory made me happy, or if it made me sad because there might not be any more.

"You all right?" Ruby was looking at me, concerned. As in, Ruby was now making conversation with me. "Been a bit of a long day?"

"Could say that." I sounded more philosophical than I meant. I had to do what I'd come here for. "Look, this is a long shot, as in super ridiculously long, but ... were you about to step in for the main stage slot?"

She nodded. "Wow, news travels fast."

"Us lobsters slash crabs are well connected." I tried to click a pincer dramatically, but it just flicked me in the face. "So, er, what exactly is stopping you?"

She nodded towards the guitarist, who was on the phone. "We're a bassist and drummer down. They were last seen heading into the adult ball pit two hours ago."

"There's a ball pit?!" Why was I only finding this out now?! "Although –" *focus, Bella* "– you can tell me about that later. What I need to know now are two things."

She looked at me, intrigued. "Go on."

"One. Would you be up for help from some other people?"

She cocked her head to one side. "And two?"

"What would you say if I said I knew those people playing now –" I pointed at the monitor " – would be totally up for playing?"

"I'd say..." she thought. "Is this a hidden-camera

show? Are you going to turn out to be Declan Donnelly or something?"

I *knew* it was too ridiculous for her to say yes to. But it'd been worth a try.

"And I'd say … no. Sadly not. I'm a person who's just had the most ridiculous weekend of her life. I've been rescued from a Portaloo, got called a slug on the internet – think you might have posted a video of me dancing in a bin bag?" Ruby's eyes widened.

"That was you?"

"Uh-huh. I've also taken life advice from a corn on the cob, been sent aubergine emojis by my own mother –" Ruby gasped "– *yes, I know*, and been trolled by a man named Brian. So, that's why I'm asking you. Because I have nothing else to lose."

But Ruby had a quizzical look in her eye.

"Brian from The Session."

"Uh-huh."

"You're not …" She clicked her fingers, as if trying to click information into place. "… one of the girls who started the protest?"

I didn't know how to answer, suddenly less sure if this was going to a good place or not. But Ruby hadn't finished.

"The Stop The Session protest that just got The Session dropped by their label?"

"Whoa." My giveaway gasp came out before I could stop it. This was HUGE?!

Ruby laughed. "I'm guessing from that reaction that your answer was yes, you *were* one of the people behind it. In which case my answer is also yes."

"To what?" The shock news about The Session had made me forget what I'd asked.

"To whatever you want?!" she laughed. And with Wet Donald coming to the end of the song. I explained the plan. The crowd wanted one final headline act and needed a band. And quickly. But the band needed musicians. And I *knew* Adam and his band knew the songs. So if Tommy K were up for figuring it out with them, maybe there was a way it could work.

And after a quick chat with her guitarist, I got the answer I'd hoped for.

They were up for giving it a go.

So now all I had to do was tell Adam.

But what if he wasn't ready to speak to me?

CHAPTER

THIRTY-FIVE

Ruby walked me up the metal steps to the side of the stage. The first few rows of the crowd were all jumping in time like a big wave of people. And right in front of me was Adam. Drumming. Sweaty. Happy. But I was terrified. I hadn't spoken to him since he'd stormed off.

And now here I was, dressed as a lobster, about to ambush him with the lead singer of his favourite band. Ruby, with her perfect bob, amazing make-up, and one-off hand-stitched bodysuit, was the hottest person at the festival. Full 10/10. And I, in this three-day-old lobster sweatsuit, was physically the hottest person at the festival. There was nowhere on my body I wasn't sweating out of.

To distract myself I pulled my camera out of one

of the claws and took a couple of close-up pictures of Adam in action as he played the last song. And more as the band walked to the front to the stage and with hands raised, clapped the people who had come to see them. They looked like proper rock stars. And even better when they group-hugged, overwhelmed by how well it had gone.

The crowd had loved it, and the cheers didn't die down for ages.

I waited for the right time to try to get Adam's attention as he headed back to his drums. But with time running out, and him in no hurry to leave the stage, I realized the right time would never happen. It was now or never.

Feeling like I might pass out, I took a deep breath and yelled his name.

As soon as he looked up and realized it was me, the smile that had been plastered on his face disappeared.

Well, this felt great.

But I couldn't give up. I shouted his name again.

"Not now," he mouthed. But he wasn't cross. He looked upset.

"Tommy K want to you play on stage with them!!!" I yelled as loud as I could, trying to point at Ruby. But he couldn't hear me or see her. And he was clearly in no hurry to speak to me either. There was only one thing for it. I edged on to the stage, trying to pretend the whole crowd couldn't see a dishevelled lobster stage invading, and put my pincers to my mouth. I yelled with everything I had.

"I'M SORRY ABOUT EVERYTHING. BUT I'M NOT HERE TO TALK ABOUT THAT." It was fair to say he looked alarmed. But I had to carry on – for him. "YOU MIGHT BE NEEDED ON THE MAIN STAGE NOW TO PLAY WITH THE TOMATO KETCHUP CONSPIRACY THEORY." I was making my mouth shapes extra big to help him understand. But he just looked scared. Panicking, I leant back and tugged on Ruby's top. She stepped nearer to me, and into view of Adam. His face fell in shock as I pointed manically at her.

And even though things were rubbish between us, and even though none of this made sense, he walked towards me. *Yes.* I had a chance of making the plan work.

But what to say first?

I needed to explain the emergency situation – but I also wanted to say sorry.

I wanted him to be on stage with Tommy K, but I also wanted him to know I'd been an idiot not just telling the girls they'd got everything wrong in the first place.

I wanted him to know that him being happy was my priority – but my biggest hope was that he could be happy with me.

And now he was in front of me waiting for me to explain what I was doing.

The crowd by the barrier were peering to see why the drummer had walked off to talk to girl in a shellfish suit.

I had no idea what to say.

He was looking me dead in the eye.

I had to say something. And I had to focus on what was important for right now.

Put his chance to play a headline gig on the main stage before me wanting to sort us out.

With my heart racing, I leant towards him. I had to keep unemotional, just tell him the facts. But without my consent my pincers threw themselves around him. And before I knew it I was pushing my face into his neck. And before I could stop them, five words fell out of my mouth.

"I'm sorry. I love you."

Woah.

Had I just verbal-hiccupped the most significant words of my life?!

I jumped back. I don't know who looked more shocked. Me or Adam.

The crowd cheered. Could I take this coincidence as a good sign?

A less good sign was that Adam hadn't said anything.

I didn't know much about love, but one person saying it and the other staring at them silently didn't seem like a classic "it's going well" omen.

He lifted his finger to his lips.

Was he shushing me?!

I'm pretty sure out of all the articles I'd ever read in preparation of declaring love, not one gave me advice on being shushed! But then none suggested doing it looking – or smelling – like I did right now.

Ruby tapped me on the shoulder. "You do know he's wearing a clip mic?"

"I don't know what that means…" It dawned on me. "Unless it means thousands of people just heard what I said because it came out on those ginormous speakers?"

Adam slow nodded, his nose scrunched in awkward, I-was-trying-to-tell-you embarrassment.

"They heard that too." Ruby was trying not to giggle. "I'll get them to turn it off."

So *that's* why he was shushing me. I would have said thanks if I wasn't dealing with every bit of my dignity slowly dying, as at least thirty people chanted, "She loves you, she loves you."

I waited for Ruby to get off the crew's walkie-talkie, wondering if it was true that what didn't kill you made you stronger, or just meant you'd die of shame an hour later alone in a tent?

But time was ticking and when she nodded in my direction, I jumped in to finish what I'd just started – my words spilling out.

"Sorry about that, but it was my only secret left. You said you wanted honesty. So there it was. I've already sorted out the stuff with those girls. Promise. Not that it's anyone business, but I told literally *everyone* who got the wrong end of the stick that I'm still a virgin."

Ruby coughed. Adam pushed his hand over his eyes in semi-horror.

"They haven't turned the mic down yet, have they?" The "Ooooooooo" from the crowd gave me the answer I needed.

"Everyone heard that, didn't they?"

Someone in the crowd shouted, "Yes, you nitwit." (I was mildly impressed they went for "nitwit" and made a note to use it more myself.) Taking matters into her own hands, Ruby reached out and unclipped Adam's mic, pulling the lead out of the transmitter.

"Seriously, you guys?!" She dangled the mic in front of us, laughing. "You're OK to speak now."

407

Adam looked totally star-struck. I took my chance to properly explain.

"Just listen for a sec. I'm sorry I'm here. I'm sorry I just ambushed you and, er … said what I said. And I'm sorry thousands of people heard it. But forget about all of that. Especially the last bit. Long story short, well not that short, but shorter, is the protest was amazing and we all sat down, and The Session stormed off, and now they're dropped and they need a band for the main stage and are you and the others up for playing the main stage with Ruby? And are you up for doing it now?"

He put his hands up to his head. "Is this actually happening?"

Ruby put her hand on his back. "Yes it is." She turned to his bandmates. "So if it's a yes, we have a golf buggy waiting. And we need you ALL to get in it. So, are you in or not?"

THiRTY-SiX

Adam wasn't just good.

He was A. May. Zing.

I already knew he was something else, but he took the whole thing in his stride, like playing on a massive stage, with a massive band, to a massive crowd was NBD.

And having the gig start, stop, be on, then off, then back on again, meant the crowd were full of next-level energy.

They played everything. Tommy K songs, covers, even a couple of Wet Donald originals. Ruby sorted it so Rach, Tegan and I could watch the whole thing from the side of the stage, all the bands we'd been seeing all weekend milling around next to us, like we were part of their world, not imposters. From up on the stage we got a glimpse of what all the flags, banners and high-vis vests must have looked like, and it made me even more proud of what we'd done. Towards the end of the set Ruby escorted me down to the photography pit at the front of the stage to take some photos. It was like an actual dream.

Maybe this was why festivals were so great – anything really could happen. As we danced along to the last song, my phone vibrated. A message from my sister in the family group.

JO: Like mother like daughter.

And a picture of me yelling into the loudhailer.

(And a 🫳 that she was trying to make her new signature sign-off).

Today really was surreal – my sister was being voluntarily nice about me to Mum!?

Mum instantly started typing back.

MUM: SO proud of my Bellington Boot!!!

A picture then attached. I clicked download.

Something hairy, and red, and warty was on the screen.

MUM: OOPS THAt s a pic of Mumbles nipple
rash Itook for the vet!!! Laugh Out Loud!!

She followed up with a short video of her grinning
face, which took up just the bottom left corner of the
picture, the rest being our kitchen ceiling. She didn't
move and just wobbled a bit, clearly thinking she was
taking a photo.

ME: Love you guys.

And I meant it.

And when the band finally came off stage they got
the biggest cheer ever. Press, photographers and celebs
all swarmed around them, trying to grab moments and
pics for Insta. Rach filmed the whole thing, including an
interview with Ruby about the protest, and uploaded it
straight to our #StopTheSession website and Instagram,
along with a gallery of pics I'd transferred from my
camera. On the homepage we put the biggest shout-
out to Brenda and Ruby (Rach and I decided they were
our new MGC) and I shared the link with Mum and Jo
immediately.

But despite being surrounded by loads of my favourite
bands, there was only one person I cared about.

Adam.

And as soon as he came off stage, he headed over.

"Bells – I can NEVER thank you enough." He shook his head, tiny beads of sweat flying off it, as he tried to take it all in. "Best. Night. Of. My. Life."

We smiled in shared celebration, before remembering that things were not OK between us.

"No probs." I shrugged. "Just please never, ever do the same for me. My idea of actual hell."

"Noted."

"Although…" I got out my camera. "When the world tour happens, remember who's up for being the official photographer?"

I flicked through some of the photos, his eyes becoming wider with each one.

"These are amazing! I love them!"

I stared at the screen like it could protect me from the fact neither of us knew what to say about my dropping the L-bomb earlier. (Which was ironic, as about a thousand other people were commenting online about it after someone posted a clip of the audio.)

"I can send you a couple?" I kept the conversation firmly on logistics, not emotions.

"Ah, yes, please, then I'll forward them on. My parents were listening to that whole thing live." He showed me his most recent message. It was from his dad.

DAD: We're listening live, son! So proud.

As we were looking, a picture of his mum, brother and dad popped up, all thumbs up and massive smiles.

"Is…" I zoomed in. "Is…"

Adam nodded. "Yup, my dad is moist of eye." He laughed. "What have you done, Bella?! It's the end of the world as we know it!"

"Adam?" A tall lady with a rolled-up T-shirt on broke into our conversation. "Have you got five? We'd love to grab a quick chat for the radio?" Adam looked at me, as if trying to get silent permission. We both knew we had unfinished business. "All your bandmates are already there."

I smiled and mouthed: "Go."

"Bella, can I see you later then?" Whoa, real name usage frightened me as it meant he was saying something serious. "We do need to talk."

It wasn't talking that was scaring me. It was the listening. To him probably saying "it's better if we're just friends". And the resulting crying and trying to permanently hermit myself in my tent even after all the

413

festival had cleared away. But he didn't need to know that, so I just said, "Sure."

With Adam off with his bandmates, I headed back to Rach and Tegan, who were loving the backstage after-party. We spent the final hours of the final night sneaking off to investigate the VIP areas (they had proper showers! Rach borrowed their hair straighteners!), taking casual photos of ourselves (entirely set up to make sure we got a celeb in the background), giving The Session crew a hand as they packed up their merch (never to be seen again!) and leaping around on the light-up dance floor. During one particularly enthusiastic rendition of "Wild Thoughts" I spotted Ruby smiling on from the side of the stage. She'd basically made my entire life. She'd even sorted Rach with the passes she needed to camp with us, so she didn't have to see ex-MGC. But the more I thanked Ruby, the more she said not to worry. And was I definitely taking on enough liquids as I was *really* sweating.

Hours later as we ambled back, I still couldn't take it all in. So much had happened. But this night with my friends had been exactly what I needed – and it was probably the only thing that could have powered me through not messaging Adam. I wanted him to know that I could give him the time and space he needed (even if in reality I couldn't, and had to get Rach to change the thumb lock on my phone to hers).

"Well, that was one *hell* of a weekend." Rach was sitting up in our tent, squashed between Tegan and me. We'd connected our two sleeping bags to form one mega-bag. It had just gone 1:30 a.m. and was freezing.

Tegan sipped on one of the hot chocolates we'd nabbed from the backstage area. It was 50% drink, 49% mini marshmallows, and 1% jelly bean (they'd had unlimited pick and mix too).

"Sure was – who'd have thunk we'd manage to actually stop The Session?"

Rach pinched one of Tegan's marshmallows. "*And* they've blocked Brian's account. And @Hey Its The Session HQ – so we are officially a no-troll zone. I've even gone public again."

"Hellooo-hah?"

The three of us looked at each other. It was Adam.

"Yessss?" I replied with as much calm as I could (zero).

"Don't suppose you've got a minute, do you, Bella?"

It really depended what the minute was for. It was for him dumping me, then no, all my minutes were taken.

"Sure." I said it casually, but had clamped my hands

on top my head, shaking it violently at the others in a "no no no, this can never happen" fashion.

Tegan nudged me in the leg, and whispered, "I think he can probably see our silhouettes."

He definitely could. I took my hands down and clambered out.

As I did, Rach's voice came up from inside the tent. "Don't forget we've still got a bag of Haribo."

We'd said we'd save it in case I needed emergency cheering up later. Her way of reminding me they were both right here, millimetres away, ready to help whatever happened.

"Maybe later…" I replied, letting her know I understood. "Won't be long." I looked at Adam, hoping he'd say, "No, she'll be ages, and absolutely nothing bad will happen." But all he did was look at the ground and say, "Shall we go to my tent?"

In silence we picked our way through the groups of people having late-night campfires. Normally I'd worry about the mix of trip-hazard guy ropes and naked flames, but I'd run out of energy to panic about anything other than what Adam was about to say.

He unzipped the tent door. "Marcus is out with the others…" He held the flap up for me to go in. "I tried to tidy as much as I could."

I shone my torch round. On one side was Adam's stuff all neatly laid out; on the other was one big bag that looked like it was exploding with empty Pringle tubes, SpongeBob boxer shorts and a book called *In Search of Lost Time* by Marcel Proust. Adam saw me do a double take.

"He wanted to 'appear intellectual if any girls came back'." I was surprised he even owned it, to be fair. "He bought it from a charity shop on the way here, and it's been great for him … as an emergency pillow."

I couldn't help but laugh (as did someone in a neighbouring tent).

I sat down cross-legged, opposite Adam's sleeping bag, making sure I didn't make any physical contact with him. I wasn't sure what the boundaries were in this new world.

On one hand, I wanted to stay here for ever. On the other, I couldn't wait to escape.

I studied a bit of my nail varnish that was coming off. "Sooooo…"

He sat down. "So."

C'mon, Bells, be brave, be breezy.

"Whaddya want to talk about then?"

Adam picked at some mud on his shoelace. "I … think it's … it's time we … had a proper chat."

I exhaled. I felt so helpless. So scared.

I didn't want to beg, I didn't want to plead – but I couldn't just let this happen without saying anything.

"Can I just say one thing first?"

He nodded. "Sure."

"I'm *really* sorry. When I said I had no more secrets, I meant it. It's you that's important to me, not what anyone else thinks." A scoff came from tent neighbour. I didn't know them, but I already hated them. Adam was still scratching at his shoe, building himself up for what he had to say.

"So why did you let everyone gossip about us like that?"

Good question.

"'Cos I'm an idiot?" I tried to laugh, but my voice was definitely nearer the crying side of the spectrum. "A really sorry idiot."

And the tears that had been in the eye waiting room finally fell. Adam looked up, not sure what to do.

"Don't cry, Bells." Why did people always say that like it's a decision you can make?! "It's not just you that's not been honest." Worrying. "I've been a bit of an idiot too." What had he done?! "I hardly saw you 'cos of my parents being all weird with us, although I guess you figured that out. Then this weekend I kind of…" He let out a little growl of frustration at not being able to find the right words. "I was kind of weird as well... Those girls, they just got to me. Always making comments, and putting pressure on us to, y'know, do stuff. I just felt like everything was one big performance." Where was he going with this?!

"And then there was what happened earlier. That 'celebration' video."

I wanted to explain but my mind was stuck on a frantic loop of *keep it together breathe keep it together breathe* and all I managed was a "sorry".

"We haven't even spoken about it, so it's kind of annoying that you seem to be talking to everyone else about it." He shrugged, embarrassed. "Well, everyone except me."

"But that's not how it was! I promise." I knew how desperate I sounded. "They were talking AT me." But I knew I should be explaining, not defending myself.

Adam shrugged. Was he even listening?

"And it all just made me think." Oh great. Here it comes. "I need to be honest with myself. And with you. About how I really feel."

Honesty – I honestly think it's overrated. Could he not just pretend to like me (regardless of how he feels) for, say, another sixty or seventy years? That could work?

419

I looked down and shut my eyes. Assume the bad news brace position.

But the only thing I heard was … a fart.

"Sorry!" side neighbour yelled.

"No problem!" I shouted back, secretly vowing to hunt him down and turn up with a klaxon to all of his important life events. But Adam didn't even acknowledge it, focused on what he had to say.

He looked up at me, worry all over his face.

"Bella … I just can't do this."

CHAPTER

THIRTY-
SEVEN

I pushed myself up. I had to get out of here. "I get it."

I needed to be back with Rach and Tegan. Now.

Adam stood up. "Don't be like that ... please?"

How was I *meant* to be? Totally fine, and say a formal goodbye with a polite handshake?

"I have to go."

Adam grabbed my hand. "Will you hear me out?"

I knew I should probably hear his reasons, but I knew I couldn't do it now. "Sorry – I have to go."

He dropped back to the floor. "I hoped you'd feel the same."

I laughed. A genuine laugh. How dare he – I'd told him exactly how I felt a couple of hours ago. A tiny bit of my soul-crushing hurt shifted into anger.

"You know full well I don't."

"How could I?" Suddenly it was him who sounded desperate.

"'Cos I told you?!"

How funny that our first big argument was also our last.

"We've never spoken about it, Bella!"

He'd officially lost me. I turned back from the door.

"Sorry – did you totally miss the conversation that we had after your gig? You know, me shouting my feelings into a microphone? Kind of a low point for me dignity-wise?"

His eyes narrowed, like *I* was being the confusing one. "You do know what I'm talking about, *right*?"

Great. Not content with keeping me tent hostage, now he wanted me to self-dump myself.

"Yes, Adam. You breaking up with me."

But he didn't react like I thought. He opened and shut his mouth, shaking his head.

"No…" He sped up the shaking. "No no no?!" He stood back up and grabbed my hand. "How could you think that?"

I had no idea what was happening.

"'Cos you walked off. And said we needed to talk?" Was I being dumped, or not?! "And that you couldn't do it?"

"Sex!!!" He shouted in my face. "I meant sex. *That's* what I wasn't ready for."

Tent neighbour spluttered.

"Oh, do one, will you?" Adam yelled in his direction.

But my brain was on overload. "So you weren't dumping me?"

Adam looked a mixture of upset and happy all at once. "No ... the opposite!" What did that mean? "I wanted to make sure you were OK with taking things slow? 'Cos I really like you."

Slow? *Slow?!* That sounded SO much better than *stopped*.

"So you're not dumping me?" I was stuck on repeat, still not able to believe it. Adam laughed, and took both of my hands in his.

"No, of course I'm not. Because, in case you hadn't noticed Bella Fisher –" he looked me dead in the eye "– I'm completely and utterly in love with you."

CHAPTER

THIRTY-EIGHT

Several things then happened in a blur.

The best kiss of my whole entire life.

Me running to tell Rach and Tegan it was all OK.

Me running back to tell Adam I 100% also wanted to take it slow.

A happy dance so violent I may have strained an elbow.

Adam picking me up outside his tent, spinning me round, and then having a new entry as best kiss of my entire life.

And when we finished kissing he leant back, looked at me, and said "I love you" one more time, before giving me the most gentle kiss on the nose. It was the best feeling in the world.

It felt so weird, naughty almost, to be able to say those words out loud to him. Like swearing in front of a parent.

Marcus texted saying he was going to stay with some other mates, so after everything I ended up spending the night in Adam's tent. And it felt amazing. Going to sleep with his arms around me, waking up with him next to me (obviously I had to have at least ten pieces of Bubblemint gum to try and shift my morning breath, but I knew I couldn't look any worse than during my peak lobster sweat).

Was it creepy to think he looked hot while he was sleeping?

"Can I come in?" I blinked out of my Adam staring. Why was Rach here? She didn't wait for an answer, and unzipped the tent, poking her head through the opening. "Morning, lovaaaars!" I think it was meant to be a farmer accent, but she sounded more like a pirate.

A noise a bit like "Maureen" rumbled out of Adam. I think he was attempting to say morning. He gave me the biggest sleepy grin as he rubbed his eyes, before sitting up behind me and putting his arms around me.

Bliss. Give or take the fact I'd slept in my bra and thought the wire might now be piercing one of my lungs.

"Can I, er, come in too?" Tegan's voice came from the

other side of the door; she was slightly less comfortable at the thought of just walking in.

Rach pushed the entrance open and tugged at her leg. "Get in here, I *TOLD* you they wouldn't mind."

Technically we hadn't actually replied, but I'm pretty sure neither of us minded.

"Sorry not sorry to interrupt, butttt." Rach plonked herself down beside us. "In fact. No words. Just. THIS."

She held her phone up, Rach and Tegan giving each other looks as Adam and I tried to work out what she was showing us.

It was the pictures I'd taken, that she'd posted last night. Adam on stage. The protest.

I'd already sent the link to my mum – maybe they'd forgotten. I engaged as much enthusiasm as I could, not wanting to disappoint them.

"Cool!"

Rach looked disbelieving. "Is that *it*?"

I looked at Tegan for some help.

"You do know what you're looking at, right?"

Was it a trap?! "Erm, our website."

Rach bounced with excitement. "Na-ha." She bounced again. "Scroll up, scroll up."

It was the website for *Worcester Daily News* – our local paper. And the entire home page was a mash of my pictures, and headlines like "Local Girls' Rebellion As Session Learn Their Lesson", and "Wet Donald Project saves the day for RebelRocks", alongside the most incredible pictures of Adam in action. I'd even been credited as the photographer.

Rach squeaked. "You're basically Liam and Miley!" She squeaked again. "But sort of totally different and better!!!!"

I couldn't stop scrolling. They'd used *my* pictures. My photography was good enough.

All the things that had felt unreal and magical last night were right here in black and white. Adam just kept repeating, "This is too much."

"I've already told my mum to buy every copy of the paper she finds." Tegan was grinning from ear to ear. "I *bet* it'll be the front cover."

"I'll do the same." Rach winked. "We need at *least* a hundred commemorative copies."

And over the next couple of hours, as we packed away our tents to catch the shuttle bus back to our pick-up point, our phones went wild. Everyone wanted to be in touch. As we trudged towards the exit with our bags on our backs (hi, Dave!), we even heard our names shouted across the hordes of people heading home. It was Ska. She ran over.

"Just wanted to say congrats on everything." She turned to me. "Saw the pics, FIRE!!!" So now the protest hasn't been the lame disaster she thought, suddenly we were cool enough to talk to? "And you?" She looked at Adam. "Smashed it!"

I didn't know what to say first. To get lost. To shut up. To ask her what happened with Derek? But I didn't have time to choose a favourite, as Rach beat me to it.

"Yeah, they both did, didn't they? And now they're SO in demand we really don't have time to stop, so, seeya." She turned to Adam, Marcus, Mikey, Jay, Rach and Tegan. "You coming?"

We all absolutely were, and laughing we pushed on up the hill, leaving Ska glaring after us.

Tegan turned to walk backwards. "I for one cannot *wait* to never have to speak to her, or Luke, ever again." It was rare for her to say a bad word about anyone.

I didn't want to buzzkill and remind her I might be at college with them both. And ex-MGC. EURGH. The real world could wait. I was going to miss hanging out with my friends 24/7. Despite all being grubby and exhausted, they even made the trek back fun. Jo met me outside the coach with a massive hug, telling me how proud she was of me, and there was a huge clap as Teeg, Rach and I climbed on board.

But all too quickly the coach had pulled into the farm shop car park, ready for us to be collected. I said bye to Adam before we got off, as we both agreed we didn't look in any fit state to be around each other's parents. I would have been more emotional about this being the end of the whole festival if I wasn't distracted by my mum, who was waving a newspaper in the air as a kind of royal greeting to the entire coach. Weirder still – and I don't know if it was sleep deprivation or the fact that my boyfriend OFFICIALLY LOVED ME – I didn't even mind (well, maybe a little, so I let Jo get off first, so everyone could assume she was her mother only).

When I eventually stepped off, Mum smothered me in kisses – and judging by Jo's face, also the bright orange lipstick she was wearing. Smelling her washed hair and seeing her non-muddy nails made me realize how dirty I was – but you must stop noticing when everyone around you is the same. I looked around – yup, it was like a group of dusty, sweaty zombies had been released back into the wild.

"Couldn't be more proud of you, my special sausage!!!!" Mum gave me another hug and pulled open the paper. "Just *look* at you!"

"No big deal," I lied completely, enjoying the moment. "Do you have anything to eat in the car?"

"Glove compartment Softmints are all yours."

Jo picked her bag up. "Shotgun the front seat!"

Damn her. I raced after her anyway (as much as you can do when you have a bag on your back that's so big you look like an upright tortoise), but she beat me to it.

I opened the back door of our little Mini, giving a final wave to Rach, Tegan and Tegan's dad. They were heading back to Tegan's for the night. But I didn't mind missing out, as I hadn't had an evening with Mum and Jo for ages. Although first we had to drop the camera back off with Mr Lutas before anyone noticed we'd borrowed it.

Mum shrieked, making me jump.

"Girls!!!" She stepped back out the car and flapped her arm. "That man I was telling you about?" I swear Jo muttered, "Oh god." "He's here!"

No. No no. NO no no. If I wasn't feeling human enough to see Adam's parents, I certainly wasn't mentally equipped to meet the man who made my mum send us the water spurt emoji multiple times. How was I meant to appear aloof and threatening when I had three-day-old glitter on my face?!

Jo and I looked round – but the area Mum was flapping towards only had Marcus, Adam and Adam's dad talking to a random man. Before we could stop her,

Mum rushed towards them, her harem pants wafting about like leg parachutes. Jo and I trundled after her, to limit the damage that was about to happen.

"Well, *this* is a coincidence," she was shouting, giddy with excitement.

Please no. Did her new man *really* have to be a friend of Adam's dad?

And was I really going to speak to Adam's dad looking part human, part hedge?

And even worse. Were the worlds of Adam's parents and mine about to collide?

I turned to Jo, only one word necessary. "HELP?!"

But what happened next made us both stop in our tracks.

The man my mum went and kissed on the cheek wasn't Adam's dad's friend.

It was Adam's dad.

CHAPTER

THIRTY-NINE

Total hyperventilation.

This could not be happening.

So what? Mr Douglas was having an affair? With my mother??

Did this make Adam … my sort-of brother?

I grabbed Jo's arm as much for solidarity as to stop me collapsing.

Adam's dad looked at me.

"Bella!" He seemed genuinely pleased, no idea I was on to him. "We can't thank you enough for what you did for Adam!"

I think he went to hug me, but backed off when he smelt me.

Jo gulped. She'd figured it out.

Did Adam's dad not realize I was my mum's daughter? I looked across at Adam, his usually smiley self. He had no idea what was about to happen. Like a lamb to the slaughter. A really fit lamb, to a real curveball of a slaughter.

"You two know each other?" Mum put her arm around me. Who was going to figure it out first? Could I somehow get us out of this?!

But the only words I managed were "Adam" and then "Dad" like I was learning to talk.

"Maybe we should go, Mum?" Jo tried to intervene, but Mum was missing the point and was firmly on cloud nine.

"Don't be silly, Joanne!" Mum was acting all girly and weird. It was gross. She was also using our full names, which meant she was trying to appear posher.

Adam put his hand out. "Nice to see you, Ms Fisher."

Mum grabbed his hand and pulled him in for a hug. "You know I hate *Ms*?! Call me Mum!"

Was she doing that on purpose? Was this legal?! Surely if you're dating someone your parent can't be allowed to swoop in on one of *their* parents? Wasn't that like parent incest or something?

Mum stepped back and looked at Adam's dad. "We've had some *right old times* this week, haven't we?"

Someone please make this end. Maybe the coach could run me over?

"Mum, we don't need to talk about it now. Let's GO," I pleaded. All I got back was a dirty look from her.

"So…" Oh no, Adam was joining in. Please don't let him ask the million-dollar question. "How do you two know each other?"

I closed my eyes and waited for my life to end.

But Mum just smiled.

"Laughter yoga!"

Sorry, *what?!*

"You know my new business?"

Adam shook his head politely.

"YOU WHAT?" I shouted a lot less politely. I looked accusingly at Jo. "Did you know about this?"

She looked a guilty. "Kinda. And I might have kinda forgotten until right this second." She threw her hands up. "Oi?! It's been a busy month?! Lots going on."

This made her equally as responsible in my eyes. The images of my mum and Adam's dad were forever burnt on to my soul.

I crossed my arms. "And you thought you'd tell me *when*, Mother?"

Mum fake laughed. "I thought I *had*, Bellington?" Oh good, she was using that name in public. "We had a great few sessions, didn't we?" She looked warmly at Adam's dad. "Really unleashed some endorphins."

"Sure did, Mary." He was smiling. *He could smile.* "All the stress of this one's exams." He pinched Adam's cheek. Adam looked mortified. Nice to know it wasn't always me. "Just got too much at one point ... Bella..." He put his hand on my arm. First contact since he Heimliched me. "Your mum is a miracle worker."

"Thanks, Cliff." Mum turned and tutted at me. "But, Bellington, please explain *exactly* what you *thought* all that noise and laughing was in our living room?"

I thought back to the "Do Not Disturb – Unless You Want To Be Disturbed" sign and shuddered. "No comment."

And, like the weirdest private joke, they both put their hands on their hips, bent forward and "ha-ha-haaad" and "he-he-heeed" until they ended up in a fit of genuine laughter.

And somehow, with a mum who sold dog ice cream and taught laughter yoga, and a boyfriend's dad who thought wearing cowboy boots on a Monday daytime was OK (yes, I'd noticed) they still thought I was the weird one.

It was definitely time to go home.

CHAPTER

FORTY

After the festival it felt like the whole summer was stretching out in front of us. If I could have paused time right then I would have done. My friends, Adam – it all added up to the best summer of my life. All I had to do was ignore the looming exam results. Which I did until the very second my alarm rang to wake me up to go and get them.

The day of reckoning. And I reckoned it wasn't going to be good news.

I munched some toast, hardly aware I was even eating it as the doorbell rang.

Jo.

She was meant to be at work today.

"Surprise?!" She passed me a tiny good luck card.

"Stayed at a mate's last night. Thought today might be the day you'd need a sister lift." She was right, I really did.

And an hour later, with good luck messages, good luck selfies, and advice about "laughing through any outcome," coming through thick and fast from Mum, I was standing at St Mary's gates with Tegan and Rach, Jo waiting in the car.

Even Mr Lutas looked nervous. He was milling about, in his normal tweed suit, but without his usual leather shoes – this must be his casual look. When he saw me he headed over.

"Ms Fisherrrrrr."

"Mr Lutas." I resisted the urge to add on ten r's to the Mr bit. "Nice trainers."

"Oh … ah." I'd accidentally flustered him. "Thank you. I suppose." He coughed, regaining his teacher-ness. "I just wanted to say the verrry best of luck to you." Out of all the teachers here, it was only really him who understood how much I wanted to get on the photography course. He'd been my biggest supporter to make it happen. I just hoped I didn't let him down. "I rrreally hope it all works out the way you want." His face softened. "The way we both want."

"Same…" I scrunched my mouth to one side. We

both knew what he meant. That I'd got the grades I needed. Not ruined my only chance. That the last five years hadn't been for nothing and I hadn't wasted my effort – or his. And I could be his first student to make it on the course. "And, er, thanks. For *everything*."

And before I knew what was happening I was giving him the world's most awkward hug. More of a wrestling move really, considering he had his arms flat against his body. I regretted it the second I did it, but had to hold for the required amount of polite-British time.

"Well, erm, yes. Let me know how it goes."

He shuffled off quickly.

It was weird that I'd spent the last five years wishing I never had to see any of my teachers ever again – and now the day had come when I wouldn't and I was wondering if I would miss them. Year Seven me was disgusted I could even allow that thought.

Tegan held my hand. She knew how terrified I was. They were nervous too, but with their brilliant marks on coursework and mocks, at least whatever happened they'd be together.

Together we walked in. Together we collected our envelopes. And together we found out the news.

Tegan had aced it with almost all top grades.

Rach had done way better than she'd hoped for.

And I had done exactly what I expected.

Totally messed up.

I wasn't going to college with my friends – and I only had myself to blame.

CHAPTER

FORTY-ONE

I closed Jo's car door and slid into the seat.

She switched the music off. "So?"

I tried to explain, but no words came out: just tears. She wrapped me in a cuddle and didn't say a word. She thought I didn't see her one-hand sneak-text Mum to tell her we'd ring later, but I appreciated her stalling her for me. Which just made me cry even more. Proper ugly crying where you give up trying to keep on top of both the tears and the mucus.

When I got my breath back I handed Jo my envelope. She passed me a tissue, and looked through the sheets of papers, with some "Uh-huh"s and "I see"s.

"So how far off were you?"

"That's the thing, Jo, if I'd only got a C in maths, I'd have got in."

Being so close somehow made it even more painful.

"OK. Don't panic. You still have options, right?"

I nodded. "Rubbish ones."

"It might feel like that now, but I promise you it will be OK."

How could she promise when the only options were all at colleges without Tegan and Rach, and none of them had the photography course I wanted to take?

"Do you just want music on?"

I nodded, and after assuring me that when I was ready she'd help me go through all my options, she let me play Wet Donald as loud as I could. She'd even bought a family bag of Revels, which I accidentally ate all of (except the raisin ones) before we'd turned off the main road.

When we pulled up home, Mum's car was on the drive. My heart sank further. I really didn't want to have to go through all this again. But when I got in, she gave me a cuddle. She already knew. Jo must have texted again when I was having round two of epic crying.

"Tea?" she asked as if that would make everything better. I flopped on to the sofa and grunted. Mumbles jumped up beside me and rested her head in my lap.

Her top lip had got stuck on one of her teeth which always made me smile – it was like she was trying to cheer me up. I·stroked her head and tried to pretend it was all going to be OK.

Mum bought three cups through, and a home-made biscuit for Mumbles.

"It's not all bad, Bells…" she said as she put them on the table.

"You don't understand!" I snapped right back, taking my disappointment out on her.

"Let her finish," Jo said, putting me back in my place gently.

Mum sat down on the armchair. I hadn't thought about it, but she must have had to have come home from work to be here.

"She nodded towards the far end of the sofa. "Why don't you look under that cushion?" Something that looked like newspaper was sticking out.

I sat forward, Mumbles shooting me an annoyed look at disturbing her relaxing time, and investigated. It was a box. All wrapped up in the newspaper front pages with my festival pictures.

I pulled it out and looked at Jo and Mum, confused. Mum grinned. "Go on then?"

I peeled off the tape and unwrapped it.

And couldn't believe what was underneath. A brand-new camera.

"W ... what's this?"

Mum sat beside me and kissed me on the head. "Just a little something from me and Jo. We thought you deserved it."

I looked at my sister. "This is from you too?"

She smiled. "Yup."

"But it must have cost a bomb?!"

She shrugged. "Is it the right one? That's the main thing?"

It was way more than the right one. It was the best one.

And it was mine.

I couldn't believe they'd done this. Mum was working two jobs with Give A Dog A Cone and now laughter yoga, and I knew how stressed Jo had been with her extra shifts at work. And they'd done it for me.

And for the third time today I cried so many tears I worried I was going to turn into a freeze-dried human. But all thanks to Mum and Jo, this time they were happy ones.

CHAPTER

FORTY-TWO

Two hours later, I still couldn't believe it. Jo said she was almost regretting it, I'd said thank you so much. I hadn't really seen Mum though, as she'd been on the phone dealing with some sort of crisis.

So I'd entertained myself taking a whole batch of photos of Mumbles wearing various summer accessories (just the classy ones – sunglasses, baseball cap, a hat that said "Beach Please"). Adam had come round as soon as I'd rung about my results, so I'd also been pretending I needed to "check the portrait settings" but really it was an excuse to get loads of amazing black-and-white pictures of him, without him realizing my cunning plan. He hated having his photo taken, but didn't complain, and then told me he had a surprise of his own – with the money he'd got from doing some gigs that had been booked since his festival appearance he'd bought a case for my new camera.

I didn't have to make a decision until the end of the day about my college choice, so I was a bit more composed by 3 p.m., when Jo, Adam and I sat down to go through everything. Everyone was being super positive but with every prospectus we opened up, a bit more of my happiness faded. My new camera was amazing, and I could totally use it to practise in my spare time, but I did have to face up to the reality of what my future held.

As we opened the last brochure, the doorbell rang. I wasn't expecting anyone. I looked at Jo but she shrugged. Probably a delivery. Me and my rabbit slippers slid our way across the floor to open the door. My two faves were on the doorstep. Tegan and Rach. And in their hands was what I can only describe as an entire newsagent's snack shelf.

"We thought you might need these." Tegan smiled.

Rach passed me a Chomp. "Love snack-tually."

We'd been messaging all day, but they'd never told me they were going to pop round. I loved my friends.

Rach squeezed past me. "Oops, sorry!" She dropped a packet of Wotsits, and I bent to pick them up. "Is he here yet?"

"Yeah, in the kitchen."

"Cooooool." She headed straight there, although she still gasped "Adam" when she saw him.

I laughed and gave Teeg a hug. "I hope she never changes."

By the time we got back to the kitchen the reams of paper about courses and pamphlets about colleges were covered in crisps. Maybe it was a sign.

I loved everyone being here for me, it meant the world to me, but it couldn't hide my rising panic about the decision I had to make.

The doorbell rang again.

This time Mum shouted down.

"It's for meeeeee!" She tromped down the stairs, jujing her hair. "A client!"

I looked at the others apologetically. "Prepare to shut off your ears and pretend you can't hear what's going on in my house." They nervous laughed, giving each other glances I didn't understand. And minutes later I realized why. Because when Mum shouted for me to bring her tea through, I recognized *exactly* who her new client was.

Sitting on the sofa was Mr Lutas.

"Oh?!" I didn't mean to react quite like that, but felt it was legitimate. "You're wearing socks."

I don't know why I said this. Why was I obsessed with his feet today? Why *wouldn't* he be wearing socks?

"I am, yes." Mr Lutas pushed his glasses up his nose and glanced down. "Pantone 1505." I think that was his way of saying orange. He looked up at my mum. "Would you…?"

She nodded. "'Course." And picked up her tea. "I'll be in the kitchen if you need me."

What was going on?

"Why don't you sit down, Bella?" He sounded more gentle than normal.

Had the world shifted? Why was my old art teacher offering me a seat in my own home?

I sat down slowly, suspiciously. "What's going on?"

He pulled a folded bit of paper out of his pocket. The newspaper with my pictures on.

"I've got a question for you." I looked at him, willing him to get to the point. Was he about to ask me if I was OK with him doing laughter yoga with my mum?! If this was how weird life got after school, I wanted to go back, please.

"Go on…"

He unfolded the paper and smoothed it out across our coffee table. "Do you think you could cope with rrrre-sitting your Maths GCSE in November?"

"Sorry – I'm not with you."

He cleared his throat.

"I've been speaking a lot to your motherrr today." So she'd lied about having a "business crisis"?! "Because I've had a word with Worcestershire College. I sent them thrrrough your porrrtfolio for another look, and with all this extrrra materrrrial –" he pointed at the paper "– if you were able to commit to studying for – and passing – your maths re-sit in November, they…" He paused. "Would be willing to offer you a place."

There was only one thing to do.

Yell a massive "YEEESSSS", and give Mr Lutas our second awkward hug of the day. So much emotion today! Especially when I finally released him and saw that he looked almost as happy as me.

"Mr Lutas, you are an *utterrr* legend!!!" He laughed. In five years I'd never heard him laugh. Today was historic in so many ways.

"No one has ever called me that beforrre." He scratched his noise, embarrassed. It was almost endearing.

"Well, they should?! You've made my life!"

He wrinkled his massive brows. "So it's a yes, then?" I nodded triple-speed. "I need to give them an answer by five, but your mother wanted me to ask you in person. Said it wasn't her decision."

"Tell them, tell them, tell them! And thank you, thank you, thank you."

He raised his shoulders. "Well, it's *your* talent I don't want to go to waste. Just don't let me down?"

"I won't. I promise." And I meant it.

"I'll make the call, then." He picked up his phone (I tried not to react that he had a picture of a painting of a pineapple as his screen saver), and I dashed to tell Mum and the others.

But when I pushed open the kitchen door, none of them were sitting at the table.

Rach and Jo were standing on the kitchen chairs waving their arms, Mum and Tegan were by the door pulling party poppers, and Adam was in the middle with a balloon in his hand.

"CONGRATS!!!" they all yelled together.

Mumbles even had a tiny dog party hat on.

They'd all known and had turned up to surprise and congratulate me in person.

I didn't know what to do. Except grin and grin and grin. Not just because I'd managed to scrape my way into college, but because I had the best friends and family and boyfriend in the world. Even my dog – who

449

was now glued to my leg, like she knew there was good news – was next level.

So I did the only thing I could think of.

Picked up my new camera, and took a photo of this moment so I could remember it for the rest of my life.

ACKNOWLEDGEMENTS

I always read these bits of a book first. Is that weird? Probably. But if you do too, then know you are not alone.

To everyone else that's taken a more traditional chronological approach, you've already read a lot of words, so I'll try and keep this short.

Wonderful Lauren, you not only make books way better, you make writing them fun. Thank you.

Gemma – best agent in the world. And so, so much more. Thank you for everything.

Pete, sorry this book made you leave the country. Thanks for all your help and DIY knowledge. Olivia – we went on tour! It was awesome – just like you. Jamie, every single cover has been gorgeous, I can't say thank you enough (*insert celebration emoji here* Or don't, cos someone would have to design it). Chie – danke! And everyone at Scholastic, thanks for being the nicest team and making me feel so welcome and supported.

A massive tent-based thanks to Pam and Ben. My first ever festival dream-team. We picked that litter good and proper. Glastonbury is still my happy place thanks to you. Pam – I'm forever grateful for your never-ending patience and friendship, especially when I was writing this. You always seem to know when it's needed the most. As do the equally amazing Tina and James. Thanks for being you.

A big 2 a.m. festival hug to all the amazing people that have supported Bella and me along the way. Rosanna – writing buddy, perpetual cheerleader. Jess – human Google, total inspiration. Dan, fellow tea towel lover. Julie – icon (say no more). Lucy R – the OG, thanks for absolutely everything. Matt, Mikey, Katie, Vivek, Lyndon, Jono, David, Robyn, Holly, Lou, Yasmine, Lisa, Jen, Aiss, Tom, Becky, Sarah, Alistair B, Smithy and Anya (global supporting superstars) – thanks for all the things, big and small. Barbara please keep an eye on Kevin – he's officially a bookshop renegade.

And a massive thank you to the incredibly supportive authors and bookish peeps I've met – Chelley, Chloe C, Neil, Jim, Kimi, Fiona, Alice B, team YALC and all the creative and dedicated bloggers who've made things even more exciting and a bit less scary (extra-big wave at Beth, Jo, Zoe, and Lois). Special funny shout-out to Simon, Perdita, Chloe S and Stephanie. And of course Team Cooper. Wow. Look at you go.

Chris. You make every adventure feel possible.

And my family, who mean the world to me. Becca, my wonderful sister. I won a best friend for life. Moomin and Daddles – a never-ending backbone of support from day one. And of course Ian and Rose. Rose – I'm your biggest fan. Keep sparkling every day – being kind is cool.

But most of all to all the people who have followed Bella, and got in touch to say they know how she feels. This one's for you.

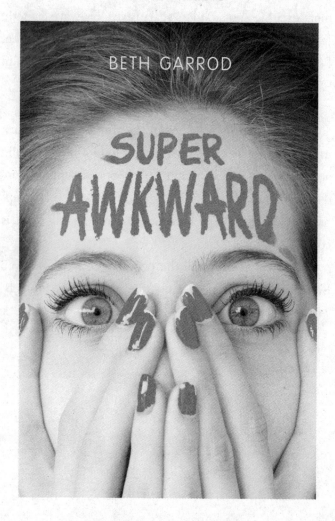

I, Bella Fisher, am absolutely
WINNING at **FAILING** at life.

BETH GARROD

TRULY MADLY
AWKWARD

I, Bella Fisher, am feeling as cool,
calm and collected as ever.
AKA: NOT AT ALL.